THE PROMISE IN POPPIES

a *Poppy Creek* novel

USA TODAY BESTSELLING AUTHOR

RACHAEL BLOOME

For film and TV rights: hello@rachaelbloome.com

Cover Design: Ana Grigoriu-Voicu with Books-Design.

Editing: Beth Attwood

Proofing: Laura Perry

SERIES READING ORDER

THE CLAUSE IN CHRISTMAS

THE TRUTH IN TIRAMISU

THE SECRET IN SANDCASTLES

THE MEANING IN MISTLETOE

THE FAITH IN FLOWERS

THE WHISPER IN WIND

THE HOPE IN HOT CHOCOLATE

THE PROMISE IN POPPIES

CHARACTER LIST

Cassie (Hayward) Davis: Co-owner of The Calendar Café. Barista extraordinaire. Married to Luke. Daughter of Donna Hayward. Granddaughter of Edith Hayward (deceased). (*Heroine of The Clause in Christmas*: Book 1)

Luke Davis: Woodworker (previously a lawyer). Owns Davis Designs. Married to Cassie. Son of Leonard (deceased) and Maggie Davis. Older brother of Colt Davis. (Hero of *The Clause in Christmas*: Book 1)

Maggie Davis: Mother of Luke and Colt. Owned Maggie's Bakery before it became The Calendar Café.

Donna Hayward: Mother of Cassie. Daughter of Edith Hayward (deceased).

Edith Hayward: Grandmother of Cassie. Mother of Donna. Left her home in Poppy Creek to Cassie in her will with a unique clause stipulating Cassie must complete 25 days of festive tasks to claim her inheritance.

Frank Barrie: Coffee roaster. Former recluse. Married to Beverly. Wrote *The Mariposa Method* under the pseudonym Richard Stanton. Co-wrote a second edition with Cassie.

Beverly (Lawrence) Barrie: Head librarian. Married to Frank.

Eliza (Carter) Parker: Co-owner of The Calendar Café with Cassie. Baker extraordinaire. Mother of Ben (Carter) Parker. Married to Grant. Daughter of Hank and Sylvia Carter. (Heroine of *The Truth in Tiramisu*: Book 2)

Grant Parker: Website designer and artist. Married to Eliza. Father of Ben. Older brother of Olivia Parker. Son of Stan and Harriet Parker. (Hero of *The Truth in Tiramisu*: Book 2)

Ben (Carter) Parker: Son of Eliza and Grant. Grandson of Stan and Harriet Parker and Hank and Sylvia Carter.

Penny (Heart) Davis: Owner of Thistle & Thorn: Curiosities & Collectibles. Married to Colt. Half-sister of Kat Bennet. Daughter of Timothy Heart (deceased) and Helena Bennet (deceased). (Heroine of *The Secret in Sandcastles*: Book 3)

Colt Davis: Chef at The Whispering Winds Inn (formerly a coffee roaster and cook at Jack's Diner). Married to Penny. Son of Leonard (deceased) and Maggie Davis. Younger brother of Luke. (Hero of *The Secret in Sandcastles*: Book 3)

Kat Bennet: Co-owner/manager of The Whispering Winds Inn. Engaged to Jack Gardener. Daughter of Helena Bennet (deceased). Father unknown. Half-sister of Penny. (Heroine of *The Meaning in Mistletoe*: Book 4)

Jack Gardener: Owner of Jack's Diner and co-owner of The Whispering Winds Inn. Engaged to Kat Bennet. Son of Richard and Elaine Gardener. Older brother of Lucy Gardener (and four younger brothers). (Hero of *The Meaning in Mistletoe*: Book 4)

Oliva Parker: Event planner and co-owner of the Sterling Rose Estate event venue (formerly Sanders' Farm). Engaged to Reed Hollis (formerly married to Steven Rockford III). Daughter of Stan and Harriet Parker. Younger sister of Grant Parker. (Heroine of *The Faith in Flowers*: Book 5)

Reed Hollis: Owner of Reed's Roses (flower farm & delivery service) and co-owner of the Sterling Rose Estate (adjacent to his flower farm). Engaged to Olivia Parker. Son of Bruce and Joan Hollis. (Hero of *The Faith in Flowers*: Book 5)

Lucy Gardener: Influencer with an inspirational lifestyle YouTube channel called Grow with Lucy Gardener. Dating Vick Johnson. Daughter of Richard and Elaine Gardener. Younger sister of Jack Gardener (and four other brothers). (Heroine of *The Whisper in Wind*: Book 6)

Vick Johnson: Coffee roaster. Dating Lucy Gardener. Former Marine. Son of Rhett Douglas (mother deceased). (Hero of *The Whisper in Wind*: Book 6)

Rhett Douglas: Cook/bartender at Jack's Diner. Father of Vick.

Sadie Hamilton: Owner of Sadie's Sweet Shop (recently expanded after Landon became an investor). Dating Landon Morris. Parents are deceased. Raised by her grandmother's best friend, Brigitte "Gigi" Durand. (Heroine of *The Hope in Hot Chocolate*: Book 7)

Landon Morris: Owner and founder of Morris Bio Tech. Billionaire philanthropist. Investor in the expansion of Sadie's Sweet Shop. Dating Sadie. Son of Irene Morris. (Hero of *The Hope in Hot Chocolate*: Book 7)

Irene Morris: Veterinarian. Mother of Landon Morris. Dating Bill Tucker.

Bill Tucker: Farmer. Widower. Dating Irene Morris.

Brigitte "Gigi" Durand: Grandmother of Sadie. Former owner of Sadie's Sweet Shop before turning it over to Sadie. World traveler. Dating Abélard Dupont.

Abélard Dupont: Frenchman. Owns a chocolaterie in Paris. Dating Gigi.

Dolores "DeeDee" Whittaker: Widow. Previously married to Arthur Whittaker, former principal at Poppy Creek High. Unofficial secretary at Luke's former law office.

Mac Houston: Owner of local grocery store, Mac's Mercantile.

Frida Connelly: Town busybody. Head of Poppy Creek's Historical Society.

Fern Flores: Owner of Hope Hideaway (a women's shelter in Starcross Cove). Surrogate mother of Kat.

Bryce Burns: Mayor of Poppy Creek.

For My Readers,
Thank you for going on this journey with me and for bringing the
characters alive in your hearts.

"If God cares so wonderfully for wildflowers that are here today and thrown into the fire tomorrow, He will certainly care for you."

— MATTHEW 6:30

LETTER FROM THE AUTHOR

Dear Friend,

No other book in the Poppy Creek series has been more nerve-racking and utterly wonderful to write. Since 2019, the people of Poppy Creek have lived in my heart and mind. The thought of saying goodbye to so many beloved characters— even temporarily—presented a daunting, bittersweet task. And yet, each time I sat down to write, the words flowed from fingertip to keyboard, as if the characters themselves knew exactly how they wanted their stories to end.

While the pages of this book are filled with surprises, twists, and turns, ultimately, I think you'll find it couldn't conclude any other way. And it's my sincerest wish that it will impart the enduring gift of hope in your hearts.

Before you embark on your return trip to Poppy Creek, don't forget to join the Secret Garden Club (www.rachael

bloome.com/secret-garden-club) **to access the exclusive extended epilogue.**

And if you'd like to chat more, you can reach me via email at hello@rachaelbloome.com, through my website, or in my private Facebook group, Rachael Bloome's Secret Garden Book Club.

Until next time,
    Happy Reading!

Rachael Bloome

CHAPTER 1

CASSIE

Cassie Davis stared at the pink and white test stick, surprisingly calm considering her entire world could change in a matter of minutes. Three minutes, to be exact.

"Cass, you ready?" Eliza Parker called from the other side of the bathroom door. "The meeting's already started."

"Almost." Cassie glanced at her phone balancing precariously on the narrow edge of the porcelain sink. According to the timer, only forty-five seconds had passed since she'd placed the cap back over the absorbent tip of the pregnancy test. How was that possible? It felt like a lifetime ago.

"Are you okay?" Eliza's concern carried through the thin crack in the doorframe. "You've been in there for ages."

"I'm fine. Be right there." She stuffed her phone and the test stick in the pockets of her long, lightweight cardigan and flicked on the faucet to wash her hands.

In hindsight, she shouldn't have taken the test at work. While The Calendar Café—a bakery and coffee shop combo she co-owned with Eliza—often felt like home since they spent so much time there, it afforded little privacy. And yet, after days spent avoiding the inevitable, too fearful of the potential outcome, she suddenly needed to learn her fate, to the point of anxious distraction. How would she be able to restrain her burning curiosity until after tonight's gathering?

The tiny strip of plastic scorched a hole in her pocket as they closed the café and headed across the town square toward the meeting hall. Cassie barely noticed the pleasant evening breeze that smelled faintly of apple blossoms or the way the setting sun painted the Western-style storefronts in a soft pinkish hue. Normally, she'd savor every sweetly scented breath, soaking in each nuanced detail that made Poppy Creek the most magical town she'd ever known—a town she'd gratefully called home for the last two and a half years.

But tonight, she couldn't concentrate on anything other than the impending test results. It felt as though a switch had been flipped in her brain, jerking her thoughts from dogged denial to a single-minded desperation. When she'd missed her period last month, she'd brushed it off. With her irregular cycle, missing one period here or there wasn't uncommon. But missing two periods in a row? That was difficult to ignore. So, that afternoon, she'd waited to take her break until Sally Hooper—an infamously unobservant cashier at Mac's Mercantile who hadn't even noticed when her husband bought all the supplies for her own surprise birthday party— came in for her shift. In a town like Poppy Creek, you could never be too careful. If anyone witnessed her purchase a pregnancy test, the news would make it to Luke before the three-minute timer had a chance to chime.

Luke...

The tangled knot in Cassie's stomach tightened as she and Eliza climbed the creaky wooden steps leading into the large one-room meeting hall. Her husband, Luke Davis, waved at them from the back row of folding chairs where he'd saved them a seat.

His warm hazel eyes shimmered with affection as he met her gaze then crinkled around the edges when he smiled. Her breath stalled somewhere in her throat, too feeble to handle the way his entire face lit up with delight at the mere sight of her. They were approaching two years of marriage, and he still looked at her with the same adoring disbelief, as if he couldn't believe his good fortune.

To be honest, *she* was the one who felt lucky. She'd never met a man like Luke, so strong, steadfast, and selfless. So full of love. He would make the most incredible father.

Guilt pricked her heart as she followed Eliza to their seats, the pregnancy test jostling in her pocket with each step. If the results were positive, Luke would be overjoyed. Like most married couples, they'd talked about having kids before, and Luke couldn't wait to be a dad. She'd tried to match his enthusiasm, hoping, *praying* her heart would change. How could she admit the idea of motherhood filled her with an intense, all-consuming fear that she wouldn't be good enough? That she'd be just as unqualified for the role as her own mother, and her mother before her?

When it came to maternal bloodlines, the Hayward women had a less-than-stellar gene pool. Her mother and grandmother had a horrible falling out shortly after her grandfather's death, which resulted in her mother skipping town at eighteen, with an infant Cassie in tow, never to speak to her grandmother again. Cassie's earliest memories were of dingy motel rooms and even worse apartments, and a parent who was rarely sober and barely keeping it together. If it wasn't for her mother's beguiling beauty and infectious charm—which inspired benevolence in both men and women alike—she wasn't sure how they would've survived.

As for her grandmother, Cassie had mixed feelings. Without Edith Hayward and the unusual terms of her will, Cassie never would've moved to Poppy Creek and met Luke, plus so many others she now considered family. Inheriting her grandmother's cottage had been the lifeline she'd needed, and she couldn't be more grateful. And yet, why hadn't her grandmother reached out to them before her death? Would their lives have turned out differently if she'd tried to make amends sooner? Cassie couldn't help mourning all the lost years… all the what-ifs.

Mayor Burns shot her and Eliza a look of annoyance as they settled in their seats, but he didn't miss a beat of his monologue. He gave the same one every year before the big Founders Day Festival, extolling the three main families who established the town of Poppy Creek in the 1800s: the Haskets, the Cunninghams, and the Burnses. As the legend goes, they'd come in search of gold but found a new, better way of life. They'd built a legacy. One that he still carries on to this day, et cetera, et cetera, and so on.

While Cassie could appreciate his familial pride, the tales grew more outlandish with each retelling, and his constant grandstanding wore on her nerves. After all, it wasn't as if he'd personally saved the town from drought, famine, and forest fires.

Nevertheless, Founders Day—which was a bit of a misnomer since the festival actually lasted three days—was an annual highlight. Under normal circumstances, she'd hang on every detail of this year's celebration with eager anticipation. But her thoughts kept drifting to the item in her pocket.

"Lastly," Mayor Burns said loudly, yanking her attention to

where he stood at the podium. His thick, dark hair glistened in the overhead light, the not-so-subtle sheen a clear sign he needed to cut back on the pomade. "I have an update on the library. As you know, the property has been in my family for generations, and I've been leasing it back to the town for a price that's more than magnanimous." He paused as if he expected praise or applause, then cleared his throat and continued. "But I've recently received a generous offer from a well-reputed developer. They plan to convert the building into a one-stop shop for affordable consumer goods, and I think it's in the town's best interest to accept."

Cassie stiffened, the life-altering pregnancy test momentarily forgotten as the room erupted in cries of protest.

"People, people, please calm down." Burns rapped his gavel against the podium a few more times than necessary, as if the action brought him personal satisfaction. "Change is hard, but it's time we think about our future. Forward progress is the bedrock of a town's survival."

"But what about the library?" Beverly Barrie, the head librarian for several decades, asked in a voice fraught with apprehension.

Her husband, Frank, squeezed her shoulder in a show of support.

"I'm sure we can find a suitable location to relocate the library," Burns said with an air of indifference. "Besides, aren't people reading more e-books these days, anyway? We can simply move the library online."

Beverly gasped in horror, her hand flying to the vintage cameo at her throat. More outraged murmurs rippled throughout the room.

Cassie's stomach clenched at the collective aura of alarm. Mayor Burns couldn't seriously be considering selling a historic piece of the town to a faceless corporation, could he?

"What about preserving the town's heritage?" Frank narrowed his bushy, silver-speckled eyebrows at Burns, his gray eyes darkening with displeasure as if a storm brewed just beneath the surface. "You let in one money-grubbing muckety-muck, you might as well turn Main Street into a strip mall."

"With all due respect, Mr. Barrie," Burns purred with practiced patience, "I hope you trust me more than that."

"Not even as far as I can throw you," Frank muttered under his breath.

Cassie hid a smile. Just a few short years ago, Frank would've been the last person to champion their bucolic way of life. An infamous recluse, he rarely left his house, let alone frequented the quaint mom-and-pop shops lining the four cobblestoned streets framing the town square. Now, despite his somewhat crusty and cantankerous exterior, he'd become a beloved member of the community. And although he was old enough to be her grandfather, he'd become the father figure she'd never had.

A sudden surge of emotion swelled in her chest at the thought. She'd never met the man who bore her DNA. She didn't even know his name. Despite her many attempts to learn more about him, her mother had doggedly kept his identity a secret, for reasons she wouldn't divulge. A microscopic seed of resentment burrowed in Cassie's heart. What would she say to her own son or daughter one day when they asked about their family tree?

"The fact is," Burns said in an authoritative tone, tearing Cassie from her melancholy musings, "the library can't keep up with its lease payments, and I've been lenient for as long as

I can. If it's not this developer, it will be someone else. I, for one, want to see Poppy Creek grow and thrive, not shrivel into a ghost town like so many others before us."

A somber hush settled over the room as his ominous words sank in, permeating the air with a thick haze of hopelessness.

There had to be something they could do. Cassie couldn't bear the thought of Poppy Creek changing, possibly losing its very essence, purely for the sake of perceived progress. While big corporations could provide jobs and cheap goods, and they weren't evil in and of themselves, there was something special about their way of life. Poppy Creek was a tiny pocket of tranquility in a tumultuous world, and now more than ever, she wanted it to stay that way.

As if driven by an internal force greater than herself, she rose from her chair. Her cheeks colored as everyone turned toward her, waiting for her to speak.

Mayor Burns glowered as if he could force her back into her seat with the harsh angle of his eyebrows, but her feet remained rooted to the floor.

"What if we use the festival as a fundraiser for the library?" Her voice shook with nerves, and she gathered a breath to steady it. "We could hold a silent auction, sell raffle tickets, and whatever else we can think of. If we raise enough money to pay off the debt and cover a rent increase, will you honor the library's lease agreement?"

The mayor's brown eyes muddied, and a muscle in his jaw flexed almost imperceptibly. Was he angry? She couldn't tell for sure, but her heart sank.

The room rumbled in support of her proposition, and the mayor's sharp, chiseled features melted into a smooth, syrupy smile.

"Of course. I only want what's best for the town."

His response was met with applause, which he accepted with exaggerated humility.

Cassie subconsciously placed a protective hand over her stomach.

Although she'd gotten the answer she wanted, something in the mayor's gaze left her feeling oddly unsettled.

CHAPTER 2

CASSIE

Cassie stared out the passenger window, barely registering the silvery, moonlit tree line as their faded red pickup rattled down the rugged two-lane road pitted with poorly filled potholes.

"Hey," Luke said, breaking the silence. "You made the right decision."

She shifted in her seat to face him, suppressing the urge to fling her arms around his neck in a grateful embrace. How did he know her so well? "Are you sure? I keep wondering if I should've accepted Landon's offer." Landon Morris, a billionaire entrepreneur and newcomer to Poppy Creek, had approached her privately after the meeting and proposed buying the library from Burns and donating it back to the town. On the surface, it seemed like a simple solution to their problem, but she'd ultimately advised Landon against making the generous offer.

"You made the right call," Luke assured her. "Having Landon whip out his checkbook every time the town has a financial need sets an unhealthy precedent for everyone involved, but especially Landon. It would change the dynamic, turning him into an ATM, and people would stop viewing him as an equal member of the community. The issue concerns all of us, and it's important we take ownership and solve it together."

Cassie couldn't help but smile. That was exactly how she felt about the situation, and hearing Luke voice her thoughts helped ease some of her doubts. "How do you always know the right thing to say?"

"I think it has something to do with the mind meld that happened when we got married. The one that lets us finish each other's sentences and read each other's thoughts." He flashed her a grin—the one that usually made her stomach flutter—but this time, her stomach lurched at the terrifying prospect. What if he really *could* read her thoughts? Would he think less of her?

"Besides," he added as if they'd never changed topics, "I have no doubt we'll be able to raise enough money. It's just unfortunate we even need to. I still can't believe Burns wants to sell the library to a developer." He briefly dimmed his head-lights for a passing car then flicked them back to brights, illuminating the shadowy silhouette of the surrounding pine trees.

"To be honest," Cassie admitted, "I'm not surprised. I don't know him well, so maybe this is uncharitable, but something's always seemed a bit off about him."

"Yeah, I know what you mean. He's never been the town's most popular mayor."

"How does he keep getting reelected?"

"Lack of competition, I guess." Luke shrugged. "There's some old bylaw that stipulates the mayor has to be from one of the founding families. Billy and Gina, the last of the

Hasketts, didn't have any children. Billy's in his late nineties now—and thinks wearing pants is optional—so that rules them out. The Cunninghams and the Burnses came to blows over something several years ago. No one knows for sure what happened. Frida Connelly swears they argued over which color to paint the gazebo in the town square, but that seems unlikely. At any rate, now the Cunninghams either raise armadillos in Oxnard or oxen in Amarillo. I can never remember which. Rod and Anne Burns only had one son, Bryce. So, I guess you could say he's our mayor by default."

"That's kind of sad. Can't the bylaw be changed?"

"Probably. Bryce took over after his dad passed away, and as far as I know, no one ever questioned it."

"What about his mom?" Cassie asked, realizing she'd never thought about his parents before. Mayor Burns had always lived in her mind as this singular entity who simply materialized into existence. Until recently, she didn't even know his first name.

"Anne?" Luke said thoughtfully. "I think she moved back to Washington after her husband died, to be near her family."

"Isn't Bryce her family?"

"Yeah…" He trailed off, his brow furrowed as if he struggled to find the right words. "Let's just say they never saw eye to eye."

"Then I'd probably like her," Cassie teased.

"You'd love her. She and my mom used to be good friends. They hosted a book club together when I was a kid. She'd be glad you stepped in to save the library." He briefly took his eyes off the road to meet her gaze. "I know I said this earlier, but it bears repeating. I'm really proud of you, Ru."

The tender way he evoked her nickname sent a pleasant ripple down her spine. Even though they'd settled into the comfortable rhythm of married life, he could still melt her in an instant with little more than a simple word or touch. Would all that change if they had a baby on the way? She reached inside her pocket, guilt making her palms sweat. She needed to tell him.

"I never want Poppy Creek to lose its heart and soul," he continued, unaware of the smoldering secret between them. "This town, exactly as it is now, is where I want to raise our kids." He cleared his throat. "You know, whenever we're ready to have kids."

"Luke, stop the truck," she blurted, unable to wait a second longer.

Startled, he punched the brakes. "What's wrong? Did you see a deer?"

"No. I—" She hesitated, suddenly at a loss for words. How did she even begin to explain? "I, uh, need to talk to you about something. It's important. Can you park up ahead?" She pointed toward a small clearing on the side of the road.

He tossed her an uncertain glance but did as she asked.

She reached for the overhead light then remembered the bulb had burned out. Or had the wiring fried? She couldn't remember. Either way, the truck had been falling apart for years and needed to be replaced, but it had belonged to Luke's father, so he refused to part with it. His sweet, sentimental side was one of the countless qualities she loved about him. And one of many that would make him a wonderful father.

Tears welled in her eyes at the thought, and she blinked them back, fumbling for her phone.

Focus, Cassie. You don't even know for sure if you're pregnant.

"Cass, what's going on?" Luke asked, concern creeping into his voice.

"I need more light." She yanked her phone from her purse,

frustrated to find another dead battery. But what did she expect when she'd spent half the day Googling everything from pregnancy symptoms to preschools?

Pulse racing, she shoved open the passenger door and slipped into the dim moonlight. The cold night air wrapped around her, making her shiver.

"Where are you going?" Luke switched off the engine, and the low growl gave way to an eerie stillness save for the quiet chorus of crickets.

Trusting him to follow, she scrambled toward the beam of the headlights, her heart pounding, her stomach swirling. For an instant, the world seemed to sway, and she closed her eyes, waiting for the ground to stop spinning beneath her.

She'd delayed the inevitable all day, afraid of the finality, but now, the urgent need to know the truth—one way or the other—seemed to suck all the oxygen from the air.

The sound of Luke's boots crunching on the loose dirt and gravel stopped a foot or so away. "Cassie?" He spoke her name softly, his question lingering on his lips.

She opened her eyes. Her husband stood before her, the ever-steady pillar she'd learned to lean on, no matter the storm. He never wavered, never faltered. And yet, she'd let her insecurities and fears keep them apart.

"There's something I need to show you." She dug her hand in her pocket and retrieved the pregnancy test, keeping her fingers wound tightly around it.

"What's—?" His voice fell away and he met her gaze, his expression searching, *hopeful*. "Is that—?"

She nodded, her throat too tight to speak.

"What does it say?"

"I don't know," she whispered. "I've been waiting to find out."

He bridged the distance between them, stopping toe-to-toe. She felt the heat from his body, felt his eagerness. He placed a hand on her upper arm, the firm, comforting pressure of his palm radiating through the thin fabric of her cardigan. Suddenly, every sound—the rustling of the wind in the trees, the rhythmic croak of the bullfrogs, even her own heartbeat—all seemed louder and more distinct.

This was it. The moment of truth. The moment that would define the rest of their lives.

Luke took her free hand in his, lacing their fingers together until their palms met. For several seconds, neither of them moved. Cassie savored the warmth of his touch, clinging tightly, afraid to let go. What if, from this moment on, everything changed? Or what if nothing changed at all? She wasn't sure which outcome frightened her more.

Ever present, ever steady, Luke stood quietly by her side, cradling her hand in his, not rushing or pressuring, simply waiting until she was ready.

Gathering a tenuous breath, she loosened her grip, uncurling her fingers.

Her heart stopped.

Even the bullfrogs and crickets seemed to pause in silent solidarity.

There, in the gleam of the headlights, were two unmistakable pink lines.

"Does that mean what I think it does?" Luke asked in a hushed breath, as if speaking too loudly would somehow alter the results.

Tears welled in her eyes, springing from a place deep within herself she couldn't explain, a mixture of joy, terror, and disbelief—a sensation so overwhelming, she could hardly find the strength to stand. "We're pregnant," she whispered, her words sounding disconnected and far away, as if they belonged to someone else.

"I can't believe it! We're going to have a baby!" Luke swept her off the ground, spinning her around before he gathered her into his arms for a kiss so passionate and all-consuming, she almost forgot her fears. When their lips finally parted, he pressed his forehead to hers. "You're going to be the best mom," he murmured, his tone raspy with emotion.

She stepped closer, burying her head against his chest as a silent tear slid down her cheek.

He seemed so confident, so certain. And for now, that would have to be good enough for the both of them.

CHAPTER 3

DONNA

Donna Hayward stretched her arms out wide and lunged forward, sinking even deeper into Warrior Two, one of her favorite yoga poses. Most days felt like a battle—against her alcohol addiction, against her regrets, against all the negative voices that often made breathing difficult.

She closed her eyes, relishing the warmth of the sun against her skin. Her daily yoga practice had become one of the only times she was able to quiet her thoughts, the only time she could silence the whispers of remorse that fed her constant heartache. In these tranquil moments on the concrete roof of her apartment building in San Francisco, when she'd drown out the cacophony of sirens and harried commuters, she'd finally experience peace. Maybe even hope.

"My thighs are killing me," Stephanie moaned. "Can we change positions yet?"

Donna suppressed a sigh, remembering she wasn't alone. Stephanie Patel, a young twenty-three-year-old she'd met in an Alcoholics Anonymous meeting two months ago, had glommed on to Donna the first night they met. Steph had still been hung over from a friend's birthday party and had a look of desperation in her dark, bloodshot eyes that Donna recognized. It was a look that said, *Drinking is ruining my life, but I don't know how to stop.*

At first, Donna had rebuffed the girl's many invitations to grab coffee or a late-night snack from the taco truck down the street from their meeting, knowing she was looking for a sponsor. What right did Donna have to counsel anyone? If Stephanie had known her two years ago, before she became sober, she wouldn't have considered Donna a decent human being, let alone a mentor.

But one night during a meeting, Stephanie had shared her deepest fear—that because of her drinking she'd continue to hurt the people she loved most. Shortly after, Donna agreed to grab coffee. She still didn't feel qualified to give advice—her own life was a mess—but she could be a chilling example of what *not* to do, which, in some ways, was even more persuasive.

She stretched her arms overhead, pointing her fingers toward the pale blue sky dotted with wispy white clouds.

Stephanie mimicked her movements, as she did nearly every morning for their regular yoga sessions. Over the past two months, they'd become an inseparable pair. Normally, Donna kept to herself. She'd spent years latched on to others —mostly men—in a futile attempt to dull her feelings of rejection and worthlessness. But her efforts to appear fun-loving and charming only made the emptiness more pronounced. Now, she preferred solitude. Except, Stephanie was still in the early days of her sobriety—the days where one slip could send you tumbling backward into an abyss that seemed impossible to escape. Her best defense? Constant supervision.

"How are your amends going?" Donna asked, folding into Downward-Facing Dog.

Stephanie bent forward, her hands and feet firmly planted, creating a perfect triangle with her slim body. Her long black hair cascaded like an inky waterfall onto her mat. "I'm done with all but one of them. That's good enough, isn't it?"

"Who's left?" Donna asked, skirting the question. She could easily say, *No, it's not enough. You have to address every offense from your past.* But she found it more effective to pinpoint the root of Stephanie's resistance.

"My parents."

Donna didn't respond right away, giving Stephanie a chance to fill the silence.

"I've been a total nightmare. They let me live at home since my part-time job at the laundromat doesn't pay enough to rent an apartment. But I was constantly sneaking out, staying out late, coming home drunk, making a mess of things. I even broke my mom's favorite vase. The one they bought on their honeymoon in Venice. And I never apologized. A real daughter of the year."

Donna listened quietly while Stephanie came to terms with her actions, allowing the reality of her poor choices to fully sink in. Confession came first. An addict needed to acknowledge the reasons for the amends before they could properly make them.

"I made a scene in front of my dad's coworkers, too," Stephanie admitted, her voice soft with shame. "He'd invited them over to watch a Giants game, and I crashed the party, drunkenly yelling something about athletes and their overinflated egos before I helped myself to their cooler of Bud Light. He was so embarrassed." She blew out a breath, her arms shaking as she held the pose.

"Through it all, they never gave up on me, though. And they never kicked me out. My mom would even leave the light on in my room so I didn't have to stumble in the dark when I came home hammered."

The comment caught Donna off guard, and her forearms wobbled, nearly giving out. She quickly shifted into Child's Pose, aware of the irony as her thoughts flew to her own mother. No matter how badly they'd fought, or how cold her mother had become after her father died, whenever Donna snuck out of the house—usually to sit in her favorite spot by the river, where her dad had taught her to cast the perfect line and choose the best lure—her mother kept a lamp lit in her bedroom window. Her room sat at the top of a turret—the bay window was her favorite feature of the pretty Queen Anne Victorian—and she could see the light glittering through the trees like a lighthouse, guiding her back home. Until the day she left for good, never once looking back.

"I owe them a major apology. I've been such an inconsiderate jerk." Stephanie collapsed to her knees and hastily rolled up her mat. "Okay if I take off?"

"Of course." Donna retreated from her painful memories and mustered up a smile. She knew Stephanie would come around eventually; she'd simply needed a sounding board. As she watched her young mentee slip her bare feet into a pair of worn sneakers, Donna's stomach clenched, a familiar knot of regret winding itself into a tight ball. If only Stephanie knew how lucky she was. Making amends was never easy, but in some cases—like hers—it wasn't even possible. What she wouldn't give to see her mother face-to-face, to say all the things she kept hidden in her heart.

Stephanie tossed a wave over her shoulder, and Donna waved back, but her yoga practice was far from over. She felt more tense than when they started. Settling back on her mat, she prepared to sink into Savasana when the loud ring of her cell phone pierced the air.

Her heartbeat stammered. This was the call she'd been waiting for—the call about the promotion. She'd been wait-ressing at Sel et Poivre, a fancy French restaurant in the Marina District, for nearly two years, slowly working her way up the ladder. When a management position finally opened up, she'd gone out on a limb and applied. Well on her way to fifty, it was time she had something to show for herself. On Friday, she'd breezed through the interview, and Marc, one of the owners, had said he'd be in touch first thing Monday morning. Which was today.

Gathering a breath, Donna kept her gaze glued to the sky, quieting her nerves as she pressed the phone to her ear. "Hello?"

"Hi, Mom."

Donna jolted in surprise. Cassie? She had a monthly phone call with her daughter on the second Thursday of every month—one of her many attempts to repair their tenuous relationship, the relationship she'd nearly destroyed countless times over. They rarely broke or veered from their fixed date. Her pulse fluttered. Was something wrong?

"Hi. Is everything okay?" She never used terms of endear-ment like *honey* or *sweetheart*. That's what other moms said to their daughters—moms who weren't abject failures. Moms who'd earned the right. She didn't even deserve to be called Mom at all, if she was honest with herself.

"Everything's fine. I'm at a doctor's appointment, and they have some routine medical history questions I thought I'd double-check with you, if that's okay?"

"Of course. Fire away." Even though Cassie had said "routine," Donna couldn't help feeling on edge as she rattled off answers—to the best of her knowledge—about her family's history of various diseases and disorders. But it wasn't until Cassie asked about gestational diabetes that her heart stopped. Why on earth would the doctor be asking about gestational diabetes unless—

Before she had a chance to confirm her suspicion, her phone buzzed with another call. *Marc.*

"Mom?" Cassie prompted. "Did you hear my last question?"

"Yes, sorry. I was distracted by an incoming call. No history of gestational diabetes."

"Great. Thanks! I'll let you get your other line. Bye!"

"Wait, Cass—" she started, but her daughter had already hung up.

In a daze, Donna accepted Marc's call.

"Donna, my love! How's my favorite employee?" Marc's smooth timbre slipped through the speakers, oozing with his trademark charm. Some might consider him unctuous, but Donna had to give the man credit. He'd made a pass at her shortly after she was hired, but he'd respected her polite refusal and hadn't let it affect their working relationship.

"Waiting anxiously," she said honestly, for more than one reason. Would Cassie have told her about the pregnancy if they hadn't been interrupted?

"Well, wait no more, *mon amie*. You have the job! That is, if you still want it," he teased.

His excitement reverberated in her ear, but she couldn't formulate a response. She couldn't stop thinking about Cassie. Her daughter was going to have a baby. Which meant she'd be a grandmother. This precious new life would have no memories of the old Donna; it wouldn't know the demons she wrestled every day. She'd have a chance to start over, to do things differently. Maybe she'd even have a chance to be there for her daughter, to be the kind of mother she should have been.

"Hello? Donna? Are you listening?" Marc chanted in a singsong voice. "I'm making all your dreams come true. You *do* still want the job, don't you?"

"Sorry, I—" She paused. What could she say? This was the moment she'd been waiting for. She'd worked so hard, paid her dues. She was finally turning her life around, and this was the professional break she needed. She'd be a manager at a five-star restaurant. No more low-level positions, scrounging to get by. And yet, she couldn't summon the one simple word that should be on the tip of her tongue.

Every fiber in her being was telling her she needed to go back to the last place on earth she ever wanted to be, the place where all her nightmares began.

CHAPTER 4

CASSIE

Cassie set a steaming cup of Earl Grey in front of her friend and sister-in-law, Penny Davis, then settled in the chair opposite her. Penny mentioned something about an email and an old diary, but Cassie's thoughts kept drifting. Sunlight streamed through the front window of The Calendar Café, glinting off Penny's long, coppery braid. The thick plait fell in front of her right shoulder, dusting the tabletop. Had Penny been born with wispy auburn curls? And what about her eyes? The burnt umber hue perfectly matched her hair color, which made for a striking combination.

Beneath the table, Cassie placed a hand on her stomach. What color eyes would their baby have? Green like hers? Or hazel like Luke's? Or maybe some other color entirely. So much about raising a child involved uncertainty. Would her pregnancy have complications? What about the delivery? Would their baby be born healthy? Would she even carry to term? She shuddered, not even wanting to consider the possibility of a miscarriage.

They'd decided not to announce their pregnancy until

they made it past the first trimester, just in case. While she understood the prudence in waiting, the last few days had been more difficult than she'd anticipated. She longed for advice, for the wisdom of experienced mothers. Was it normal to be riddled with worries, to have doubts about motherhood, while also being hopelessly in love with a child you'd never met?

The instant she'd heard their baby's heartbeat, the tears fell, unbidden. Luke had wrapped his arm around her shoulders, holding her close against his side, his own eyes glistening as they processed the intense, unfamiliar emotions. The doctor had given them a moment of privacy, as if she'd witnessed similar scenes countless times before.

"Okay, I'm ready to hear your big news, Penn." Eliza plopped onto the chair next to Penny, nearly spilling her tea and plate of snacks in the process. "I had to pull a tray of cappuccino truffle cookies out of the oven, but Ryder said he'd get the next one. Although, he may eat them all before they make it to the display case." She tossed an affectionate smile over her shoulder at their part-time employee who happened to be "sampling" one of her mocha almond scones at that precise moment.

The husky senior had the typical bulky build befitting his defensive lineman position on the high school football team, and he packed away more baked goods during his four-hour shift than his paycheck could possibly cover. But his cheery, affable disposition made up for the constant trail of crumbs, and they were grateful for the help.

"What are you drinking?" Penny, an avid tea lover and aficionado, sniffed the ribbon of aromatic steam curling from Eliza's cup. "Raspberry leaf and… nettle?"

"Good nose!" Eliza applauded Penny's olfactory prowess. "And red clover."

"Interesting combination." Penny eyed Eliza's odd culinary assortment, adding, "And speaking of interesting... What are you eating?"

"Let's see, I have lentils, sunflower seeds, quinoa, pineapple, and liver."

Penny wrinkled her nose, and Cassie fought back a sudden wave of nausea. So far, her morning sickness had been mild, but certain smells triggered an immediate adverse reaction. She could now add liver to her list of foods to avoid, along with scrambled eggs—poor Luke had to sacrifice his favorite breakfast—tuna fish, and, sadly, the bergamot perfume he'd given her for their last anniversary.

"Feel free to help yourselves." Eliza nudged the plate toward the center of the table, and it took all of Cassie's self-control not to scoot her chair away.

"Tempting," Penny said with a teasing smile. "But I think I'll grab one of those scones before Ryder polishes them off." As she stood, the skirt of her vintage peasant dress swung around her ankles. "Cass, can I get you anything?"

"No, thank you," she said, before considering the implications.

"Nothing?" both of her friends asked in unison, clearly surprised.

Cassie glanced at the bare tabletop in front of her, realizing her critical error. Whenever she sat down to chat with friends, she at least had a cup of coffee, if not one or more of Eliza's delicious desserts to go with it. A bit impulsively, she'd decided to avoid caffeine and sugar as much as possible during her pregnancy, despite her doctor's assurance that both were safe in moderate amounts. How would she explain her new dietary restrictions? In hindsight, she should've made herself a decaf latte as a decoy. "I'll, uh, get something later."

Luckily, Penny didn't press further and turned the attention back to Eliza when she returned with her scone. "What's with the strange smorgasbord?"

"They're supposed to help with fertility." Eliza shoved a pineapple spear into her mouth, licking the juice off her fingertips as she added, "I figured I'd give this a try before being stabbed by a thousand needles."

"You mean acupuncture?" Cassie hid a smile at Eliza's exaggerated description. She always did have a flair for the dramatic.

"Tomato, tomahto." Eliza waved her hand before snagging another spear. "It's torture, however you say it. But we haven't had any luck for almost a year, so I'm desperate enough to try anything."

"I'm so sorry, Liza." Penny placed a hand on Eliza's arm in a show of sympathy, but Cassie sat frozen, guilt gluing her in place. How was it fair that Eliza, who wanted another child more than anything, couldn't get pregnant, while it had happened to her unintentionally?

"Thanks." Eliza's petite shoulders slumped forward as if she was unburdening herself of a massive weight. "I've been trying to stay positive, because I know how much this means to Grant, but there are days I worry it won't happen for us again." Unshed tears illuminated her large chocolate-brown eyes, and Cassie could tell she was exerting a great amount of effort to keep them at bay. Sniffling, Eliza asked Penny, "What about you? Have you and Colt thought about having kids yet?"

Cassie squirmed. Somehow, she needed to derail this line of questioning before it became her turn.

"Once or twice," Penny admitted. "But honestly, I can't see it happening any time soon. Colt spends every waking second at the restaurant." Her sweet, soft-spoken voice trailed with a twinge of sadness, which surprised Cassie. Penny always seemed so happy and content, blissfully enjoying married life —they'd tied the knot shortly after Cassie and Luke—and running the quirky antiques store she'd inherited from her late father. "Don't get me wrong," Penny added. "I'm happy he's found his calling and finally settled into something he loves. But…" She chewed her bottom lip, searching for the right words. "He doesn't seem like himself. He's gone from being spontaneous and carefree, always whisking me off on wild adventures, to living in the kitchen, pouring all his creative energy into new recipes."

"We're talking about Colt Davis?" Eliza asked in disbelief. "The same Colt Davis who barely graduated high school because he kept ditching class to pull some kind of prank? Colt Davis, who's never kept the same job for more than six months?"

"That's the one," Penny conceded with a sigh. "I swear, Kat sees him more than I do."

Cassie offered a small, sympathetic smile. When Colt first accepted the position as head chef at the Whispering Winds Inn—a luxury inn run by Penny's half sister, Kat Bennet— Colt's family couldn't have been more proud… and relieved. He'd had a habit of gallivanting around the globe, running from responsibility, and pushing the limits with one extreme sport after the next. But they'd only wanted him to settle down—to plant roots—not alter his entire personality. What had spurred the sudden change?

"Wow." Eliza expelled a breath of incredulity. "I never thought I'd see the day when Colt became a workaholic."

"He's probably just excited to finally have a career he's passionate about," Cassie said, hoping to ease some of Penny's concern. "It might take time to find a healthy work-life balance, but he'll get there."

"You're probably right." Penny attempted a smile, but it didn't quite reach her eyes. "Shall we get to our main topic for today?"

"Yes! I'm dying to hear about this diary." Eliza sprinkled sunflower seeds and quinoa on a slice of liver—presumably to get it over with all at once—and crammed the hefty bite into her mouth, making a face as she chewed.

Poor Eliza... A few days ago, Cassie would have traded places with her friend in a heartbeat, gladly handing her the baton of motherhood. But now? Cassie subconsciously rested a hand on her stomach. Now, she wasn't sure what she wanted.

Penny pulled a laptop from a worn leather briefcase, her eyes brightening. "I've been brainstorming ideas for a special exhibit piece for the library, something that would draw interest. And I remembered my dad talking about a diary written by Lydia Burns." Turning to Cassie, she explained, "Lydia was the wife of the town's founder and first mayor, Chadwick Burns. Her diary documents the early days of settling in Poppy Creek, first the gold mining camp, then constructing the town."

"Sounds fascinating. And the perfect item to showcase for the fundraiser. Maybe we could even auction off the chance to read it?" Cassie wouldn't mind bidding on it for herself. She'd always been intrigued by the town's history. "Where's the diary now?"

"That's the thing. I have no idea." Her fingers fluttering with excitement, Penny flipped open her laptop and logged into her email. "The diary remained in the Burns family for years, until Bryce finally sold it."

"Typical." Eliza rolled her eyes. "No qualms about selling off family heirlooms to the highest bidder."

"And not just any bidder," Penny said with an air of reverence. "Edwin Mackensie, an eccentric billionaire. I think he's even wealthier than Landon."

Eliza whistled, duly impressed.

"My dad brokered the sale," Penny continued. "Although, he tried to talk Burns out of it, since he believed that kind of history should stay with the town."

"I agree with him," Cassie said, once again perturbed by the mayor's questionable moral compass. Did he really have the town's best interest at heart?

"Why did Edwin even want a diary about an obscure small town, anyway?" Eliza asked, struggling to stomach another bite of liver.

"He collects historic diaries. He's never confirmed or denied the claim, but as legend goes, he even has one of Princess Diana's diaries in his personal collection."

"*The* Princess Di?" Eliza gasped. "I don't believe it."

"I don't know if I do, either," Penny admitted, "but I also wouldn't put it past him. Edwin and my father forged a casual friendship while they negotiated the diary deal, and eventually Dad went on to find a few other items for him, too. He said Edwin was the most interesting man he'd ever met and had an uncanny way of getting exactly what he wanted."

"Wait." Cassie frowned, trying to connect the dots. "You said you don't know where the diary is?"

"Not exactly." Penny clicked on a recent message, expanding it to fill the screen. "After the town hall meeting, I found Edwin's contact info in my dad's old Rolodex, and I sent an email asking if he'd be willing to loan us the diary for the festival. This is what he wrote in return.

"You asked for a favor, and I'll happily oblige.
Your father was a friend, a truly great guy.
He liked solving riddles, hiding treasure to find.
Let's see if his daughter is of the same mind.
If you can solve all the riddles to a count of four,
Then the diary you seek will surely be yours.
But be warned, lest you quit before you start.
These clues of mine aren't for the faint of Heart."

Cassie leaned back in confusion. "I don't understand… What does it mean?"

"I think," Penny said, eyes sparkling, "if we solve all the clues—sounds like four in total—and find the diary, he'll give it back to the town."

"It's a treasure hunt!" Eliza cheered, bouncing on the edge of her chair.

Cassie glanced between her friends. Their excitement radiated across the table. A real-life treasure hunt organized by an eccentric billionaire? She supposed stranger things had happened. But would they have time to solve all the riddles before the festival in three weeks?

CHAPTER 5

DONNA

Donna parked on Main Street but remained in the driver's seat, cocooned in the safety of her run-down Corolla. Townspeople shuffled past her dusty windshield carrying boxes of colorful streamers and bunting, no doubt preparing for some festival. In Poppy Creek, there was always another festival.

Starry-eyed tourists strolled the cobbled streets, gazing in awestruck delight at the charming window displays of cute and quirky establishments like Thistle & Thorn, an oddball antiques store, and Sadie's Sweet Shop. The chalkboard sign out front advertised an afternoon taffy-pulling demonstration and something called a nitrous ice cream sundae. Today's flavor? Grenadine and Gold Dust.

Strange how so much could change and yet, inexplicably, stay exactly the same. The town, with its historic brick, stone, and shiplap buildings and slow, sleepy tempo, still felt trapped in time.

Of course, she realized that was part of the allure. Most people viewed Poppy Creek as this idyllic slice of heaven tucked into the northern California foothills, a secluded pocket of small-town hospitality. A respite from life's weariness. A home away from home. And maybe to some people—like her daughter—Poppy Creek really *was* all of those things. But to Donna, the town held nothing but painful secrets. It had left scars as deep and real as the one on her knee. The one from the serrated edge of the drain pipe. From the night she'd climbed through her window, too drunk to notice the slicing pain followed by the trickle of blood down her leg. The night of her father's funeral. The night that changed everything.

Donna drew in a steady breath, trying to recenter. The day would be hard enough without a macabre trip down memory lane.

In over three decades, she'd only been back home—could she even call it that?—a handful of times. The first visit had been an unmitigated disaster, a relapse for the record books. She'd been so ashamed, and still was when she allowed herself to think about it. The subsequent visits were for her daughter, to make amends and reconnect. The trips never got easier, and she could barely believe she was considering staying for an indeterminate amount of time. That was, as long as Cassie didn't mind.

She winced, recalling Marc's hurt and anger when she'd not only turned down the promotion but asked for time off. His entire demeanor had shifted. He'd ranted about how he couldn't believe she would throw away her future and how he regretted investing in her professional growth. To add insult to injury, he admitted his business partner had wanted to hire someone else for the management position, but that he'd personally vouched for her. Every word felt like a knife twist. She seemed destined to continually disappoint. In the end, he'd asked her to cover her next few shifts until they could rearrange the schedule, then collect her final paycheck. In one conversation, she'd lost a supposed friend, a dream promotion, *and* her job.

After all that, what if Cassie didn't want her to stay? What if she had to return to San Francisco, to the apartment she'd lent Steph—with strict rules to check in every evening and attend daily AA meetings—and a job she no longer had?

Her heart started to hammer. The seat belt seemed to constrict, cinching tighter across her chest. Suddenly feeling trapped, she struggled to release the clip with her trembling fingers. Once free, she leaned back against the headrest, expelling a pent-up breath, and her gaze fell on a wooden sign.

Jack's Diner.

Underneath, in smaller print, it read: Patio Seating and Bar.

Her mouth watered, triggering an all-too-familiar urge. Well-rehearsed thoughts swam through her mind. *Just one drink. One small sip to calm my nerves. One glass to forget.*

Except, it was never just one.

She pushed through the heavy oak door, welcomed by the tangy, smoky scent of barbecue. Marc would've had a conniption at the simple rustic interior with mismatched plaid and leather upholstery, but the handful of customers dotting the cozy booths looked happy and content.

Swallowing the lump lodged in her throat, she strode toward the bar.

"Welcome to Jack's." The bartender had the kind of wide, friendly smile that deepened the creases around his eyes and mouth, softening the rough edges marked by his slightly crooked nose and the jagged scar along his jawline.

"Thanks." She perched on the leather barstool, sitting halfway on the edge.

"What can I get for you?" He set down the glass he'd been drying and tossed the dish towel over his shoulder.

As their eyes met, she couldn't help noticing his were a blueish-gray, like the sky after a storm.

"Root beer, please."

"Bottle or glass?"

She bit her bottom lip, wavering, then asked, "Can you put it in a tumbler? On the rocks. I mean, with ice."

He cast her a curious sideways glance then grabbed a short, stocky glass. "Coming right up."

She watched as he prepared her unusual request, feeling self-conscious. But sometimes, merely feeling the smooth, familiar contours in her hands helped ease her anxiety. And right now, she had ample reason to worry.

She hadn't thought through her plan at all. She had no job, no place to stay, and no clue if Cassie would welcome her presence. Somehow, despite her appalling parenting, her daughter had become the most kind, compassionate, and forgiving person Donna had ever met. But although she always made her feel welcome, a weekend visit wasn't the same as an indefinite one. What if she'd made a huge mistake coming here? And perhaps even more worrisome, what if her past collided with her present, causing irrevocable harm?

Her hands shook as the bartender passed her the soda.

"Are you okay?" His voice—a velvety baritone—carried a hint of concern.

"Yes, thanks. Just a bit nervous." Why was she telling *him*? She downed a quick gulp before she could say anything more, wincing as the carbonation burned the back of her throat. Not quite the same as whiskey, but it still had a kick.

He nodded in the amiable, understanding way befitting most bartenders. *Empathetic ear* must be in the job description.

"Let me guess." He studied her for a moment then speculated, "You're visiting family and you don't always get along."

She cracked a smile. "You're pretty good at this."

"Comes with the territory." He returned her smile, and she once again observed how it transformed his entire face, elevating his objectively attractive features to downright handsome. Was he forty-nine? Fifty? Maybe a little older? And why did she suddenly care?

"I'm visiting my daughter," she blurted, running from her unwelcome train of thought. "I'd like to stay for an extended visit, but I haven't asked her yet. She doesn't even know I'm here. We get along, but…" She trailed off, not sure how to explain their complicated history. How did you tell a perfect stranger that you used to be a drunk who didn't deserve her daughter's forgiveness?

"You haven't always," he finished for her, putting it simply.

"You could say that."

He studied her again, glancing from her glass back to her face, his expression thoughtful. "How long's it been?"

"What do you mean? Since I last saw my daughter?" She shifted beneath his gaze. This man she'd never met before could see far too much, making her feel uncomfortably exposed.

"Since you got sober." He said the words without judgment, as casual as offering her a refill.

Her cheeks burned, and she gulped another sip of soda. "Is it obvious?"

"Not many people order a root beer on the rocks," he said with a kind smile. "Besides, it takes an addict to know an addict."

Sitting up straighter, she blinked in surprise. "But you're a bartender." She hadn't meant to sound accusatory, but the contradictory combination didn't make sense.

"Alcohol was never my vice." He let the statement linger without further explanation and immediately piqued her interest. If not alcohol, then what? Drugs? Gambling? Why was she so eager to know?

"Two years," she answered honestly. "You?"

"Twenty."

The number hung between them for a silent moment, both weighty and ethereal. "How?" she breathed, admittedly in awe.

"You know, same as I do. One day at a time."

Her heart sank. Not the magic hack she'd hoped to hear.

"The meetings help," he added. "Which makes living here tough sometimes."

"No meetings?" One more thing she hadn't considered before making her rash decision.

"I've considered starting one." He grabbed the old-fashioned soda glass he'd been holding when she arrived and ran the rag along the sloping curves, although it was clearly dry. "A catchall group, for anyone in recovery."

"Why haven't you?"

"I wasn't sure anyone would come." He cast a sideways glance in her direction, still polishing the same glass. "It would help to know at least one other person would be there."

Her stomach swirled, and she abruptly drained the last drop of root beer, setting the tumbler back on the bar. "How much do I owe you?" She dug inside her purse for her wallet. Had his statement been some kind of invitation? And if so, why did she find it so disconcerting? Men had hit on her in stranger ways, and she'd deftly avoided their advances without a second thought. Why did this feel different?

"It's on the house. Think of it as my way of welcoming you to town."

She lifted her gaze to protest, but her breath quickened when their eyes locked, catching her off guard.

Time to go. She snapped her purse shut and hopped off the barstool. "Thank you."

"My pleasure." He tipped his head in her direction, flashing a sexy half grin.

Flustered, she scrambled for the front door.

What was wrong with her? If she stayed in town, she *should* attend a meeting. She'd just passed up a perfect opportunity simply because the man made her stomach flutter.

Which was ridiculous. She didn't even know his name.

CHAPTER 6

RHETT

R hett Douglas set the soda glass back on the shelf. It sparkled in the overhead light, not a single spot or speck in sight. How long had he been drying it? *Too long.* He wondered if the mysterious—and undeniably attractive—brunette had noticed. Most likely. She'd acted a little spooked when she left. Why hadn't he asked for her name?

Despite how it sounded, his remark about the recovery meeting hadn't been a pickup line. At least, not entirely. He'd mulled over the possibility several times, but something about Root Beer on the Rocks had renewed his motivation. Which, admittedly, should be a red flag. He'd moved to Poppy Creek to reconnect with his son, not meet women. Especially not a recovering alcoholic with only two years under her belt.

She's off-limits. Don't even think about it.

Of course, they could still be friends, couldn't they? Before he had time to dismiss the terrible idea—befriending a beautiful woman he already found far too appealing could only end badly—the cowbell above the entrance jangled. For a split second, he hoped she'd come back.

Luckily—since he apparently couldn't heed his own advice —his son, Vick, walked through the front door instead. Vick *Johnson*. Under different circumstances, the fact that his son chose to go by his mother's maiden name might have wounded his pride. But at this point in his life, after his myriad of mistakes, he didn't have much pride left. His son could go by whatever name he wanted. Rhett was simply grateful he'd given him a second chance.

Vick tossed a wave in his direction before heading to an open booth, followed by his boss and mentor, Frank Barrie.

Rhett buried a sharp pang of envy, reminding himself that Frank and Vick's relationship was a good thing. A *great* thing. Until recently, Vick had wandered aimlessly around the country, taking one random job after another, running from his ghosts like so many haunted veterans before him. Now, his son had a promising career as a coffee roaster, a sweet and supportive girlfriend, and a close-knit community who cared about him. What more could a father ask for?

At the internal question, a powerful longing pierced his heart, and not for the first time. What he wouldn't give to finally hear Vick call him Dad. A title both simple and monumental, taken for granted by so many. But in truth, a title he had yet to earn.

Carlos Hernandez, a hard-working college-aged kid and whiz with a chef's knife—the guy could julienne a stack of carrots in seconds—finished marrying the ketchup bottles and grabbed two menus.

"Mind if I take this one?" Rhett asked.

Carlos glanced at the booth, recognized Vick and Frank, then handed him the menus. "Be my guest. Frank nearly bit my head off the last time he ordered." He flashed a wry smile before slipping behind the bar. "But to be honest, I'm more afraid of Beverly."

"Me, too." Rhett laughed. Ever since Frank's heart attack, Beverly had her husband on a strict heart-healthy diet. Except, she knew he couldn't be trusted outside her own kitchen, so she'd enlisted the loyalty of every server in town, much to Frank's chagrin.

Rhett left the menus on the bar, knowing he wouldn't need them. Between Vick and Frank's frequent visits and the fact that Jack, the owner, didn't like change, they had every item memorized. "What'll it be, gentlemen?"

"I'll have the BoomTown Burger." Vick ordered the triple patty, triple cheese, bacon, and fried jalapeño monstrosity nearly every week and still managed to stay fit. Oh, to be in his twenties again, able to inhale a day's worth of calories in a single meal without breaking a sweat. At fifty, he got heartburn merely by looking at trans fats.

"I'll have the Motherlode," Frank said brusquely, referring to the smoked tri-tip plate with a bacon-smothered baked potato, cheesy creamed corn, and a behemoth-sized biscuit dunked in garlic butter.

"Not so fast, Jesse James," Rhett teased. "You might like to play fast and loose with the law, but I've already served my time in the slammer, and I ain't going back." The joke slipped out before he could think better of it, and he shot a sideways glance at Vick. His son kept his gaze glued to a scratch in the wooden tabletop. While Rhett had learned to poke fun at his sordid past—like doctors with their gallows humor, it helped add levity to an otherwise dehumanizing experience—Vick wasn't ready to laugh about it yet.

"What's the warden got on you, son?" Frank asked.

"She threatened to revoke my library card."

Frank chuckled. "That sounds like my Bevy. Sweet as a peach, unless she's protecting someone—or some*thing*—she loves. Ole Burnsy Boy better watch out. Between Cassie and my Bevy, he doesn't stand a chance." The old man's eyes glinted with pride and affection, softening his prickly appearance. Rhett pegged him to be somewhere in his late eighties, and despite the wonky heart and the walking stick, he still looked pretty good. Distinguished, in a rugged kind of way.

"Cassie has us working on an exclusive blend for the silent auction." Vick appeared relieved at the change in conversation. "Frank just ordered these insanely expensive beans from Molokai."

Rhett nodded, recalling an article he'd read recently on the Hawaiian island's coffee production. "There's something in the red soil that gives the coffee a richer flavor profile, right?"

Vick's eyes widened in surprise, the same gray-hued eyes as his own. The one visible contribution he'd made to his son's life. "How'd you know that?"

"Just a random fact I picked up somewhere." Rhett hid a smile, not ready to reveal he spent hours on the internet in the library researching anything and everything about coffee, hoping for even one second of connection.

"Hey, Douglas," Jack Gardener bellowed in his loud, jovial baritone, swapping Rhett's last name for his first—a sign you'd made it into his close circle of friends.

"Yeah, boss?" Rhett grinned. Jack, who was closer to his son's age than his own, refused to be called boss, which Rhett conveniently forgot on a regular basis. Although they gave each other a hard time—always in good fun—there were few men Rhett respected more. And not just because Jack had given him a job when most people tossed his résumé in the trash—once, right in front of his face. Jack's big heart matched his hulking six-foot-four frame, like a big ole soft teddy bear with surprisingly muscular biceps.

"Can you hold down the fort? I have to put out another wedding-related fire." The moment Jack noticed Vick and Frank, his perpetually cheerful features broke into an even bigger smile. "Well, if it isn't two of my favorite customers. What're you having?"

"A burger for this one." Frank jerked his thumb toward Vick. "And rabbit food for me."

"What do you think?" Jack placed an enormous palm on Rhett's shoulder. "Can we add some lean steak to that rabbit food?"

"I think I can make that happen."

"Great. I'm leaving you guys in good hands. I shouldn't be gone more than an hour."

"How bad's the fire this time?" Rhett asked. Ever since Jack proposed to his fiancée, Kat, on Thanksgiving, they seemed to deal with one issue after another, most of them involving Jack's mother, Elaine.

"Let's just say I'm feeling the heat." He turned to Vick. "Do me a favor, Johnson. Propose to Lucy so my parents can start fussing over your wedding and leave ours alone." Jack's chuckle rumbled from deep inside his chest, making it clear his suggestion was only a joke, but Vick squirmed.

Interesting... Rhett studied his son with masked curiosity. He'd been dating Jack's little sister less than six months. Was he considering marriage already?

Rhett pressed his lips into a tight line. He'd rushed into marriage before he could handle the responsibility, and he'd wound up ruining more than one life, including his own. But how could he discern if Vick was ready for that level of commitment when his son would barely discuss the weather with him, let alone a potential engagement?

CHAPTER 7

DONNA

By the time Donna reached The Calendar Café, she'd managed to shove all remaining thoughts of the enigmatic bartender out of her mind. In their place, her subconscious reeled with all the ways her daughter could react to her visit, from indifference to pleasant surprise to irritation. Why hadn't she called first?

Knowing Cassie, she would've told her not to come, not wanting to be an inconvenience. But in her gut, somewhere deep down—latent maternal instincts, maybe?—Donna knew her daughter needed her. Even if she purely filled in at the café so Cassie could rest and prepare for the baby.

Gathering a deep breath, Donna pushed through the front door. A welcoming bell chimed overhead, and not for the first time, a sense of awe and pride swept over her. *Her* daughter had created this warm, inviting atmosphere. She'd decorated the walls with local art, hand selecting each piece, from the watercolor wildflowers sweeping across the canvas to the close-range photograph of poppy petals unfurling in the sunlight. She'd arranged the comfy chairs and couches by the fireplace and helped create the coffee blends lining the display shelves, ready for customers to take home. Her daughter had envisioned this idyllic space, making it a reality for others to enjoy.

This particular afternoon, thanks to the post-lunch lull, Donna counted only a handful of customers and didn't see anyone behind the counter. A tourist couple and their two children commandeered a far table, the young kids stuffing their mouths with enormous, caramel-drizzled brownies while their parents studied a slew of brochures and a map on their iPad. A pretty redhead sat at a small table by the register, filling out the kind of order form they'd used at the restaurant for whatever breads and baked items they didn't make in-house. Donna had a vague feeling they'd met before but couldn't remember her name.

As if she'd read her thoughts, the girl glanced up from the form, flashing a friendly smile when she met her gaze. "Hi, Miss Hayward! It's so nice to see you again."

Donna hesitated, the girl's name on the tip of her tongue. Kit? Katie?

"Kat," the girl offered, coming to her rescue. "Kat Bennet. I'm a friend of Cassie's. We met at Christmas."

"Of course. Hello again. And please, call me Donna." Donna smiled and nodded toward the slip of paper on the table. "Ordering wholesale?"

"Yes. I run the Whispering Winds, an inn outside of town. Cassie and Eliza supply all our coffee, pastries, and basically any baked goods we use at our restaurant."

"They're definitely the best. They make a great team." Since the moment she'd met Eliza, Donna liked the petite, spunky woman who'd become more than her daughter's closest friend. She'd become the sister she'd always wanted. Eliza had sat by Cassie's side, holding her hand in a show of support the afternoon Donna had arrived to make her amends, two days before Cassie's wedding to Luke. Donna still remembered Eliza's large brown eyes watching her, wary and protective. But they'd also held a softness, a glint of compassion Donna had rarely received in life. She supposed, in a way, they had an unspoken bond. Two teen moms who'd experienced firsthand how unkind and unforgiving the world can be when your biggest failing is on display for all to see and judge.

"Mom?" Cassie's startled voice yanked her from her thoughts.

Cassie and Eliza emerged from the kitchen, each carrying a tray of round, fluffy profiteroles, fresh from the oven. The room flooded with their sweet, buttery scent.

Donna stood still, merely staring at her daughter as an unexpected wave of emotion washed over her. To a casual observer, Cassie looked exactly the same as the last time Donna saw her—the same dark waves spilling around her shoulders, the same graceful features and full lips that always appeared slightly arched, poised to smile. Today, her skin seemed to glow from the inside out, and the light reached all the way to her eyes, making the rich green hue bright and luminescent. Her daughter had always been beautiful, but now? Tears sprang to Donna's eyes before she could stop them, and she inhaled sharply, determined not to cry.

"Is everything okay?" Cassie set the tray on the counter, her countenance cloaked in concern.

"I'm fine, I just—" She hesitated, her words tumbling

together. Now that she was here, facing her daughter, she realized she had no idea what to say. "I—I thought I could help."

"Help with what?" Cassie cocked her head, sounding genuinely curious, which added to Donna's nervous reservations.

Once again, she opened her mouth to speak, but the words wouldn't come. It had all seemed so straightforward back in San Francisco. Come to Poppy Creek, learn the ropes at the café, cover Cassie's shifts, cook meals, help around the house, and simply be present for whatever her daughter needed. Between morning sickness, acid reflux, back aches, swollen feet and ankles, and fatigue, she remembered long stretches during her pregnancy when she barely wanted to get out of bed.

Donna's gaze fell to Cassie's stomach, hidden behind an apron. As far as she could tell, she still wasn't showing. It had to be early on in the pregnancy. Too early, perhaps? She'd been so single-minded in her eagerness to see her daughter, she hadn't considered the possibility that Cassie hadn't told anyone yet. She glanced at Eliza, who studied Cassie, her brow furrowed, as if a million thoughts whirred through her mind. Surely Cassie had confided in her best friend?

"To help with—" Donna tried again, her gaze flitting back to Cassie's stomach. With what? What if no one knew? She should ask to speak to Cassie privately. But the idea came too late.

Eliza followed her gaze, the pieces clicking into place. "Wait a minute... You're not drinking coffee, you haven't touched a sliver of dessert in days, you nearly vomited when I had liver for lunch..." Her eyes widened. "Cass, are you—?"

Cassie's cheeks flushed a shade Donna recognized—the scarlet blush of shame. But why would Cassie feel guilty about being pregnant? "I'm so sorry, Eliza. I was going to tell you."

For a moment, neither woman spoke or even blinked. Donna could almost see a ribbon of tension pulled taut between them. But why?

"I—I'm so happy for you," Eliza stammered, her hands trembling as she tried to slide the baking sheet onto the counter. But it slipped off the edge, crashing to the floor, scattering the round, puffy pastries at her feet. "I—I'm so sorry." Biting back a sob, she turned and fled to the kitchen, Cassie mere steps behind.

Donna stood frozen in horror, too mortified by the scene she'd caused to move. Once again, she'd wreaked havoc in her daughter's life, extending the destruction to her friends, as well. She hadn't wanted to hurt Cassie or Eliza, and yet she'd skillfully wounded both. A quiet, cruel voice whispered in her ear, *You want to help your daughter? Then leave. She's better off without you.*

Donna turned on her heel, smacking into a tall teenage boy who towered at least six inches above her five-foot-seven frame.

"'Scuse me, ma'am." He ducked around her, halting behind the counter when he saw the pile of profiteroles on the floor. "What happened?"

"Ryder." Kat stepped forward, startling Donna, who'd forgotten she was there. The young family must have left sometime during the debacle. "Can you clean up and cover the register for a bit? Cassie and Eliza had to take care of something."

"Sure." He stooped to pluck one of the plump pastries off the floor and popped it into his mouth.

Kat placed a hand on Donna's arm. "Don't feel bad. It was clearly an accident. Cassie and Eliza will work it out."

"I hope so." Donna dragged her gaze back toward the kitchen, wondering what to do next. At the very least, she should apologize to Cassie, shouldn't she?

"Where are you staying?" Kat asked. "With Luke and Cassie?"

"No, I don't want to impose. I'll probably find a room for the night and head home tomorrow." Even as she said the words, her stomach twisted. Was that the right thing to do? Or was she simply running away again?

"I have an empty room at the inn. I'd love for you to stay with us. No charge."

"That's very kind, but I couldn't—"

"Don't be silly. Of course you can." She set the pen and completed order form on the counter. "I hate for rooms to go to waste. You'd be doing me a favor. Besides, the only other accommodations in town are at the Morning Glory Inn, and they're full with a bird-watching group from Sausalito."

Donna wavered. In the past, she would've jumped at the offer of a free room. For years, she'd survived off the generosity of others, often taking unfair advantage. But in recovery, she tried to balance learning to take responsibility and ownership of her problems while also discerning when to accept help. Perhaps this was one of those times?

"Are you sure? I really don't mind paying for the room." It wasn't much, but she had some money in savings.

"I'm positive. I'd be thrilled if you'd stay as my guest."

Kat sounded so sincere and earnest, as if she meant every word, and Donna briefly wondered why she seemed personally invested in someone she hardly knew. "That's very kind. Thank you. I accept, but just for tonight."

"We'll see." Kat's emerald eyes sparkled with a hint of a smile. "Why don't we give Cassie and Eliza some time to talk, and I can show you the inn? I'm parked out front. You can follow me there, if you like. It's not far."

Donna let her gaze flicker back toward the kitchen one last time before she fell in step beside her eager hostess.

Several minutes later, Donna parked behind Kat's silver sedan. Kat slid out of the driver's seat and mouthed *I'll be right back* before heading toward a battered blue pickup. A man Donna recognized as Cassie and Luke's friend Jack—who'd been a groomsman at their wedding—leaned against the truck, petting a beautiful white husky perched on the passenger seat. The dog wiggled and licked Kat's face in greeting.

Donna climbed out of her car, marveling at the majestic inn while she waited for Kat. The two-story, Georgian-style structure with regal white columns flanking the entrance stood proudly at the end of the circular drive. It was somehow both imposing and inviting, and Donna had never seen anything quite like it. Even the snootiest of customers she'd served at Sel et Poivre would happily stay here without a single snide comment or complaint.

"But she's gone too far this time." Jack's agitated voice carried in the breeze, breaking through her thoughts. "I'll call her right now and tell her she needs to back off."

"Please, don't," Kat said in a calm, soothing tone.

Were they arguing? Jack gruffly shoved the sleeves of his flannel shirt up to his elbows, his rigid posture betraying his frustration. Kat placed a gentle hand on his muscular forearm, and he melted at her touch. "I honestly don't mind," she told him. "Your mom is just trying to help."

"But this is what they do, Kat. My parents take over everything. Today, it's our wedding. Tomorrow, it will be where we're going to live after we get married. Then, it'll be when we have kids—"

"Jack," Kat said softly, taking his hands in hers. She looked so delicate and small next to the blond-haired, blue-eyed giant, yet she carried herself with a strength and confidence Donna admired, as if she'd taken care of herself from a young age, rising to the challenge instead of spiraling out of control, as Donna had done. "I appreciate you rushing over here because you thought I'd be upset, but I'm fine. Really. I don't care where we have the wedding. Or what color the flowers are. Or whether we serve chicken or fish—"

"Or tri-tip," Jack interjected.

Kat smiled. "Or tri-tip. I only care that our friends and family are there to celebrate with us, whether it's here in Poppy Creek or in Primrose Valley."

"But—" Jack protested, and Kat hopped onto her tiptoes to cup his cheek with her palm.

Donna looked away, granting them as much privacy as possible given her close proximity.

"Please, don't let this ruin your day. It'll all work out. We'll talk more about it later, okay?"

Donna couldn't hear his reply, but when she stole a quick glance, he'd stooped to kiss Kat tenderly before climbing back inside his pickup truck.

Kat waved as Jack made his way back down the driveway while the husky hung his head out the window, his fluffy ears fluttering in the wind.

"Sorry about that," Kat said, joining Donna by her car. "Weddings tend to make everyone a little tense, don't they?"

"Except you. You're remarkably calm for a bride."

Kat shrugged. "I've never been one of those girls who daydreamed about the perfect wedding." She led Donna up the broad brick steps decorated with potted peonies in pinks, yellows, and reds. "And I don't have much family, apart from my sister, Penny, and Fern, the woman who raised me, and they don't really have any preferences or expectations, either, beyond seeing me happy."

Donna followed Kat through the double doors into a stunning foyer with a sweeping staircase and elegant vintage decor befitting the building's historic heritage, but she barely noticed the carefully preserved details. *The woman who raised me...* Such a telling phrase that spoke volumes about Kat's upbringing yet made Donna want to know so much more. Like what had happened to Kat's mother?

"There's a sitting room and library on the left that's open all hours." Kat directed her attention to a pair of French doors. "To the right is The Westerly, our in-house restaurant. It serves breakfast, lunch, and dinner, and there's a menu in your suite if you'd like room service."

Suite? Kat had mentioned an empty room, not a suite. "Everything is lovely," Donna told her, impressed with the level of care and forethought. "I don't remember Poppy Creek having anything like this."

"This used to be a personal estate owned by Jack's parents," Kat explained, leading her out back to a large patio surrounded by a sprawling garden fragrant with lavender, hyacinths, and roses in every color and variety imaginable. "His parents put the property in his name when they moved to Primrose Valley, hoping to tempt him into the family real estate business."

"Is that why Jack said his parents want to control his life?"

she asked without thinking, then smiled sheepishly. "Sorry, I couldn't help overhearing."

"It's fine." Kat gave a lighthearted laugh. "In a town like Poppy Creek, I've become accustomed to everyone knowing everything. And yes, I think that's part of it. Among other things. Jack and his parents have a complicated relationship and only recently reconnected after years of barely speaking to each other. It takes time to work through old wounds."

"Yes, it does," Donna said softly, suddenly somber. Occasionally time ran out, leaving your wounds open, raw, and unable to heal.

Kat paused her tour by a white gazebo clothed in climbing clematis vines. The sweetly scented pale pink blossoms created an aromatic canopy dotted with contented butterflies and the occasional hummingbird.

"This spot is stunning." Donna inhaled deeply, savoring the heady perfume. "Have you thought about having your wedding here?"

"That was the original plan, but Jack's mother, Elaine, just texted us both that she secured a venue in Primrose Valley."

"And you're okay with that?"

"Strangely, I am. I love the inn, but it's a lot of work, too. Most of my time and effort goes into running this place. There's something nice about having Elaine take on the bulk of the wedding planning. Jack thinks it's overbearing, but honestly, it's a relief. I don't care about the details. I just want to marry the man I love."

Kat's expression was so sincere, Donna didn't doubt her words, and she couldn't help smiling at her sweet, simple desire. There was something about the younger woman that intrigued her, like a gentle tug on her heart. Kat had an easy, open, and friendly air about her, and yet, there was something else—a depth to her eyes—that hinted at a harder life, that she'd seen, maybe even experienced, things most people couldn't fathom. But instead of being cold and callous, she radiated warmth. And was it her imagination, or did Kat seem particularly keen on forming a friendship with her?

CHAPTER 8

CASSIE

Cassie draped her arm around Eliza's shoulders as her friend cried softly, her face buried in her hands. Her heart aching, Cassie longed to say something to ease the pain threaded between them but knew even the most eloquent words of wisdom couldn't assuage Eliza's sadness. So, instead, she waited in comforting, companionable silence.

Two years prior, they'd sat in this very spot, on a secluded bench in the tranquil, tucked-away courtyard, perched beneath the same wisteria-covered arbor, cocooned by the sweet, honeyed fragrance of violet-hued blooms.

Cassie recalled listening quietly while Eliza tearfully revealed her long-kept secret: that her ex-boyfriend, Grant, who'd returned for Luke and Cassie's wedding, was indeed the father of her son, Ben. While she'd had her reasons, Eliza knew, in her heart of hearts, that she'd made the wrong decision and had deeply wounded the people she loved most in the world.

The confession had been painful, but it had also been healing, and cemented their friendship in a way that couldn't be shaken, no matter what they faced. At least, Cassie prayed that would be the case.

"I'm so sorry, Cass." Eliza lifted her tear-filled eyes to meet hers. "And I'm so embarrassed. I really am happy for you. *Truly* happy. I hope you know that."

"I know." Cassie swept aside a strand of Eliza's silky blond hair that clung to her damp cheek. "It's okay to be sad, too."

"You would say that. Because you're a good friend. And I'm a self-centered drama queen." She attempted a rueful grin, trying to make light of the situation, but Cassie could still hear the twinge of grief in her voice.

"No, you're not. You're a good friend, too. The best, actually. And I'm grateful you're in my life because if I'm honest, I find this whole pregnancy slash motherhood thing a little terrifying."

Eliza squeezed her hand. "You're going to be an amazing mom."

"How can you be sure?"

"Because I know you. You're the most caring, loving person I've ever met. And that little bean in there"—she gestured to Cassie's stomach—"is one lucky kid."

Tears pricked Cassie's eyes, and she flung both arms around Eliza's petite frame, pulling her into a hug.

"I wish we could be pregnant together," Eliza murmured.

"So do I."

Eliza leaned back, wiping her eyes. "I keep hoping Grant and I will get another chance to do it right. With Ben, Grant missed everything, and I know he mourns the loss. I do, too. Even though I had my parents, Luke, Maggie, and a community of support, there were still moments I felt alone. Moments I missed Grant so much it hurt. Hearing Ben's heartbeat for the first time, feeling him kick." Her voice caught, and she gathered a steadying breath. "I want to share those memories with him. I want to share the happiness, heartache, exhilaration, and exhaustion. There's something special about going through it all together, you know?"

She did know, and her heart ached for her friend and all the regrets she carried with her. She couldn't imagine exactly how Eliza felt, but she did know the sorrow of living life looking over your shoulder, focused on what could have been.

Cassie reached for her free hand, hoping her touch could speak the words that wouldn't come. What could she say? That the future couldn't undo the past, but you could still find joy in the present? That you could be grateful for the life you have while also grieving what may never be? Both nebulous concepts that offered little solace in the present sorrow.

As if sensing she needed a tangible reminder of life's blessings, Eliza's son, Ben, bolted through the back door, bursting with youthful excitement.

"Mom! Aunt Cassie! Guess what?"

"What?" Eliza straightened, swiping beneath her eyes to dispel the lingering traces of her tears.

"Sorry, he got away from me." Grant chuckled, stepping into the courtyard. He adjusted his glasses, squinting in the glare of sunlight. "By the way, did you know Ryder is eating profiteroles off the floor?" His grin faltered when he noticed their red, puffy eyes. "Is everything okay?"

"Better than okay." Eliza conjured a smile. "Luke and Cassie are having a baby."

"No way!" Grant beamed. "Congratulations, Cass. That's incredible news."

"Thank you." Cassie returned his smile. For the first time in days, she felt a wave of relief. By accidentally spilling the news, her mother had inadvertently afforded her the support she craved. "Luke is beyond excited, and I'm sure he'll appreciate talking to you about it, but please don't mention it to anyone else yet. Now that the secret is out, we'll start telling people. But Maggie doesn't get back from her trip until tomorrow. I don't want her to find out through the grapevine before we get a chance to tell her."

"My lips are sealed." He mimed tugging a zipper closed, and Cassie fondly observed the globs of dry paint on his fingers. He'd become quite the artist lately, designing fewer websites in favor of spending more time at his easel. They'd sold several of his pieces in the café, and he'd even taken on some commission work. His entire life had changed since moving back to Poppy Creek, and yet he made the shift from workaholic bachelor to full-time dad look effortless. Enviable, even. Did he ever have doubts? Did he ever miss the version of himself that existed before becoming a father? Or did he like this amalgamation better?

"Does that mean I'm getting a cousin?" Ben asked, interrupting her thoughts.

"Sure does." Eliza ruffled his shaggy blond hair.

"Cool! A boy cousin or girl cousin?"

"We don't know yet," Cassie told him. "But we should find out soon."

"I hope it's a boy. I've always wanted a brother to play catch with me."

Cassie's chest squeezed as she caught Grant and Eliza's quick, wistful glance. She forced a brightness into her voice. "I'll see what I can do, but you can play catch with a girl cousin, too."

"That's true, I guess." Ben shrugged, his nine-year-old attention span already on a different topic. "Guess what? I get to be the blacksmith apprentice for the festival!"

"That's wonderful, Bug!" Eliza stood to give her son a congratulatory hug.

Cassie nodded along, trying to match Ben's enthusiasm as he raved about all the cool tools he'd be able to use under the watchful supervision of Mac Houston, who'd be trading his title of town grocer for head blacksmith for a day.

Among the children in town, the blacksmith's apprenticeship was the most coveted role on Reenactment Day, followed closely by candle maker and bread baker. Her heart warmed at Ben's animated ramblings, and she wondered if she'd be sitting here listening to her own child one day.

Before she met Ben, she had zero experience with kids and had felt completely clueless when tasked with babysitting him on her own. But she'd quickly fallen for his innocent sweetness and had loved their time together. She'd also learned that they shared a special kinship, since they'd both grown up without a father. Watching him now, with Grant's hand resting on his shoulder in such a simple yet intimate gesture, her heart hummed with happiness for Ben, while also harboring her own deep-rooted longing, still unfulfilled.

Her thoughts drifted to the private conservation she'd had with Landon several weeks earlier. His friend had created a proprietary software that could locate a person of interest anywhere in the world with minimal data. It sounded like the kind of spyware technology limited to Hollywood's imagination, and yet, she'd seen it work first-hand when it reunited Sadie's grandmother, Gigi, with her former flame, Abélard Dupont. The two lovebirds were now inseparable. But in their case, the program had access to a wealth of information found in Abélard's handwritten letters, not to mention the samples of the handwriting itself.

In Cassie's case, she had next to no details to share, other than her own suspicions that her father had either lived in Poppy Creek or a nearby town. She'd also supplied Landon's friend with personal data that could be used to narrow down possible genetic markers, but even so, the odds weren't in her favor. Unless she finally convinced her mother to reveal more about her past, she had little hope of finding her father.

As if privy to her thoughts, Eliza placed a hand on her arm, startling her back to the present. "Cass," she said gently. "I think you should talk to your mom."

CHAPTER 9

DONNA

Donna stood on the balcony of her suite, overlooking the picturesque garden below. As she scanned the lush, verdant lawn, she noted several spots that would be ideal for her morning yoga practice. At the thought, a melancholy suspicion cinched around her chest. Would Stephanie continue to practice on her own? She'd laid out a simple routine she could follow in her absence, but she had niggling doubts that Steph would be disciplined enough to follow it.

Donna stepped back inside and plucked her phone off the nightstand. No missed calls or messages. Why hadn't Stephanie called yet? She tried to keep her thoughts from drifting down dark and twisty alleyways, which all led to Stephanie slumped on the floor with an empty liquor bottle in her hand.

"She's fine," she said aloud, hoping to convince herself. "She said she'd phone after the five-thirty meeting, and it's only—" Donna glanced at her phone again. "Six forty-five." Her pulse skipped a few beats, guilt seeping through the cracks of her carefully assembled armor. What if Stephanie ditched the meeting? What if she'd gone to a bar with her friends instead? What if—

Donna closed her eyes, inhaling through her nose then exhaling slowly through her mouth, allowing the heat of her breath to warm her from the inside out. *Stephanie needs to take responsibility for her own sobriety. You can't babysit her every second of the day.* The mental reminder made sense, but Donna still couldn't shake the heavy weight in the pit of her stomach. What if Stephanie needed her and she wasn't there?

Her phone vibrated in her palm, and she jumped, nearly losing her grip. Her daughter's name appeared on the screen, yanking her thoughts from Stephanie but cementing the feelings of guilt. "I'm so sorry," she blurted in lieu of a greeting. "I shouldn't have been so careless. I never meant to—"

"Mom, it's okay," Cassie interrupted, her words tempered with kindness. "I know you didn't mean for that to happen. I should have realized that my phone call from the doctor's office the other day would've sparked questions. I was so caught up in myself and the baby, I didn't give much thought to anything else."

Donna's heart melted at the mention of her grandchild, and she sank onto the edge of the four-poster bed. "How is the baby?"

"About the size of a prune." Cassie laughed softly, and Donna suddenly ached to see her, to hold her.

"How are you feeling?"

"Exhausted." Cassie paused a beat before adding, "And nervous."

There was something in her voice—a fragile vulnerability—that reminded Donna of when Cassie was a little girl, and a long-forgotten memory popped into her mind. Cassie was seven, about to attend a new school for the second time that year, and she'd been so afraid, she'd locked herself in the bathroom of their studio apartment. Donna—still hung over from the night before —hadn't known what to do. She'd knelt on the other side, using her most soothing tone, but couldn't cajole Cassie out of hiding. Impulsively, she'd unclasped the pendant from around her neck —a gift from her father and the only reminder of her former life that she'd allowed herself—and slid it under the door.

"This is a magic necklace," she'd said, making it up as she went along. "As long as you wear it close to your heart, everything will be okay." She'd held her breath, her head throbbing, until the door cracked open. Cassie tiptoed out of the bathroom, her large green eyes tentative but hopeful, the tiny silver silhouette of a sparrow tucked beneath her T-shirt. Every day afterward, Donna recalled seeing the thin metallic chain peeking from her collar, until one day—she wasn't sure when exactly—it disappeared, vanishing into the void like every sliver of happiness before it.

Shaking away the memory, she said, "It's normal to be nervous. A lot of things are going to change. But it's going to be okay. Better than okay. It's going to be great." She was a little rusty with the pep talks, but she meant every word.

"About what you said... about wanting to help... what did you have in mind?"

"I don't know exactly. I'd thought I could stay a while and help out any way you need. Maybe I can learn to cover some of your shifts at the café so you can rest and get things ready for the baby?"

"What about your job at the restaurant?"

"I told my boss I'd be visiting you for a while." She kept her tone light. Cassie didn't need to know how that conversation had ended.

"And your apartment?"

"I've sublet it to a friend."

"And you're sure about this? I know Poppy Creek isn't your favorite place…"

Donna swallowed. While she had her fears and reservations, she didn't see any way around it. If she wanted to be near her daughter, this was where she'd have to be. "I'm sure. I'd really like to be here for you, if that's okay."

A long, agonizing silence followed, and Donna held her breath. Cassie had every reason to refuse her offer. She didn't deserve her trust or respect, and she certainly hadn't earned the right to be involved in her life. All she could hope for was grace.

"I'd like that, too," Cassie whispered.

The feather-soft words brought tears to Donna's eyes, and she lifted her gaze to the ceiling, keeping them at bay.

"We'd love for you to stay with us," Cassie continued. "Unfortunately, our guest room is in shambles at the moment, since we're turning it into a nursery, but we can set up an air mattress in the office until we figure out something more suitable."

"I don't want to create any more work for you and Luke. I already checked in to the Whispering Winds Inn." She glanced around the room again, still finding it hard to believe her good fortune. The spacious suite seamlessly paired luxury with comfort, and she adored every detail, from the cozy reading nook alcove to the deep clawfoot tub. The nightly rate had to be astronomical, but when she'd searched the website, she couldn't find the suite listed anywhere.

"In the Zephyr Suite?" Cassie asked.

"Yes, how'd you know?"

"Just a hunch." Cassie's tone hinted at a smile. "Can we have you over for dinner, at least? I need to run to the store, but I could whip up—"

"Why don't you and Luke come here?" Donna interrupted, not wanting Cassie to go to any trouble on her account. "The Westerly has an impressive menu, and I'd like to treat you both to dinner."

"Honestly, that would be lovely. I was bluffing. I had no idea what I'd cook for dinner." Cassie laughed, and Donna didn't think she'd ever heard a sweeter sound. "I'll check with Luke, but we can probably be there in thirty minutes, if that works for you?"

"That would be perfect." They exchanged goodbyes, and Donna hung up the phone feeling more hopeful than she had in a long time. But her optimism evaporated the instant she eyed the blank screen. Still no call from Stephanie.

Donna hopped off the bed and paced the room, twisting the phone in her hand until she couldn't stand another second of silence. Stopping abruptly on the balcony, she bit her bottom lip and jabbed the redial button.

"I know, I know. Don't be mad," Stephanie rambled after answering on the third ring. "I should've called."

"I was starting to worry." Donna could hear the motherly admonition in her voice but was too relieved to care about maintaining a more reserved response.

"I'm sorry," Stephanie said, sounding sincere. "I lost track of the time. I've never had a whole apartment to myself before. And…" Her voice trailed off, taking on a more apologetic tone when she admitted, "I got sidetracked trying on all your clothes. It's like you're renting out your closet to someone who actually has taste," she teased. "I've never seen you in anything other than jeans or yoga pants. How come you never wear any of this other stuff?"

"That's a wardrobe from another life."

"Well, I bet you looked hot."

"A hot mess. Christian Louboutins are hard to walk in when you're hammered."

"Good point. I've sprained my ankle too many times mixing high heels and Hairy Navels."

"Speaking of," Donna said, taking advantage of the segue. "How was tonight's meeting?"

Her heartbeat quickened at the unusually long pause. "Steph?" she prompted.

A loud, resigned sigh filled the speaker. "I didn't go. And before you get all lecturey, I know I shouldn't ditch. I'll go tomorrow. Cross my heart."

"You'll go tonight. There's a seven-thirty meeting at Marina Bible Church."

Another sigh. "Fine. I'll go. But that meeting always has the worst snacks."

"You should've thought of that two hours ago. Wasn't it Sharon's turn to bring snacks tonight?"

Stephanie groaned. "Yeah. And she said she was baking those fudgey nut brownies I like. Darn. See what happens when you're not here to keep me in line?" Her tone was playful, but Donna couldn't help the twinge of guilt. Steph had missed a meeting, but it could have been so much worse.

"Call me the second the meeting ends, okay?" She might still be at dinner with Luke and Cassie, but she needed to make sure Steph followed through this time. "It might not seem like a big deal to miss one or two, but consistency is important."

"Yes, ma'am."

They chatted for a few more minutes, and when they finally got off the phone, the whispering voice in the back of her mind grew louder, its accusatory tone unmistakable.

If she didn't want to be a hypocrite, she knew exactly what she needed to do. And it required another trip to Jack's Diner.

CHAPTER 10

CASSIE

Cassie stood off to the side, watching her mother angle the stainless steel carafe beneath the frothing wand for the third time that morning. The antique copper espresso machine hummed as pressure built, then released when Donna turned the knob, expelling hot steam into the cold milk. With practiced, measured movements, Donna mimicked Cassie's frothing technique, creating a perfect pillowy cloud.

"Hey, that looks pretty good." Eliza peered over Donna's shoulder, balancing the tray of warm lemon-glazed biscotti at her hip. "Much better than the last time."

"Who would've thought frothing milk would require Olympic-level skill?" Donna teased, briefly taking her eyes off her task. Unwittingly, she lowered the carafe half an inch, and the tip of the frothing wand bubbled on the surface, spurting and spewing milk.

"Look out!" Eliza cried, laughing as Donna fumbled with the knob, cutting off the supply of steam.

Both women laughed at the mess of splattered milk and foam, and Cassie marveled at the lighthearted, carefree sound.

How many times had she prayed for a moment like this one? A moment of pure, silly fun with her mother. A moment without turmoil, tension, or tainted by too much alcohol.

At dinner last night, they'd almost seemed like a normal family, brainstorming possible baby names and decorating ideas for the nursery. Not once did she worry her mother would order a bottle of wine and consume the entire thing, culminating in a drunken scene.

Even more unexpectedly, her mother had taken a call during dinner, and when she returned, she'd told them all about a young woman named Stephanie. When she spoke, her mother's eyes glinted with affection, her care and concern for the girl apparent in every syllable.

For a brief, embarrassing moment, a wave of envy had washed over her, shadowing their pleasant evening. Her mother obviously shared a bond with this girl that she could never fully understand, a disheartening thought. But she'd quickly dismissed the unwelcome realization, concentrating on the present truth: her mother was here now, with her, making up for lost time.

The more Cassie considered the magnitude of her mother's offer, the more grateful she felt. Between her fatigue, preparing for the baby—plus grappling with the accompanying emotions—and organizing the library fundraiser, she'd been more overwhelmed than she'd anticipated.

"You're really getting the hang of it." Cassie grabbed a wet rag to help mop up the mess.

"Fourth time's the charm." Donna smiled, wiping a glob of froth off her cheek.

The bell above the front door chimed, and Cassie turned to see Landon Morris stroll inside. He'd traded his typical suit and tie for jeans and a lightweight pullover; the pale periwinkle blue made his dark eyes pop. She noticed he seemed more relaxed since he'd moved to Poppy Creek. Small-town life clearly suited him. Or maybe it had more to do with his rapidly blossoming relationship with Sadie Hamilton. The former rivals turned sweet-shop-owning sweethearts certainly brought out the best in each other.

Cassie set down the damp cloth and moved behind the register to take his order. "What can I get you today? Eliza made these amazing saffron and sun-dried tomato focaccia rolls this morning that I think your mom will love." Since Landon and his diabetic mother, Irene, avoided sweets, they'd made an effort to include more savory items on their menu.

"Sounds delicious. I'll swing by for some this afternoon. I actually stopped in to give you an update on the search."

Cassie stiffened and cast a furtive glance at Donna, who was busy preparing another shot of espresso. Had she overheard?

"You know what," Cassie said, thinking quickly, "I was just about to head to Penny's. I promised I'd help her with something. Care to walk with me?" She didn't wait for a response before asking Eliza, "Think you two can handle things for a few minutes?"

"Absolutely." Eliza tucked the last lemon biscotti in the large glass jar with the others, creating a tantalizing pattern as chocolate almond, tart cherry, and pepper pistachio all comingled. "Ryder will be here soon, too."

"Perfect." Cassie whipped off her apron and folded it neatly behind the counter. "And you're okay on the espresso machine?" she asked her mother.

"You tell me." Donna presented an expertly extracted shot. Cocoa-brown and honey-colored swirls decorated the thick crema.

For a moment, Cassie merely stared. She'd been moved by coffee before—like the first time she saw Frank Barrie perform his proprietary roasting process, the Mariposa Method—but this felt different. More personal. As a child, she'd made coffee for her mother as a hangover cure. Of course, as an adult, she now knew it was an old wives' tale more than scientific fact, but at the time, she'd felt comforted, less helpless. She didn't realize coffee would grow from a lifeline to a lifelong passion. And she certainly never expected to share it with her mother like this, on positive terms, apart from a desperate remedy.

She swallowed past the tightness in her throat. "I couldn't have done it better myself." Before the tears came, she turned away, calling, "I'll be back shortly" over her shoulder as she followed Landon into the bright, crisp morning air.

"Must be nice to have your mom around," Landon said casually, falling in step beside her.

"It is." Cassie smiled. As a newcomer to town, Landon didn't know about her mother's past, and there was something refreshing in the innocent simplicity of his comment.

"You have news?" she asked, trying not to get her hopes up. What if the software had worked after all? What if she no longer needed to prod her mother for more information and risk ruining the delicate rapport she'd coveted for so long?

"Not good news, I'm afraid." Landon offered an apologetic grimace. "Steve's program keeps hitting a wall. He needs more information. I know it was a long time ago, but is there anything your mom can tell you about your dad?"

Cassie's heart sank, although she knew she shouldn't be surprised. "I'll try to find an opportunity to ask her." She'd invited her to Maggie's for dinner that night, but her mother already had other plans, the details of which she hadn't volunteered. Previously, Cassie would've suspected the worst. But these days, she tried to give her the benefit of the doubt. She didn't mind if her mother kept a *few* secrets, but some details —like the identity of her own father—she had the right to know. Didn't she?

"Great. Let me know what you find out, and I'll pass it along to Steve."

"Thanks, Landon. I really appreciate it." They paused in front of Thistle & Thorn, and Cassie did a double take at the display of vintage baby items in the window. Silver rattles and glass bottles sparkled in the sunlight. It had to be a coincidence. Surely the news hadn't made it around town yet.

She glanced at Landon, but he appeared completely unaware as he bid her goodbye, promising to stop by the café later that afternoon for the rolls. As he strode toward Sadie's Sweet Shop, he passed two men unloading an an ultramarine chaise lounge from the back of a delivery van.

With one man positioned on either side, they lugged the hefty piece of furniture toward the antiques shop, and Cassie tugged the bright teal door, holding it ajar as they maneuvered the awkwardly shaped item through the opening.

"Delivery for Penny Heart," one of the men grunted, starting to lose his grip.

"Over here, please." Penny sprang from behind the register and directed them to an open space near the back of the shop that she'd prepared beforehand.

The two men unceremoniously plopped the chaise lounge on its delicate, hand-carved legs, and Cassie waited for Penny to sign and pay for the delivery before rushing over to admire it.

"Penn, it's gorgeous." She ran a hand along the sloping

back, relishing the feel of the silky upholstery beneath her fingertips. "Is it yours?"

"Sadly, no. I tracked it down for a client. But it is beautiful, isn't it?"

"It's stunning. But why did the man say the delivery was for Penny Heart? Didn't you change your last name to Davis?"

"Legally, yes. But I use my maiden name for some business transactions. My dad's reputation still carries weight with some dealers and collectors, and I don't want to lose the advantage. The world of antiques and collectibles can be surprisingly competitive."

"That makes sense." Cassie sat down, letting her weight sink into the soft cushion. "It's a shame you can't keep it, though. This might be the most exquisite chaise lounge I've ever seen."

"It's technically a fainting couch. They're similar, but the armrest is one of the big distinctions."

"Fainting couch?" Cassie echoed, the term tapping on her brain for some reason.

"Historians believe the name originated in the Victorian era, back when corsets restricted oxygen flow and caused women to faint frequently," Penny explained.

"Faint…" Cassie murmured, filtering through her thoughts. When she suddenly connected the dots, she dug her phone out of her back pocket, brimming with excitement.

"What?" Penny asked, peering at her quizzically. "You look like you just picked the winning lottery numbers."

"Better than that." Cassie opened her folder of recent photos, scrolling until she found the snapshot she'd taken of Edwin's riddle. "I think the clue we've been missing is in the last line," she said, then read aloud.

"'You asked for a favor, and I'll happily oblige. Your father was a friend, a truly great guy. He liked solving riddles, hiding treasure to find. Let's see if his daughter is of the same mind. If you can solve all the riddles to a count of four, then the diary you seek will surely be yours. But be warned, lest you quit before you start. These clues of mine aren't for the faint of Heart.'"

She turned her phone around so Penny could see the screen. "Look at the last word. The *H* in Heart is capitalized like a proper noun."

Penny frowned. "How come I didn't notice that before?"

"I didn't notice, either, but I bet it's referring to your last name."

"I think you're right, Cass." Penny's eyes brightened. "Not for the faint of Heart..." she repeated. "Do you think it's referring to the fainting couch?"

"It's a theory, at least."

"I suppose it's possible," Penny said thoughtfully. "Since my client wanted something so specific, I put feelers out to several dealers. And the collector community can be pretty small. With Edwin's connections, I suppose he could've found out about the delivery." She slid her palm into the crease between the cushions. "Still, it seems far-fetched, doesn't it?"

"You said he has an uncanny knack for making the impossible possible." Cassie crouched, feeling underneath. "It's worth a look."

They searched for several minutes without any luck, and Cassie's enthusiasm faltered. She'd been so certain she'd solved the riddle. If this didn't work, she doubted they'd ever figure it out.

Seconds away from giving up, Cassie grazed a small tear in

a seam with her fingertips. Her heartbeat skipped. Wiggling her fingers farther inside, she widened the opening. Her breath caught when she felt a thin, sharp edge. "I think I found something."

Penny dashed to her side, her coppery eyes wide in anticipation.

After dislodging the folded slip of paper, Cassie leaned back on her heels. This was it. Another clue! It had to be. She gingerly peeled back the corner, her pulse thrumming. The black typed font stood out against the stark white backdrop in four even lines.

"You solved the first clue, now for number two.
When the time is right, you'll know what to do.
But before I grant you your request,
All the birds must leave their nest."

Cassie met Penny's gaze, completely at a loss. "What do you think it means?"

Penny sighed and sank to her knees, crestfallen. "Honestly? I have no idea."

CHAPTER 11

CASSIE

Cassie removed the baking sheet of cauliflower from the oven, inhaling the rich, spicy scent. The lightly browned florets were a deep yellow hue and smelled of turmeric, cumin, and garlic. Cassie smiled. In her retirement, Luke's mother, Maggie, had taken a shine to traveling the world, and her newfound adventurous spirit had translated into her cooking. At first, Luke had worried about his mother gallivanting across the globe alone, but she'd found a company called Twilight Travel that specialized in all-inclusive tours for the over-sixty crowd. Or as the company's tagline described it: Luxury Tours for Your Twilight Years. She'd just returned from Costa Rica and seemed eager to compare travel notes with Colt, who'd visited the Central American country several times. But her youngest son had yet to arrive.

"Anything else I can do?" Cassie asked after scooping the cauliflower into a colorful serving dish.

"Can you arrange the naan in the warming basket?"

Maggie handed her a woven bread basket with a heated stone on the bottom, tucked beneath a cotton cloth.

"I'd be happy to."

Maggie lifted the thick, pillowy flatbread off the skillet with a large spatula and gently slid it into the basket Cassie held aloft. Her movements seemed smoother and more spritely than ever. Traveling suited her. In the few years since she'd retired and sold her bakery to Cassie and Eliza, she'd gone on an Alaskan cruise, toured Greece, India, the Netherlands, and Costa Rica. In addition to smiling more often, her formerly round, soft figure looked leaner and stronger, and her skin glowed with a rosy hue.

For a brief moment, Cassie wondered if a grandchild would put a damper on her travels, which clearly made her happy. This baby would impact more lives than hers and Luke's.

"Sorry I'm late." Penny swept into the kitchen carrying a large cardboard box. "I was waiting for Colt, but he's still at the restaurant, so I decided to drive separately." Her tone was apologetic with a whisper of disappointment. She set the box on the counter.

"That's all right, dear." Maggie welcomed her daughter-in-law with a kiss on the cheek.

"Maggie, you look fantastic." Penny admired the older woman's flowy pant suit printed with a pretty floral pattern. "Costa Rica suits you."

"Thank you, dear. Must be all the sunshine and tropical air." She patted her short-cropped ebony curls. "But the humidity did a number on my hair." The dark coils shimmered with streaks of silver and had a little extra flounce than usual.

"Your hair looks wonderful, as always." Penny slipped

around the kitchen island to give Cassie a hug. "Long time no see," she said with a smile.

"Any more thoughts on the riddle?" Cassie asked, returning her embrace.

"Not yet."

"Riddle?" Maggie slid a cinnamon coffee cake out of the oven and set it on the counter to cool.

Taking turns, Cassie and Penny regaled Maggie with the details of their treasure hunt, ending with the most recent clue.

"How curious," Maggie mused. "It sounds like a tricky one, but you girls will figure it out." She gazed at them with motherly affection. "I'm really proud of you both for stepping in to protect the library. Bryce's mother, Anne, would be mortified that he even considered selling it." She shook her head, clicking her tongue to make a *tsk-tsk* sound. "I blame the father for how that boy turned out. Two peas in a pod, those two. I could say more, but it's not polite to speak ill of the departed."

"How about some good news, then?" Penny opened the flaps of the cardboard box. "Wait until you see what I brought."

"What is it?" Cassie took a peek inside.

"Maggie's cuckoo clock. It had been acting up, so I sent it to a repair shop I've worked with before. I used my dad's name, and they not only fixed the mechanism, they refurbished the entire thing. It looks brand-new. It took two weeks, but I didn't think you'd mind, Maggie, since you weren't home."

Maggie wiped her hands on her apron before coming over to take a look. Her full heart-shaped face broke into a smile. "Penny, it looks beautiful! Like the day I first stumbled upon it in the *Weihnachtsmarkt*." Her features softened at the memory. "Leonard used to fix it whenever it went on the fritz, even though the noise drove him batty. He'd be pleased to see how well they took care of it."

For a moment, Maggie seemed to travel back to the past, and not for the first time, Cassie wished she'd been able to meet Luke's father. His parents had shared a special bond, one she hoped she and Luke would emulate for their own children one day.

Their first Christmas together, Cassie had gifted Luke a cuckoo clock as an expression of her unconditional love. In return, he'd given her a hand-carved ornament shaped like her grandmother's cottage. Inside, she found a dainty gold necklace. Her fingertips instinctively found the small pendant at her throat, tracing the outline of the solid gold coffee cup, landing on the tiny diamond in the center.

These early years of courtship and marriage had been filled with romance and thoughtful gestures. Would all that change when long strolls by the river and intimate, late-night meals became midnight feedings and the constant consoling of a crying infant?

"Luke, dear," Maggie called to her son in the adjacent dining room where she'd tasked him with setting the table.

Cassie's pulse stuttered as he strode into the kitchen. He'd worn her favorite forest green button-down that highlighted the gold flecks in his hazel eyes.

He caught her staring and tossed her a wink, making her stomach flutter. He'd been giddy all evening, eager to share the news with his family. Once Colt arrived, they'd all be present, ready for the big reveal. Well, everyone except her mother.

Not for the first time, Cassie wished her mother could be a

part of these gatherings. She wanted to share this piece of her life with her, to merge her two families, new and old. It had never seemed possible before, but maybe now, there was hope?

"Will you hang this back on the wall for me?" Maggie asked, gingerly removing the clock from the cardboard box.

"Sure thing." Luke lifted it from his mother's hands, flashing a grin at Penny. "You had them remove the sound box, right?"

"Sorry, that cost extra," Penny teased.

Everyone, including Maggie, shared a lighthearted laugh.

"What'd I miss?" Colt Davis breezed into the room as if he weren't almost forty minutes late.

"Nothing," Penny quipped, stiffening as Colt bent to kiss her hello.

Cassie immediately sensed Penny's annoyance at her husband's tardiness, but the second their lips met, she melted in his arms. Whatever issues they had, clearly no love was lost.

Colt's hand slid around Penny's waist, resting on the small of her back, and when their lips finally parted, he appeared to whisper "I missed you" before lightly kissing her temple.

Cassie's heart warmed at the intimate exchange. For all their differences—and the sparks that occasionally ignited as a result—they made an incredible team and an endearing couple who loved each other fiercely.

"Hey, Mom. You look great." Colt stooped to kiss his mother's cheek next. "Sorry I'm late. I'm working on a new salad for the inn utilizing local, in-season produce. I've brought some for you guys to try." He set a large Tupperware container on the counter then tapped a box of candy tucked beneath his arm. "I also grabbed some of Sadie's triple-chocolate truffles to celebrate your triumphant return."

Luke grabbed her hand and gave it a quick squeeze. From the look on his face, he couldn't wait a second longer.

"We have some big news to add to tonight's celebration." His grin grew wider, as if he couldn't contain his excitement. "We're having a baby!"

Penny squealed and launched herself at Cassie, throwing her arms around her in unbridled delight while Maggie gasped and covered her mouth with both hands. Tears glistened in her eyes as she glanced from Luke to Cassie then back to her son.

"Congratulations, old man." Colt clapped a hand on his brother's shoulder. "I've always thought I'd make an awesome uncle."

"A decent one, at least," Luke teased, and Cassie watched the two brothers in amusement, both playing it cool while the shimmer in their misty eyes betrayed their soft, gooey centers.

"How are you feeling?" Maggie asked when it was her turn to hug the mother-to-be.

"Pretty good, all things considered. Tired, mostly. And constantly hungry."

"Oh, goodness. You poor dear. Let's eat, let's eat!" Maggie gestured for everyone to grab one of the serving dishes then herded them into the dining room. "I want to hear all the details!"

Luke quickly mounted the cuckoo clock before joining Cassie at the table. With one arm slung across the back of her chair, he filled in the gaps of the story whenever she paused to take another bite. By the time they'd finished dinner and moved on to dessert, they'd made plans to host a gathering at the café the following evening to announce the news to all their friends.

For the first time since seeing those two pink lines, all of

Cassie's fears and apprehensions slipped into the background, muffled by the outpouring of love and support. For the first time, she didn't worry about being good enough. And for the first time, she felt nothing but pure, unsullied excitement for the adventure that lay ahead of them.

"We should probably get going." Luke glanced at the clock. "It's almost nine, and I try to get these two in bed before ten."

These two... Cassie smiled. Her husband couldn't be more adorable.

"I'll pack up some leftovers." As Maggie scooted back her chair, the cuckoo clock struck nine.

Colt released a good-natured groan as the tiny door sprang open, followed by the trademark sound.

Cuckoo, cuckoo, cuckoo.

Cassie stared, suddenly captivated by the clock's unique design. Instead of one bird springing forward at regular intervals, two small lovebirds sat on a single nest.

"You noticed it, too?" Penny leaned across the table, her voice breathy.

"Noticed what?" Colt asked.

"You think the next clue is in my cuckoo clock?" Maggie's eyes widened, her gaze darting between Cassie and Penny in disbelief.

"What clue?" Colt turned to Luke. "Do you know what's going on?"

Luke shook his head.

"It's possible," Cassie told Maggie, taking out her phone. Her fingers trembled slightly in anticipation. What were the odds that they'd solve two riddles in one day? "'You solved the first clue, now for number two,'" she read aloud. "'When the time is right, you'll know what to do. But before I grant you your request, all the birds must leave their nest.'"

"Wait." Colt glanced at his wife. "Is this the scavenger hunt you were talking about the other day? The one with the nutty billionaire and some old diary?" He didn't wait for a response before adding, "You think he hid a clue in my mother's clock?"

"We found this clue in a fainting couch I had delivered today," Penny told him. "But that's not even the craziest story. I did some research this afternoon, and learned that once, when Edwin wanted a particular diary that supposedly belonged to Amelia Earhart, he tracked down the owner on a private island in the South Pacific. And it was completely off-the-grid."

"I don't like it." Colt's turquoise-blue eyes flashed with a protective glint. "I don't like the idea that this guy has access to Mom's clock and your couch. It's creepy."

"He's harmless, I promise," Penny assured him. "He was friends with my dad."

This news seemed to only marginally mollify his concerns.

"Should we see if the clue's even in there?" Luke stood and carefully lifted the clock from the wall.

They all watched with bated breath as Luke gently laid it facedown on the table. Taking out his pocket knife, he removed the tiny screws keeping the protective backing in place. An astonished hush settled around the room as he retrieved a small slip of paper.

"Well, I'll be," Maggie breathed.

"Am I the only one who finds this a little stalkery?" Colt asked, crossing his arms in front of his chest.

"Shh," Penny quieted her husband with a wave of her hand, then asked, "What does it say?"

Luke unfolded the note and cleared his throat. "'Roses are red, violets are blue. But sometimes it's nice to mix the two.'"

He looked up, baffled. "Does that mean anything to any of you?"

"Not to me," Penny confessed.

"Me, either," Cassie admitted. "But I know someone who might be able to help."

CHAPTER 12

DONNA

D onna tightened her grip on the steering wheel as her car rattled down the dilapidated dirt road, lurching violently at every pothole and protruding rock and root. What was she doing here? Maybe she should've accepted Cassie's invitation to dinner at Maggie's. After all, wasn't it time she overcame her issues with Luke's mother?

The last few days in Poppy Creek had been an exhausting exercise in avoidance. She constantly looked over her shoulder, afraid of who she might find. How much longer could she live like this? That much anxiety couldn't be healthy. And the desire to drink, to escape and forget, weighed more heavily each day. She needed a meeting now more than ever.

When she reached the end of the road, she nudged the gear shift into park and sat motionless, too stunned to even unbuckle her seat belt. She should have suspected the enigmatic bartender lived somewhere unusual when Jack's directions consisted of a left turn off Old Highway onto Quail Road, followed by another left past the hollow log, then a precarious ramble down an unpaved road until she reached the big boulder. But she'd expected to find a small cabin, maybe even a yurt, not *this*.

The edge of the river hugged the grassy bank, framed by cattails swaying in the breeze. A striking figure stood by the water's edge, fishing rod in hand, his lean frame highlighted by the burnished glow of the setting sun. A few yards away, a vintage Airstream—with more scrapes and dents than her decrepit Corolla—sparkled in the soft golden hue. A long strand of string lights stretched between the awning and two pine trees, creating a twinkling canopy over a pair of battered camping chairs neatly patched with duct tape. Smoke curled from a simple charcoal grill, and Johnny Cash's gravelly baritone rippled through the reeds.

To some, the scene might evoke a sad, almost pitying sentiment. On the surface, the man had very little to call his own. But to Donna, the serene simplicity beckoned to her soul, conjuring emotions she hadn't felt in a long time.

The man responsible for the idyllic setting turned, his face registering surprise, then delight when he spotted her. He reeled in his line, and Donna gathered a breath, summoning the courage to exit the car.

"Are you stalking me?" His voice held a teasing quality, but she supposed tracking him down and showing up at his house unannounced did seem a little strange. She really needed to start thinking before she acted.

"I asked for you at the diner, and Jack sent me here." She cringed then quickly added, "I didn't ask *for* you. I asked to speak with you. And Jack gave me directions. I hope you don't mind." Why did she suddenly sound like a nervous schoolgirl? When it came to men, she usually held all the cards. Whatever this feeling was—the flustered, discombobulated, falling-through-the-air-without-a-parachute feeling—she wasn't a fan.

"I don't mind at all." He grinned, and she couldn't tell if it was merely friendly or flirtatious. "Are you hungry?"

"Oh, um…" The savory smell of grilled fish filled the air, and Donna's stomach released a loud growl. *The traitor.*

He chuckled. "I'll take that as a yes."

Her cheeks heated. She'd planned to eat at The Westerly again since Kat had insisted she stay, claiming the room would sit empty otherwise. And once again, Kat had refused her offer to pay, asking for yoga lessons instead. It hardly seemed like fair compensation, especially since she actually enjoyed her company.

"I don't want to intrude on your dinner," Donna told him. She'd simply say what she came to say, then take off. "I would've called first, but Jack said you don't get reception out here."

"You wouldn't be intruding. Especially if you have to catch your own meal." His eyes held a mischievous glint as he offered her the rod. "You know how to fish?"

She accepted his challenge with a smile. More at ease with the foam grip in her hand, she strode to the water's edge. Fixing her gaze upstream, she swept the rod over her right shoulder, then, with a swift, fluid motion, flicked it forward, releasing the line. The lure sailed through the air, effortlessly hitting her target.

He whistled. "I'm going to go out on a limb and say you've done this before."

"I've been casting reels since I could walk. My dad taught me." Her chest tightened at the unwelcome flood of memories.

"Think he'd give me a lesson?"

"He... died." It had been over three decades, yet the words still lodged in her throat.

"Sorry to hear that." His tone bore the soft edges of someone who'd experienced a similar loss.

She met his gaze, and his eyes held hers, unguarded and unwavering. In that split second, she felt more seen and understood than she had in years. How could someone communicate so much in one simple glance? A strange warmth burned in her chest, radiating outward. She wanted to look away—to sever the disconcerting connection—but she couldn't move.

A tug on the line yanked her back to safety. Focusing her thoughts on the task at hand, she cranked the reel, grateful for the distraction.

For the next several minutes, they took turns with the fishing rod, exchanging innocuous anecdotes about their biggest catches. As they moved from catching fish to cooking them, she finally learned his name and that he'd recently moved to Poppy Creek from southern California to be near his son.

"It's a big change," he confessed, flipping the freshly caught trout to sear the other side. "But I like it here. I like the slow pace and the honest, down-to-earth people. They're real salt of the earth folk, you know?"

Not sure what to say, Donna took a sip of water from the tin mug and shifted slightly in the folding chair set near the crackling campfire. The flickering flames did double duty—dispelling the cool, evening air and roasting their baked potatoes wrapped in tinfoil.

"How are things going with your daughter?" he asked as if sensing the need for a topic change.

"Honestly? Better than I could've hoped for. She's giving

me the second chance I don't deserve." She took another sip and swallowed her nerves. She'd talked about her past before, mostly in AA meetings, but she'd always managed a degree of separation, like a safe perimeter, allowing outsiders a brief glimpse without ever inviting them inside. And yet, something about Rhett—an intangible quality that extended beyond their shared struggles—had unlocked a hidden door. "For most of my daughter's life, I was an unbearable drunk. It's a miracle we both survived. You can't even imagine the pain I've put her through."

"I think I can," he said softly, his gaze never leaving the grill. For a moment, he seemed lost in his own regrets, and the gentle rush of the river filled the silence.

Something in his expression—the mixture of empathy and anguish—struck a chord. Maybe they had even more in common than she thought?

"As desperately as I'd like to fix the past, I know I can't." She swallowed again, this time finding it more difficult. "But I can move forward, praying I don't repeat it. Which is why I'm here." Taking a deep breath, she said, "If your offer still stands, I'd like to start a recovery meeting in Poppy Creek. For anyone who needs it. I've learned the hard way that I can't do this on my own." As she said the words, she realized she meant so much more than her sobriety.

CHAPTER 13

RHETT

R hett studied Donna's features in the firelight, finding it hard to look away. She was beautiful, there was no denying that. But there was something else about her he found even more alluring. She had this soft strength paired with a raw humility and gritty resilience. The kind of resilience born from brokenness, from facing the ugliest part of yourself without flinching. The kind of resilience bred on your knees, head bent, soul bared. The kind of resilience he recognized.

"I spent most of Vick's life in prison." His confession hovered in the air like an apparition, ghoulish and grim, and he fixed his gaze on the flames. "We met for the first time last fall. My own son. Born with his father behind bars." He shook his head, leaning forward toward the edge of the chair, fighting the urge to stand and pace. "After my incarceration, his mother filed for divorce and told Vick I'd abandoned them. Not that I blame her. In a way, I had."

He stole a glance in Donna's direction, fully expecting to see a look of disgust. Maybe even horror or apprehension.

But he saw only compassion in her eyes. "I served time for armed robbery. My gun was fake, but my buddy's wasn't. He shot a security guard who almost died." The words scratched against his throat, but he pressed on, needing her to know the whole story.

"Before that moment, if you would've asked me if I'd ever rob a bank, I would've laughed at the absurdity. I had no idea what I was capable of, given enough fear and desperation. When we ripped off that first ATM, all I could think about was my pregnant wife and how we could barely afford food, let alone formula and diapers. I didn't think about the innocent victims or even the consequences of getting caught. After the third ATM, reality had started to sink in. I couldn't sleep. Couldn't even look at myself in the mirror, let alone face my wife, who had no idea what I'd done. When I told Hank I wanted out, he convinced me to do one last job. A cakewalk, he'd said. No one would get hurt. The bank's insurance would cover the losses. And I could walk away for good and go back to being Mr. Family Man, as he so sarcastically put it. As if I could simply forget who I'd become." Rhett's lips contorted in a sad, sardonic smile. "That day didn't just change my life. It impacted everyone. The guard. His family. Every single terrified person in that bank. My son. And my wife—" His throat closed around her name. He hadn't been able to voice it since the day she died, as if passing the syllables through his undeserving lips would sully her memory.

He hung his head, no longer able to lift it. He'd come to terms with so much about his past, learned to let go, to use his story to help others. But some things... some things sank like a hook in your soul, penetrating too deep to dig out.

For several seconds, neither of them made a sound. When Donna finally spoke, her words rang faint and familiar. "God, grant us the serenity to accept the things we cannot change, the courage to change the things we can, and the wisdom to know the difference."

Recognizing the well-known serenity prayer recited by recovering addicts worldwide, he glanced up and met her gaze. Her eyes shimmered with a soft, intimate understanding, as if she could relate to his unspoken thoughts.

"Is this our first unofficial meeting?" he teased, his heart lifting.

"All we're missing is the stale coffee."

"Not much I can do about the stale part, but I've got coffee?" He let his raised inflection act as an invitation.

"Coffee would be nice."

He stood, struggling to settle his racing heartbeat as he hopped inside the Airstream to grab his AeroPress and bag of beans. "I guarantee you're about to have the best coffee you've ever tasted. And I'm not just saying that because my son roasted it." He set a kettle on the makeshift grill over the flames. "They serve it at the café in town. Have you been yet?"

"My daughter owns it." Her smile radiated motherly pride. "Well, co-owns it with Eliza."

"You're Cassie's mom? She's a great kid."

"Thank you. I agree. No thanks to me."

"I can say the same thing about Vick," he admitted. "He's everything a father could hope for. Brave, strong, selfless, kind. He's an ex-Marine. He risked his life for our freedom while I gave all my freedom away." The freshly roasted beans released a rich, heady aroma as they crackled in the old-fashioned, hand-crank grinder.

"Like you said, we do a lot of things we regret out of desperation. Desperation to survive. Desperation to forget." She spoke the last words softly before nudging one of the smoldering logs with the heel of her shoe. It crumbled into glowing coals and sent sparks skittering into the night sky.

He wanted to ask what she'd hoped to forget, but something in her pained expression told him to leave it be... for now. Instead, he finished preparing the coffee and handed her a steaming mug before rejoining her by the fire. "Black okay?"

"That's perfect, thanks."

They sipped in silence for a few minutes, serenaded by the crackling logs and soothing cadence of croaking bullfrogs.

"This is a nice setup. It's peaceful." Her body relaxed into the chair, and she leaned her head back, gazing up at the glittering assembly of stars scattered across a black canopy striped with deep violet hues.

"It's not much, but it's what I needed. To be immersed in nature, to see the stars." He reclined, following her gaze toward the heavens. "It's funny what you suddenly miss when you no longer have access to it. I never gave constellations much thought before prison, but now I can name and find most of them."

"I'm jealous. They're beautiful, in concept. But I can barely find the Big Dipper."

"It's not hard when you know what you're looking for." He set his mug on one of the flatter stones circling the firepit. "Come on. I'll show you." Leading her several feet away from the glowing flames, he stopped by the river's edge. A bullfrog splashed into the water, creating a wake of moonlit ripples. "Let's start with Ursa Major, the largest constellation you can see in the northern hemisphere. It looks like a bear, and the Big Dipper makes up the bear's back and tail, so we can start there."

"Okay..." she said slowly, not sounding convinced. After squinting at the sky for several seconds, she pointed toward a formation of stars resembling a bowl and handle. "That's the Big Dipper, right?"

He took a step closer, until they stood shoulder to shoulder, and followed the tip of her finger. "Yep. That's it. Now, trace from the bottom of the bowl down, and you'll make out the bear's back legs. See?"

"No." She frowned. "It just looks like a bunch of tiny dots to me."

"Here." Shifting to stand behind her, he reached for her hand to help guide her finger but froze the second his skin touched hers. An unexpected surge of adrenaline raced up his arm, sending his pulse into overdrive. He swallowed. *Get it together.* "Start here, then connect the dots."

She tilted her head back slightly, and her hair brushed his chin. Her soft, silky hair that smelled like mint and sweet basil. *Focus.* "The hind legs are made up of four stars. Tania Borealis, Tania Australis, Alula Borealis, and Alula Australis." He recited the scientific names, hoping to distract himself with something cerebral and technical, since her nearness had his thoughts whirling in other directions. "See it now?"

"I think so." Her voice rose with excitement. "That's the head. And the front leg is there, right?"

"Right."

"I can't believe I found it!" She flashed a grateful smile over her shoulder. "Thank you."

"You're welcome." The words escaped on autopilot. He couldn't focus on anything other than the close proximity of her mouth to his. Her lips looked full and soft, and for a fleeting moment, he wondered what they'd taste like. The thought startled him. He hadn't even considered kissing another woman since his wife. After her death, he'd resigned himself to a life alone, the life he deserved. So why did he find his head tilting downward and his body leaning, inching closer?

Donna met his gaze, her eyes wide and wary, but she didn't back away.

Somehow, his hand found her waist, but before he could draw her into his arms, a twig snapped.

His head jerked toward the sound, and his heart lurched.

The shocked features illuminated by moonlight belonged to his son.

CHAPTER 14

CASSIE

As Cassie approached the Sterling Rose Estate, she rolled down her driver's-side window, inhaling the sweet, ambrosial scent carried on the breeze. To her right, fragrant apple blossoms stretched on for miles, while on her left, rows of vibrant blooms in every shape and color imaginable created a rainbow on earth.

Visiting the flower farm and event venue always had a knack for settling her nerves, as if the fresh, floral air had healing properties. Her thoughts kept tumbling between the festival and the fate of the library, all the uncertainty surrounding their rapidly changing lives, and the strange behavior of her mother that morning.

Her mom had arrived at the café a few minutes late, and her eyes were dry and bloodshot as if she'd lain awake all night crying. Or worse. Cassie hated that her mind still jumped to alcohol, but some habits were hard to break. Like drinking.

When she'd asked her mother if she was all right, she'd been assured that everything was fine. She'd even managed a smile to assuage her concerns. And yet, Cassie couldn't shake the feeling that something had happened last night. Something her mother didn't want her to know about. Was it possible that while she'd been celebrating with friends, rejoicing over the new life growing inside her, her mother had returned to her old ways?

Battling her mounting worries, she breathed deeply, winding along the gravel road until she reached the end and parked her Prius by a potted conifer. A stunning Victorian-era greenhouse rose up before her, its glittering glass windows framed by oxidized iron, the green hue an unexpected and arresting sight against the pale blue sky.

Her spirits lifted at the pleasant sound of laughter, and she followed it around the back of the greenhouse. She paused, smiling at the adorable vignette.

Olivia Parker knelt before a row of bright red ranunculus, laughing as her fiancé, Reed—who already bore a muddy stripe across his forehead—wiped a smudge of dirt on her cheek. Not to be outdone, Olivia scooped a handful of loose soil and smeared it across the front of his white T-shirt. In turn, Reed playfully tackled her to the ground, tickling her mercilessly while Olivia swatted him with her wide-brimmed sun hat.

Cassie covered her mouth, stifling a laugh. Although they'd been dating for less than a year, she admired the couple's sure-footed yet fun and playful relationship, which had been built on a lifetime of friendship. And the fact that Reed Hollis —a sweet, sentimental soul with an uncanny affinity for flowers—had pined for Olivia since his youth, and helped repair her broken heart after a painful divorce, made their story all the more beautiful.

Olivia managed to wriggle free and sprang to her feet.

Spotting Cassie, she shouted breathlessly, "Quick! Pass me the hose!"

Grinning, Cassie tossed her the nozzle then manned the faucet. "Just say the word."

As Olivia wielded her weapon of choice, Reed stood and raised both hands, chuckling as he said, "Okay, I surrender."

"Good." Beaming triumphantly, Olivia dropped the hose. "You showed up just in time, Cass."

"Happy I could help. And I actually have a favor to ask in return."

"Does this favor include me?" Reed asked, brushing the dirt from his torso. "If not, I'll go grab a clean T-shirt."

"It may, but I'll give Olivia a crack at it first. Feel free to change."

"Thanks." As he passed them on the way to his vintage VW van, he gave Olivia a quick kiss.

Cassie couldn't help noticing the way her friend's fair complexion flushed with happiness, accentuating her faint smattering of freckles. Or the way her gaze followed Reed to his van, never wavering until he disappeared down the gravel drive.

Cassie looped her arm through Olivia's. "You two are the cutest couple. I can't wait for your wedding."

"Me, either." While her words matched the sentiment, her wistful, somber tone gave Cassie pause.

"Is there something wrong with the wedding?" Cassie found it hard to imagine. As an event coordinator—who ran a successful business in New York for several years before moving back to Poppy Creek last spring—Olivia had planned more weddings than flowers filled the field. Surely whatever hiccup she'd encountered wouldn't be too much of a hurdle. At least, not enough for serious concern.

"Not wrong, per se. But something about it doesn't feel quite right."

"What do you mean?"

"To be honest, I don't know." Olivia twisted her bare foot into the ground, her expression pensive. "I thought I knew exactly what I wanted. After all, I'd planned the wedding of my dreams when I married Steven, then had to change every single detail to fit his idea of the perfect calling card for our event-planning business. Suddenly, our wedding went from elegant and timeless to showy and over-the-top. When Reed and I got engaged, all my old, original ideas came rushing back, but now I'm not sure if it feels like *us*." She breathed a heavy sigh. "I don't know, Cass. The wedding will be beautiful, there's no doubt about that. Maybe I'm overthinking it?"

"Maybe. But it's also okay to change your mind."

"You're right and ever the voice of reason, per usual." Olivia smiled. "I'll give it some more thought. Now, what's this favor you mentioned?"

Cassie briefly explained the situation then recited the riddle, which she'd committed to memory. "'Roses are red, violets are blue. And sometimes it's nice to mix the two.'"

"How curious. It's not much information, is it?"

"No, it's not. But since it mentions violets and roses, I thought you or Reed might have a few ideas."

"You know what it makes me think of…" Olivia trailed off and shook her head. "No, that would be impossible."

"What? Believe me. Nothing you can think of will be any more impossible than what Edwin's already pulled off."

"Do you remember the hybrid rose Reed created? The one that won the competition at the Primrose Valley festival?"

"I do." Cassie smiled. The petals were the same color as Olivia's eyes—an exquisite and unusual shade of violet. As the connection hit, she asked, "Did Reed ever make more than one?"

"No. And it was featured in a few magazines and online publications, so it's possible someone like Edwin would know about it."

"Where is it?"

"In the greenhouse."

As Cassie followed her inside, her heartbeat quickened. If they got this right, they would solve two more clues in less than twenty-four hours, which would leave only one left. At this rate, they had a decent shot of finding the diary before the festival. She couldn't wait to tell the planning committee during their meeting in a few hours.

Olivia wove through the rows of seedlings and potting stations, stopping at a cozy seating area in back. A small patio set sat tucked into an alcove bathed in sunlight. On an antique marble table in the center, a single rosebush served as a focal point. Although she'd seen it before, Cassie froze, mesmerized by the extraordinary pigment of each petal. "I always forget how striking the color is."

"It is beautiful, isn't it?" Olivia flushed again. Her friend must feel so loved each time she laid eyes on it—a one-of-a-kind rose created just for her. "But I don't know where someone would hide a diary or another clue."

Cassie came closer, studying the cupped blooms from every angle. Olivia had a point. "What about in the pot? Or the dirt?"

"The dirt?" Olivia frowned.

"I know it sounds crazy. But humor me."

"Okay…" Olivia dug her bare hands into the warm earth, sifting through clumps of dirt until her eyes widened.

"What? Did you find something?"

"I think so." Dumbfounded, Olivia lifted a clear plastic bag. "There's something inside." She shook off the grainy flecks of soil before breaking the seal. "I can't." She passed the bag to Cassie. "This is too weird."

"You have no idea." Cassie chuckled, pulling out the note.

"You've made it this far, the end is in sight. You'll find the diary second to the right. Keep going till you reach morning light. Then I'll bid you farewell; it's been a delight."

"And I thought it couldn't get any stranger," Olivia said with an incredulous shake of her head. "What do you think it means?"

"I'm not sure, but we've had pretty good luck solving them so far."

"Maybe someone at tonight's get-together will be able to offer some insight?"

"Good idea. I'll be sure to ask around."

"What's the impromptu gathering for, anyway?"

"Do we really need a reason?" Cassie kept her tone light, but she could barely contain the news.

"I guess not." Olivia laughed. "It will be nice to have an evening to relax. Between work, wedding planning, and organizing the festival, I could use a night off. And speaking of the festival, are we still meeting with the historical society at the café? If so, I'll have Reed meet me there afterward rather than riding over together later tonight."

"Yes, we are. My mom has been helping out so I can focus more of my time on the fundraising efforts. I've already garnered commitments for several silent auction items as well as some impressive prizes for the raffle. I just need to collect them all."

"That's wonderful. I look forward to meeting her. According to Kat, she's quite a remarkable woman."

"She is." Cassie managed a smile despite the faint whispers of worry worming their way into the forefront of her mind.

What happened last night? And why wouldn't her mother talk about it?

CHAPTER 15

DONNA

Donna wiped the frothing nozzle, watching her daughter from the corner of her eye.

Cassie sat at a large round table with several women from the historical society. Although many of them were decades older than Cassie, Donna couldn't help noticing their obvious fondness and respect. Cassie was the kind of woman everyone admired. What must it be like to live that kind of life?

A heaviness settled around her as she recalled her almost-kiss with Rhett last night. At least, she'd thought he was about to kiss her. But when his son arrived, Rhett jumped away like he'd been caught doing something he shouldn't. And the look on his face... Was it guilt? Shame? Her heart squeezed at the vivid image permanently imprinted in her mind.

Of course he'd been embarrassed. She wasn't the kind of woman men bragged about dating. At least, not good, honorable men. The kind of men she dated loved her for her appearance and what they thought she could offer them—a fun time without strings attached. Strings like human decency and consideration for her feelings. Why would someone like her have feelings?

She rubbed her eyes with the back of her hand, wincing at their tenderness. Why had Rhett's reaction affected her so deeply? She hadn't cried like that in years. And only once over a boy. She didn't get emotionally involved. She didn't get her heart broken.

But with Rhett, something had felt different. She'd thought he understood her. That he could see the *real* her, past her failings and flaws, beyond her brokenness to the heart of who she was—someone redeemable. But if a man like Rhett, who'd forged his own second chance, couldn't see any good in her—anything worthwhile—then maybe it wasn't there at all.

The only silver lining from the ordeal? Despite every urge, every need to dull the pain, she'd resisted the temptation to drink. And for that reason alone—to maintain her promise of sobriety to herself and her daughter—she'd face Rhett again. She'd attend the recovery meeting tonight and pretend she hadn't even noticed his blatant rejection.

Feeling an uncomfortable tingle in the back of her throat, she shoved the hurtful memory aside and grabbed the tray of drinks she'd prepared. Forcing a smile, she strode to Cassie's table. "Here you are, ladies."

"Thank you! These look fabulous." Cassie surveyed the selection. "Let's see, the lavender rose latte is for Olivia."

"It smells heavenly! Thank you." The tall brunette with dirt beneath her fingernails flashed a friendly smile as she wrapped her hands around the large, round mug. "It's a pleasure to finally meet you, Miss Hayward. I've heard such wonderful things about you."

Donna blinked in surprise. She was used to people

gossiping behind her back, but never about anything good. "It's nice to meet you as well. And please, call me Donna."

"Donna, got it." Olivia smiled again and sipped her latte while Cassie reacquainted her with the rest of the women.

Dolores, who'd ordered the peppermint tea, looked familiar, and not simply because she bore a shocking resemblance to Mrs. Claus. Donna recalled briefly meeting her during one of her previous visits last year. And, if she wasn't mistaken, her husband had been her high school principal.

Donna recognized the elegant woman with silver hair twisted into a loose chignon from the library. As a child, when she'd go there to study, Beverly regularly offered her a new book recommendation. Of course, Donna never read any of them, preferring to spend her free time outside climbing trees or fishing with her dad, but she never forgot how the kind, persistent woman kept trying. Even after Donna became the pregnant teen pariah and everyone else had given up on her altogether.

"And Maggie," Cassie said, interrupting her thoughts, "you have the decaf cinnamon mochaccino."

"Thank you, dear." Offering Donna a warm smile, Maggie asked, "Won't you join us? I'm sure Ryder can help the next few customers."

Donna glanced over her shoulder, catching Ryder midbite as he shoved an entire red velvet cupcake into his mouth. "Thanks, but I should probably keep an eye on him before we don't have anything left to sell." As she returned behind the counter, she couldn't shake a tiny pang of guilt for rebuffing Maggie's invitation. The woman had never been anything but gracious and kind, extending her every opportunity to be friends. Why couldn't she accept her offer? After all, they weren't merely in-laws anymore. They were co-grandmothers. She couldn't avoid her forever.

The bell above the entrance chimed, and the second Frida Connelly strode through the front door, Donna was relieved she hadn't joined them. The older woman's cold gaze zeroed in on her like a laser pointer, turning her perpetually sour expression into an even deeper scowl.

Donna turned away, busying herself with the stack of napkins by the register. Frida had never been her biggest fan, and she didn't need another reason to question her self-worth. She was still trying to claw her way back from rock bottom.

"There's our lovely chairwoman." Cassie greeted Frida with her trademark unconditional kindness. "What would you like to drink before we get started?"

"I only drink water," Frida said stiffly. "Anything else is merely a gateway to the devil's brew." She shot Donna a pointed glare before taking her seat at the head of the table.

"One water coming right up." Grateful for an excuse to escape, Donna slipped into the kitchen. Although they had a self-serve jug of ice water on the counter, she had a feeling the persnickety woman would insist on being served.

In all her years waiting tables, she'd only been tempted to spit in someone's beverage once, when a handsy hedge fund manager had slapped her backside in front of his leering colleagues. He'd had the audacity to quip, "They sure don't make 'em like they used to, do they, boys?" before belting out an abrasive laugh. Although appalled, she'd refrained from tampering with his order, albeit *barely*.

While Frida Connelly might not be a boorish womanizer begging for a sexual harassment lawsuit, she didn't endear herself to many people, either. As the town gossip, judge, and jury, she delighted in doling out her disapproval. And over the years, Donna had received more than her fair share.

"Is Frida here?" Eliza asked as she poured pink batter into a scalloped-edged cupcake liner.

"How did you know?"

"The look of terror on your face is a dead giveaway." Eliza grinned.

Donna grabbed a freshly washed glass from the drying rack and filled it with filtered water. "You're lucky you can hide in here."

"You're welcome to join me. I'm almost done with the strawberry cream cupcakes, but I still have to make the blue raspberry ones."

"Pink and blue cupcakes. What else would you serve for a pregnancy reveal party?" Donna teased.

"Isn't it fun?" Eliza beamed. "The whole theme of tonight's party will be who can guess the news first. I've asked Jack to bring baby back ribs from the diner. And I'm also serving baby new potatoes, baby carrots, baby peas, and Babybel cheese."

"Subtle." Donna laughed.

"And that's not all! I asked Reed to bring bouquets of baby's breath to decorate the tables. And I asked Sadie and Landon to create a special dessert using molecular gastronomy, although I didn't tell them why."

"Molecular what?"

"Gastronomy. Don't worry, I don't really get what it is, either. Basically, they used some kind of scientific wizardry to transform Baby Ruth candy bars into bite-size balls of fluff that resemble the texture of cotton candy. It's surprisingly delicious."

"I wish I could try it." She'd told Cassie she couldn't stay for the party since she had her first Poppy Creek recovery meeting that night. While her daughter had expressed disappointment that she wouldn't attend the gathering, Donna hadn't missed the look of relief when she'd learned the reason why. Not that she blamed her. Having an alcoholic parent meant constant uncertainty, never knowing if and when they'd fall off the wagon. The unending anxiety was just another one of the many gifts she'd given her daughter over the years.

"I'll be sure to save some for you. But you'd better bring Frida her water before she calls out the hound dogs," Eliza warned playfully.

"Good point." Donna grimaced. "Wish me luck."

Donna delivered Frida's water—getting off easy with only a silent sneer—and quickly retreated back to the kitchen to help Eliza prepare for the party, which turned out to be a much larger gathering than she'd expected.

All the women from the meeting stayed afterward, except for Frida, who claimed to have other plans. Donna also recognized Cassie's brother and sister-in-law, Eliza's husband, Grant, and Jack and Kat, who immediately came over to say hello. She also met Olivia's fiancé, Reed, and another young couple who were so smitten, they hadn't stopped holding hands since they walked inside. She recalled meeting Sadie before—she owned the Sweet Shop—but Landon she knew only by reputation. Poppy Creek seemed like an unusual homebase for a billionaire philanthropist, but she understood his motivation. Love could make a person do crazy things. Like revisit ghosts from the past best left undisturbed.

A stylish blonde swept through the front door, immediately brightening the room with her wide, winsome smile. "Sorry I'm late. I had to finish uploading a video to my

YouTube channel, and the Wi-Fi was spotty. I keep telling my landlord he needs to get an extender out at the cabin. I might as well be living in the 1800s out there."

"Considering you don't pay rent, I'd say it's a fair arrangement," Jack teased.

"See, and I thought that was a special rate since I have to live next door to you," the girl fired back with a laugh.

She must be Jack's little sister, Lucy. Cassie mentioned she was some kind of social media influencer—a newfangled career Donna still didn't understand. And wasn't she dating—

Donna's heart ricocheted into her throat when a stoic, broad-chested man with tattoos and piercing gray eyes appeared by the girl's side.

"I don't know how you put up with her." Jack tossed him a good-natured grin.

"I think what you *mean* to say is, you don't know how I got so lucky." He slung his arm around the girl's shoulders, his expression bathed in a blissful glow. The kind of proud, doting glow of a man in love. The kind of glow she'd never inspired in anyone before. And likely, never would.

His smile instantly faded when their eyes met, replaced by a flicker of surprise. Similar to the startled expression she'd glimpsed last night when he'd arrived at Rhett's to return a book he'd borrowed. And the way he'd held her gaze—like a soldier assessing a potential threat—felt eerily familiar.

Vick's jaw flexed, and he looked poised to say something, but the bell above the front door jingled, drawing his attention.

Frank and Beverly Barrie ambled inside, Frank aided by his walking stick and his wife's arm. He took one glance at the odd assortment of food and decor and blurted, "Someone's got a bun in the oven?"

Gasps, squeals, and cheers of excitement exploded around the room, creating a celebratory cacophony of unrestrained delight as Luke and Cassie confirmed Frank's suspicion. The beaming couple disappeared in a sea of congratulatory hugs and tearful embraces, and Donna suddenly felt miles away, as if observing the scene from a great distance.

Taking advantage of the distraction, she removed her apron and slipped outside into the still night air. The street lamps had turned on, casting a soft blanket of light around the silent, sleepy town.

Glancing over her shoulder, she stole one final glimpse of the happy vignette of smiling, loving faces framed by large backlit windows.

Her daughter had built a life here, a family. And as she stood there on the quiet cobbled street, on the outside looking in, an overwhelming sense of loneliness settled around her like a heavy yoke she couldn't escape.

CHAPTER 16

DONNA

D onna briskly crossed the town square, hugging herself against a sudden nip in the air. With all the shops closed and the streets empty, she should have felt alone. And yet, she couldn't shake the unsettling premonition of being followed, of being watched.

She quickened her pace, nearly breaking into a run by the time she reached the meeting hall. The ancient steps groaned beneath her weight as she mounted them two at a time, hastening toward the door, a barrier to whatever—or whomever—lurked just beyond her sight.

A rush of warmth and light greeted her inside, along with the comforting aroma of freshly brewed coffee. For a fleeting instant, she felt safe. Until a familiar voice sent her pulse racing again.

"Hey. Glad you could make it." Rhett filled a paper cup with dark, velvety coffee from a silver urn and handed it to her like a peace offering, his expression both apologetic yet reserved. Something had definitely shifted since last night, as if he'd spent the moonlit hours erecting a wall around his heart instead of sleeping.

"Thanks." She gave a slight smile, accepting the coffee along with the new status quo.

"We were just about to get started." He gestured toward the modest gathering of members already seated. The circle consisted of a woman in a wheelchair she didn't recognize, Mac Houston, owner of the local market, and— Donna did a double take. Frida Connelly? What on earth was she doing here?

Frida sipped from her water bottle, her placid gaze fixed on a glossy show bill advertising Sylvia Carter's one-woman performance of *Macbeth in Mime* as if Donna didn't exist.

Stunned, Donna sank into the vacant seat beside the woman in the wheelchair while Rhett took the one between Frida and Mac.

"I want to thank you all for coming tonight," he said, glancing around the circle. "When I posted the flyer on Mac's bulletin board at the market this morning, I had no idea if anyone would show up, especially on such short notice. But I'm grateful you all took the time to be here and give this meeting a chance. While we aren't officially affiliated with any particular recovery group, I would like to follow a similar format. Specifically, the anonymity. Whatever you share in this room will stay in this room, including your attendance and your reason for being here. This is a safe space for support and accountability. And while how much you decide to share is up to you, I'd like to encourage all of us to be as open as possible so we can get the most out of the experience. Sound good?"

They all nodded and voiced their agreement. Except for Frida. She took another sip of water and continued to stare blankly. Under other circumstances, Donna would've assumed Frida attended simply to gather ammunition she could later spread in gossip circles. But there was something about her tense posture and the guarded glint in her eyes that hinted at a more personal motivation. Was it possible Frida Connelly—with all her self-proclaimed perfection—had a secret vice?

"Who would like to share first?" Rhett asked.

After a long pause—during which everyone shifted in their seats and suddenly had a keen interest in the weathered floorboards—the woman in the wheelchair raised her hand. "I will." She tucked a strand of dark hair behind her ear. "I'm Irene and I'm addicted to sugar. I have been for as long as I can remember. When I was little, my mom would reward me with a Ho Ho or Oatmeal Cream Pie. And when I had a bad day, out came the Twinkies and Swiss Rolls. If I was really sad, I got ice cream with fudge sauce. Whipped cream and sprinkles were reserved for special occasions like birthdays and solid report cards. Basically, sweets became the norm for all of life's ups and downs, a way to celebrate as well as cope. Before I even knew how to verbally express my feelings, I had become an emotional eater."

Irene twisted the paper cup in her hand, her nervous energy vibrating across the cluster of chairs. Donna's heart went out to the woman as she relived all the angst and discomfort from her first AA meeting. It took guts to spill your soul for all to see.

After gathering a breath, Irene continued. "I didn't realize I had a problem until I was diagnosed with type 1 diabetes. I knew I needed to stop eating sweets for the sake of my health, but no matter how hard I tried, I couldn't break the habit. I'd abstain for a little while, but I'd inevitably slip, resulting in a mortifying sugar binge. In those moments, I felt outside my own body, as if I'd literally lost control. As if I lacked the ability to save myself. To be honest, it terrified me."

Her voice lowered to just above a whisper, and Donna leaned forward to catch the last word, her heart breaking. She wanted to reach out and take the woman's hand, to let her know she wasn't alone. Everything Irene described—the shame, fear, and helplessness—she'd experienced them all. The substance might be different, but the vicious cycle was the same.

"Because of my addiction, I lost my leg and almost lost my life." Irene's gaze flitted to her right pant leg that was hemmed below the knee. "But you know what hurts the most?" Her voice wavered with emotion. "I watched it tear apart the people I love. People I would willingly die for. And I still couldn't stop. My husband left, and my son took it upon himself to fight my battle for me. A regret I don't think I'll ever be able to fully reconcile in my heart." Her eyes glistened with tears, and yet she managed to smile. "It took moving here, and meeting people who offered love and friendship in a way I'd never experienced before, to find the courage I needed. The courage to admit I couldn't do it on my own, that my own willpower would never be enough. Now, I take my addiction to the Lord in daily prayer, I have friends to lean on, and—" She blushed, adding, "A good man who reminds me that I'm so much more than my worst moment."

Irene caught Donna's eye, and a look of instant, unquestioned camaraderie passed between them. To her own bewilderment, Donna actually wanted to befriend this woman. A genuine, unguarded, two-way-street kind of friendship. The kind of friendship she'd never had.

"Thank you for sharing, Irene," Rhett said, drawing her

attention back to the meeting. "Would someone else like to go next?"

Before she knew what she was doing, Donna raised her hand.

Rhett blinked, mirroring her own surprise. He nodded, giving her the go-ahead, and suddenly all eyes turned in her direction.

She shrank back into her chair, immediately regretting her impulsivity.

Irene offered an encouraging smile, and Donna inhaled deeply, summoning the calming effects of yogic breathing.

"Hi, I'm Donna and I'm an alcoholic." She picked a point on the opposite wall to focus on, letting their faces blur into the background. She'd given this speech countless times before, but this time she felt more vulnerable and exposed, as if being back in the place where it all began heightened every excruciating detail. "I've always been a bit rebellious," she admitted, trying to separate her words from her emotions. "A wild child, people used to say. I never really fit in. I was more my father's daughter, preferring to go fishing or tinker with engines. I wasn't like the other girls my age." An invisible rope around her chest tightened as she recalled all the times her mother had tried to pressure her into "normal" girl activities like baking, dolls, and tea parties. At the time, she'd resented her mother, upset that she couldn't accept her for who she was. Now, she wondered if her mother's attempts were purely to spend time with her, to bond over a similar interest.

She cleared her throat, trying to concentrate on the present. "I'd acted out a few times, getting involved in school pranks, skipping classes, and I tried a cigarette once. I had my first drink when I was seventeen. The night of my father's funeral." An icy chill slithered up her spine at the memory, and she involuntarily shuddered. "A boy from school invited me to a late-night wake that was supposedly in my dad's honor. Normally, I wouldn't have gone. I was more of a loner, but—" She hesitated, briefly closing her eyes. She could still hear her mother sobbing in the kitchen as she lay in bed, huddled beneath the covers, trying to muffle the sound. The deep, bone-racking wails had frightened her, solidifying in her heart what she already knew to be true: her father—her best friend and the only person who understood her—was gone forever, and her life would never be the same. "I wanted an excuse to leave the house," she continued, recalling the cool metal of the drainpipe as she'd climbed out her window.

"The wake was held at an abandoned hunting blind in the woods a group of seniors regularly used as a hangout. The boy who'd invited me handed me a red plastic cup. I never asked what was in it." The familiar flush of shame crept up her neck, but she pressed on, blocking out the haunting images crowding her mind. "I remember it burned my throat, and the sharp, unpleasant odor reminded me of my mother's nail polish remover, but that didn't deter me from guzzling every last drop. He handed me another drink. And another. And for a while, the bleary, dizzy, drunken haze became a refuge, a place to hide. But the very thing I thought would rescue me became a prison I couldn't escape. That was the night I gave my life over to alcohol. The night everything changed."

Donna paused. Her mouth felt dry, and she took a sip of lukewarm coffee. The room had become unbearably silent, but she couldn't bring herself to meet anyone's gaze. Especially Frida's, who must be regarding her with a cold, disdainful glare. "From that moment on," she said, digging deep for her last ounce of courage, "I turned into someone I didn't recognize. Someone I didn't like. And no matter how desperate I became to stop drinking, to keep the addiction from destroying everything that ever mattered to me—" An image of her daughter darted into her mind, dragging unwelcome tears to the surface. She concentrated on her breathing again, determined to get through her story without a messy display of emotion. "I couldn't quit. Apart from the months during pregnancy when I couldn't stomach alcohol, even if I'd wanted to, the overpowering urge usurped every semblance of control. Until a letter from my late mother gave me the wake-up call I needed." She still kept the letter neatly folded in a thin slot in her phone case. It never left her side. "That was two years ago, and I've been sober ever since."

At the conclusion of her introduction, Donna held her breath, suddenly feeling ill-prepared to face their reaction. Would they be appalled? Disapproving? In AA, they were told not to compare their journey to someone else's, but she couldn't help feeling like the biggest failure in the room. Like her secrets were too dark, too unseemly. That she hadn't come far enough in her recovery to warrant anyone's respect. Deep down, she feared she never would.

At the unexpected sound of applause, her gaze jolted toward Irene. The woman's kind smile radiated warmth and admiration, and Donna blushed as Mac and Rhett joined in.

"Please, you don't need to do that." She shrugged away their plaudits, not sure how to handle the praise. It didn't feel deserved. "In the grand scheme of things, two years is nothing."

"Don't be silly!" Irene insisted. "It's a big deal and an impressive accomplishment. You should be proud."

"Thank you," Donna mumbled, eager to hand over the spotlight. She made the mistake of catching Frida's eye. The woman's penetrating gaze tore right through her, but she couldn't read her expression.

Thankfully, Rhett rescued her from Frida's scrutiny by reading a quote from a well-known recovery handbook, which prompted several minutes of open discussion. Afterward, everyone except for Frida—who'd excused herself the second Rhett had concluded the meeting—milled about over coffee and the fancy charcuterie board Irene had brought. Donna sampled the colorful array of cured meats, expensive cheeses, and caviar, wishing Stephanie were there to enjoy it with her. Once again, Steph had missed their scheduled phone call, and Donna had sent a text, imploring her to at least call before she turned in for the night.

"I really appreciated what you shared tonight." Irene popped a kalamata olive stuffed with feta cheese into her mouth, grinning as she said, "It made me feel less exposed after I shared, like we'd both forgotten to put pants on this morning instead of just me."

Donna laughed. "I know what you mean. It's intimidating to be the first one to share."

"You know," Irene said thoughtfully. "I didn't realize how much I needed something like this until I heard about it this morning. But the second I did, I knew I had to come. Therapy has been a huge help, but there's nothing quite like talking to other people who can relate to what you're going through."

"I completely agree."

Irene tilted her head to the side, studying her for a moment. "Would you care to come over for some pie? The night is still young and my boyfriend—is that what we call it at our age?" She chuckled before adding, "Bill makes the best rhubarb pie."

She must have looked confused because Irene quickly clarified. "Don't worry. He made a sugar-free pie for me. And it's almost as good as the real thing. *Almost*." She flashed a playful grin, and Donna found herself smiling, too.

Despite her deep-rooted struggles, Irene had the kind of easy, lighthearted attitude Donna found infectious. And refreshing. She was the kind of person who made you feel better about life simply by being in their presence.

The creaking door caught her attention, and Irene's eyes sparkled with delight. "Speaking of Bill, my chivalrous chauffeur is here. Please say you'll join us. You can follow us back to Bill's place right now, if you don't have plans."

Unbidden, Donna's gaze flew to Rhett at the other side of the room. He smiled at something Mac said, and she couldn't help noticing how it illuminated his entire face. Why did the man have to be so distractingly handsome? She shifted so he disappeared from her sightline. "Thank you. I'd like that very much."

Besides wanting to get to know Irene better, she hoped to put as much distance between herself and Rhett as possible.

CHAPTER 17

RHETT

Rhett pushed his heels against the pinewood planks, more as a nervous tick than because he found the gentle sway of the rocking chair relaxing. Donna hadn't looked at him once all evening, almost as if she wished he wasn't there. But in his defense, when Bill asked him over for a slice of pie, he hadn't known Irene had invited Donna, too. If he had, he wouldn't be here.

When she'd shared her story during the meeting, he'd been alarmed by how badly he'd wanted to comfort her, to wrap his arm around her and smooth back the dark waves that brushed against her cheeks. He wasn't short on empathy, and cared about others, but it felt different with Donna. More personal. More immediate. More visceral. He wanted to be the one to soothe her pain, to make her smile again.

He knew the knight-in-shining-armor gig was outdated and old-fashioned. He also knew he was woefully, embarrassingly unqualified for the position. But the desire lingered all the same. And sitting beside her on Bill's wide veranda, with the romantic hum of crickets and gleaming moonlight casting a silver glow over the sprawling farm, wasn't helping matters.

Determined to wrangle his unwanted thoughts into submission, he focused on a small structure in the distance, tucked into the back corner of the property. The metal siding of the renovated grain silo glinted like a warning beacon, conjuring an image of the quirky home's inhabitant—his son, Vick.

Lucky for him, Vick had plans with his friends that night and would likely be home late. Which meant he wouldn't run into him and Donna hanging out for the second evening in a row. He could tell from Vick's shocked expression last night that he'd witnessed their almost-kiss. To his son's credit, he'd recovered quickly and returned the book he'd borrowed without saying a single word about it. But Rhett knew his own guilt had registered all over his face. How could it not? After the way he'd devastated Vick's mother, shattering her heart and hopes for the future, there was no way Vick would forgive him for falling for another woman.

Not that Rhett had fallen for Donna. He barely knew her.

Even as the thought sailed through his mind, he knew it wasn't true. He may not have known Donna for long, but they'd connected on a level many couples didn't reach even after months of dating.

Dating... The word conjured a sharp longing in the pit of his stomach. He wanted to ask Donna on a proper date, with all the bells and whistles and clearly communicated intentions. He also wanted a solid, unshakable relationship with his son. Two opposing desires that, at times, felt equally unattainable.

"What brings you to Poppy Creek?" Irene asked Donna.

She set her empty plate on the table by the flickering kerosene lamp and reached for her coffee mug.

"My daughter, Cassie."

"You're Cassie's mom?" Irene smiled. "I should have guessed. She has your eyes." Irene took a sip, leaning back against the headrest of the rocking chair where Bill had helped her get situated earlier. Rhett couldn't help noticing how the rugged, soft-spoken giant of a man treated Irene with the utmost care but also with a deep and abiding respect.

"I moved here to be with my son, Landon," Irene shared. "But in my case, I didn't have much choice, since we live together." She laughed softly. "At first, I thought he'd lost his mind. Who moves from a mansion in Pacific Heights to some hole-in-the-wall most people have never even heard of? Reginald was absolutely appalled." She smiled at her portly dachshund, who snoozed in a large, luxurious dog bed beside Bill's pudgy pink pig, Peggy Sue. The two lay snout to snout, both snoring in a staccato rhythm. "And yet," she said fondly, "it turned out to be the best thing that ever happened to me." Her gaze flitted to Bill, and they shared an intimate glance. "This town gave me my life back," she told Donna. "And I have a feeling it will do the same for you."

Donna shifted in her seat as if she didn't know what to say.

An awkward silence ensued, interrupted by the urgent ring of Irene's cell phone. Bill dug it out of the side pocket of her wheelchair and passed it to her.

"So sorry," Irene said, holding up the phone. "This is my work cell. I have to take this." While she answered, Bill helped her back into her wheelchair, and she slipped into the kitchen for some privacy. Rhett caught only snippets of the conversation, but Irene sounded concerned. Cementing his suspicion that something was wrong, she returned a few minutes later with an apologetic expression. "I hate to do this, but I have to make a house call. Bill, would you mind driving me to the Nelsons'? Their rooster got stuck in the doggy door again. He might have some mild abrasions on his sides when we get him out."

"Happy to." Bill's eyes brightened, and Rhett recognized the look of a man who enjoyed being involved in his partner's endeavors. There was something special about being a team. Not that Rhett knew from personal experience. When they'd had money trouble, he'd cut his wife out of the equation, not wanting to worry her. At least, that was part of it. In hindsight, he realized it had also been about his own pride. He'd wanted to solve the problem himself. And look where that got him.

As Bill stood, so did Rhett and Donna.

"No, no." Irene waved her hand, shooing them back into their seats. "You two stay. Finish your coffee. No reason to ruin the night on our account. Right, Bill?"

Bill tipped the brim of his cowboy hat. "You folks make yourselves at home. There's more coffee in the pot. Stay as long as you like. No need to lock up."

"Thank you, but that's really not necessary," Donna said hastily. "If you're leaving—"

"Stay. I insist." Irene wasn't taking no for an answer. "I'd hate to see such good coffee and a beautiful evening go to waste."

For the first time that night, Donna met Rhett's gaze. They were both trapped and knew it. Except, he wasn't quite as bothered about it as she was.

"Thanks, Bill." Rhett shook the man's hand. "I appreciate the hospitality. You bake a mean pie."

"The secret's in the crust," Bill said with a straight face.

They exchanged goodbyes, and Rhett found himself alone on the veranda with Donna, save for their slumbering companions. An owl hooted in the distance, filling the silence.

Rhett rocked his heels, setting the chair in motion again, and Donna did the same. They swayed in tandem, communicating in the creaking of the rails. Every time he opened his mouth to speak, only one thought came to mind. One question he couldn't bring himself to ask. What else had happened the night of her father's funeral? He could tell she'd left something out. Something that had plummeted her even deeper into the abyss of addiction than her father's death. She had wounds, raw and bone-deep, that she kept so well covered, they could never heal. He knew because he had one of his own. Maybe it was time they both peeled back the bandages? "Donna, I—" His words stopped short at the squeaking of a wooden slat.

A throat cleared, and his gaze darted toward the back steps. His son glanced between them then offered a sheepish smile. "Guess I need to work on my timing, huh? I'm a third wheel two nights in a row."

"We were just—" Rhett paused. Just what? At a loss, he switched gears. "I thought you were out with friends."

"I was. But I have an early morning. Frank wants to finalize the special blend for the festival." He turned to Donna. "Congratulations, by the way."

"Thank you." Donna's discomfort and unease melted away, revealing a genuine smile. What had he missed?

Off his blank expression, Vick explained, "Luke and Cassie announced they're having a baby." His son's tone resonated with all the warmth of a close friend who would undoubtedly dote on their child with the fierce love of a favorite uncle.

During the years after his release, when he'd searched for

his son, Rhett had wondered about Vick's life—was he married with kids? What kind of husband and father would he be? A better one than he'd been, he hoped. He'd spent late nights, when he couldn't sleep, praying his son had built a happy life, full of love, laughter, and purpose. That prayer had been answered tenfold. But was Vick ready for the next step?

He pushed the thought aside, turning his full attention to Donna. Suddenly, her impromptu visit to Poppy Creek made even more sense. His chest swelled with happiness on her behalf. He could see the hopeful delight splashed across her face, heightening her beauty to such a degree, he found it difficult not to stare. "Congratulations."

"Thank you." She'd given him the same simple response as his son, but there was something in her gaze—an unguarded, vulnerable glimmer—that communicated so much more. The news of her grandchild had been a gateway, an unlocked door leading to a second chance she'd long deemed impossible. He wanted to move toward her, to take her hand and tell her he understood, but he didn't.

"I'll let you kids get back to your evening," Vick said with a smile. "Have you seen Bill? I was hoping he could give me a quick hand with something."

"He had to take Irene on an emergency vet visit," Rhett told him, hesitating to add the next thought that came to mind. *Can I help?*

As if reading his mind, Donna said, "I actually have to head back to the inn. I'm expecting a phone call. Maybe your dad can help you?"

Rhett shot her a grateful glance, once again communicating without the need for words. She gave him an almost imperceptible nod.

"Are you sure?" Vick asked. "I don't want to cut your night

short. It's only a water pressure issue. It can wait until tomorrow."

"I really need to get going, anyway," she assured him. To cement her point, she started collecting the dirty dishes. "You two go. I'll clean up here and let myself out."

"If you're sure, thanks." Vick lingered off to the side, giving them an opportunity to say good night, but Rhett had no idea what to say. Part of him didn't want their evening to end, but his son rarely asked for his help. He couldn't pass up the opportunity. Feeling pulled in two different directions, he stood frozen in place.

"Good night." Her eyes met his—a gripping shade of ever-green that dragged him further into their depths with each glance.

His temperature rose by several degrees, and he cleared his throat, grappling with his emotions. In all his life, he'd never felt so out of control around a woman, so consumed by the desire to know her ins and outs, the way she thought, felt, and viewed the world. He was more than infatuated. He was fasci-nated. And he wasn't sure he'd ever be satisfied with the surface level.

"Good night," he echoed, forcing his feet to turn and carry him down the steps, away from the last thing he needed—another elusive, unfulfilled longing.

"So, Donna seems nice," Vick said casually as they walked the worn, moonlit path softened by stray stalks of straw.

"She is." Rhett kept his tone light and noncommittal, not wanting to give too much away.

"Been spending a lot of time together?" It sounded more like a question than an observation.

"Some."

They walked the rest of the way in silence, Rhett's stride

burdened by his hypocrisy. More than anything, he wanted to be his son's confidant, to earn his trust and respect. And yet, when presented with an opportunity to be open, he'd held back. Did he expect their relationship to be a one-way street? Or was he simply too ashamed of the truth to be honest with him?

When they reached the modest front stoop of Vick's home, they were welcomed by an unusual houseguest.

"Hey, Buddy." Vick dropped to one knee to greet the miniature goat with a scratch behind his ears. "What are you doing out here? You should be asleep in the barn."

Buddy nudged his hand with the top of his head, and Vick laughed. "Hankering for a late-night snack, huh? All right." He expelled a good-natured sigh. "You know I'm a sucker. Let's go." Vick opened the door, and Buddy trotted inside.

Rhett followed, watching with amusement as Vick plucked an apple from a bowl on the counter while Buddy wiggled his backside with all the enthusiasm of a Labrador puppy.

Vick grabbed a knife from the only drawer in the compact kitchenette, granting Rhett a glimpse of the contents.

He couldn't help an involuntary intake of breath, and Vick quickly slammed the drawer shut.

But not before Rhett got a good look at the jewelry catalog featuring one item in particular: diamond engagement rings.

CHAPTER 18

RHETT

R hett followed Vick back outside, rounding the side of the silo to the outdoor shower. Even as he took in the details—the cedar plank privacy walls, smooth stone pavers, and open roof with a view of the stars—he couldn't shake the image of his son on bended knee, ring box in hand.

He liked Lucy and thought they made a great pair. Eventually, they'd make a great husband-and-wife team. But too many marriages failed because couples rushed into wedding vows before they were ready, before they knew they could weather the storm. He doubted that Vick and Lucy had even experienced their first fight. And how well could you really know someone in a matter of months?

Even as the thought entered his mind, another one crowded in beside it: He'd known Donna for mere seconds compared to his son's relationship, and yet, he felt more connected to her than any other person in his life. They'd each shared parts of themselves they'd kept hidden, too afraid or ashamed to reveal to anyone else. They'd lowered walls and invited each other into the dark places. What did that say about them? About their future? Did they even *have* a future?

He shook away the thought, trying to concentrate on what his son was saying. Something about a clog in the shower-head. Vick had shown him the main water valve and given him instructions. Instructions that he hadn't heard. But he could probably figure out the gist.

Rhett turned off the valve, still lost in his thoughts as Vick stepped inside the shower to remove the nozzle and examine the blockage. He'd have to broach the topic gently, maybe even indirectly. His son had been running his own life long before he'd entered the picture, and he doubted Vick would appreciate unsolicited advice. Especially on matters of the heart.

A suffocating heaviness settled across Rhett's chest at an unbidden memory. His own father had never been big on emotions—showing them or discussing them. According to his old man, feelings belonged to the womenfolk.

The day his father left, he'd sat him down on the scorching concrete steps of their apartment building in Stockton. A group of neighbor kids had dragged a sprinkler head into the middle of the asphalt parking lot, and their screeching laughter had permeated the silence between them. All the while, his father's new girlfriend had watched them from the passenger seat of their family sedan, the smoke from her cigarette curling out the window. His mom never let anyone smoke in the car.

"Son," his dad had said. "There are some things you won't understand until you're older. Things like love. No one really knows how it works. But sometimes it's messy. Sometimes you make a mistake and don't get it right the first time, so you have to try again. But I want you to know that me leaving has nothing to do with you, okay?"

Rhett had nodded. He knew it didn't have anything to do with him. Because if it had, if his dad had cared about him and had calculated him into his decision at all, he never would've left.

His father had given him one pat on the head, stood, and slid into the driver's seat. Rhett waited on the steps, his basketball shorts sticking to the sweat on the backs of his legs. He watched, waiting for his father to look back or catch his eye in the rearview mirror. But he didn't.

Even at ten years old, he knew something wasn't right. Family shouldn't be an *if at first you don't succeed, try and try again* kind of thing. If he ever fell in love and had a family of his own, it would be for life. Ditching them to start over wasn't an option. He didn't want to be like his father. The kind of man who thought leaving his son money after his death—money Rhett refused to touch—would somehow atone for abandoning him in life. He wanted to be the kind of man who stuck around.

Rhett's lips quirked in a sad, sardonic smile. For all his laudable, ten-year-old intentions, he'd wound up exactly like his father, just for different reasons.

"Ready!" Vick shouted as if he'd tried to get his attention before and Rhett had been too engrossed in his thoughts to notice.

Startled into the present, Rhett wrenched the lever all the way to the left. At the sound of his son's yell, he quickly yanked it the other way, shutting off the water flow.

Vick stepped out from the shower, sopping wet. "I said turn it back on *slowly*." He swiped water from his eyes, flinging the droplets onto the ground.

"Sorry about that." Rhett flashed a sheepish grin then sensed an opening. "I guess slow and steady is the way to go. Clearly, too much too fast is a recipe for disaster." He gestured to his son's soaked clothes. "I should've been patient and waited for the right time, not gone full force right out of the gate, huh?"

Vick cocked his head. "Please don't tell me you just tried to drown me to prove a point."

"Not intentionally. But why let a good object lesson go to waste?"

Vick sighed and grabbed a towel off a makeshift clothesline. "Fine. Let's get it over with." He briskly ran the towel over his hair, which he still wore in a high-and-tight military cut. "I got the ring catalog from a jewelry store in Primrose Valley. I took a look around, then they gave me the catalog and told me to go home and think about it."

"That's good advice. Marriage is something you should think about. *Hard*." Rhett paused, debating how much more he should say. He'd already come this far… "Maybe," he said cautiously, "if you can't decide on a ring, you're not ready to make a decision as big as marriage." As soon as the words left his mouth, he knew he'd been too harsh.

Vick met his gaze, unflinching, and tossed the towel over his shoulder. "Two carat canary diamond, radiant cut in a yellow gold setting with pave diamonds down the sides. It's bright, cheerful, and beautiful, just like Lucy."

Rhett blinked in surprise. "I'm confused. If you know what you want, why the catalog?"

"They thought I couldn't make up my mind, but the truth is…" For a brief moment, Vick dropped his gaze. "I can't afford it yet," he murmured. Then, almost immediately, he straightened, lifting his head. "But I will. Soon."

Rhett studied his son. He stood tall, determined, and sure-footed. He was a man of honor. The kind of man who lived and died by his commitments. The kind of man you could count on. And in that moment, he realized a hard truth: his fears had more to do with his own failings than his son's.

In tune with his thoughts, Vick's features softened. "I don't think this is about me and Lucy."

"What do you mean?"

"You still feel guilty about what happened between you and mom. About the choices you made. It's why you won't admit that you like Donna."

"I don't—" The words stalled in his throat. He couldn't deny it. Not anymore. Not to his son.

"Yeah, you do," Vick said kindly. "But for some reason, you think falling in love with someone else will be another betrayal. Like you owe it to Mom to stay single for the rest of your life. How am I doing so far? Am I close?"

Rhett marveled at his son's perceptiveness. Or maybe he didn't hide his emotions as well as he'd thought. "That about sums it up."

Vick nodded sadly. "Here are a few things you should know. First, it's not your fault Mom died. It was cancer, not a broken heart. And secondly—" He took a breath, as if his next words were a long time coming. "If she could see you now, see how you've changed, I think she'd forgive you for what happened. And I think she'd want you to be happy." Vick hesitated before adding softly, "I know I do, Dad."

A tightness in his chest rose to his throat as he stared at his son, unable to grasp what he'd heard. *Dad...* He'd all but given up hope that he'd ever hear Vick say that word.

Rhett bridged the space between them and drew Vick into a hug, burying his face in his son's soggy shoulder. He expected Vick to stiffen or pull away and nearly wept when he put his arms around him. How many times had he prayed for this moment? For a chance to hold his son? He'd been missing this piece of his heart for so long, he'd become accustomed to the emptiness. Could he handle this much happiness all at once?

"Hey, Dad. It's getting kinda hard to breathe," Vick teased.

Rhett chuckled to mask his burgeoning tears and took a step back. "And my shirt's soaked." He tugged the damp fabric away from his torso, using humor to temper his emotions.

"Whose fault is that?"

"Touché."

"So," Vick said with a meaningful glance. "What are you going to do?"

"About what?"

"About Donna."

The question hung heavy in the air, as if it carried the weight of his future. And yet, at the same time, he felt as though a huge burden had been lifted. A grin swept across his face as an unorthodox idea sprang to mind. "Do you have a fishing pole I can borrow?"

CHAPTER 19

CASSIE

C assie refilled her cup of Colombian decaf, stifling a yawn. Most of their guests had gone home for the evening, but a few friends lingered around the long table. Colt and Jack playfully argued over which one of them would be the favorite uncle, while Lucy told Penny and Kat about her latest YouTube video series featuring the upcoming Founders Day Festival. Today's video gave background information on Poppy Creek's conservation group and their efforts to protect the local monarch butterfly population, which led to the beloved tradition, the Butterfly Stroll. Cassie tried to listen in, curious about the history, but she found her thoughts wandering.

Tonight's gathering had been special. She'd never felt more loved, and she'd once again been reminded that she and Luke wouldn't be raising their child alone. They literally had an entire village of support. But something was missing. Or rather, *someone*.

During every conversation, each shared laugh, smile, and embrace, she couldn't shake a lingering, deep-seated desire:

She wanted her mother to be there with her. Despite everything they'd been through—the years of heartache, disappointment, and dysfunction—she wanted her mother to be a part of the life she'd built in Poppy Creek. Permanently.

She knew there were people in the world who would consider her foolish. Too forgiving. Too naive. Her ex-boyfriend, Derek, had tried to convince her to cut her mother out of her life completely. He'd called her toxic and a lost cause, claiming no good could come from staying in contact.

To be fair, he wasn't entirely wrong. Her mother *had* been toxic at times. And there probably were situations similar to hers where it would be healthier for the family members of an addict to keep their distance. But in her case, that had never felt like the right decision—for herself or her mother. Almost as if part of her could glimpse a tiny window to the other side of her mother's addiction. To a world where the prison doors swung open and she could finally walk through them, free and unencumbered. Free to experience a more whole and fulfilling life.

The vision had been vivid enough to keep her hope alive, even in their bleakest moments. And despite the odds, it had come to fruition right before her eyes. Although, there were still occasions she wondered if she'd wake up and realize it was all a dream.

"It's a shame your mom couldn't be here tonight," Kat said with uncanny timing. She lifted the insulated carafe of decaf, refilling her mug.

"It is. I was just thinking about how much I missed her tonight. And Kat, I've been meaning to thank you."

"For what?"

"For inviting my mom to stay at the inn as your guest." When Kat opened the Whispering Winds Inn with Jack's help, she'd vowed to reserve one suite for a woman in need. Most of the referrals came from Hope Hideaway, the women's shelter where Kat grew up, although a few had come from other connections. Kat loved providing a place of calm, relaxation, and luxury to someone who needed an escape or a chance to recharge, and Cassie admired her generous, compassionate heart. She had no idea her friend's kindness would eventually extend to her own mother.

"It's been my pleasure," Kat said warmly. "I love having her around. And I'm starting to wonder if I should offer morning yoga sessions at the inn. I think some of our guests would really enjoy it. I know I have."

"That's a wonderful idea." For a brief moment, Cassie pondered if a job opportunity in Poppy Creek would inspire her mother to stay. Perhaps she could teach yoga in the morning and then work at the café afterward? At the prospect, a tingle of hopeful optimism rippled through her.

"Plus," Kat added, her tone softening, "spending time with your mom has made me think about my own."

Cassie's chest squeezed at Kat's confession. How come the correlation hadn't occurred to her before? She should have been more sensitive to the similarities. Kat's mother had been an addict, too. Until the addiction took her life when Kat was only a child. "I'm so sorry. I didn't realize. I should have—"

"There's no need for you to apologize. I didn't mean to imply that it's a bad thing. It's been cathartic, actually. During the past year, I've worked through a lot of the hurt and anger I carried toward my mom. And I can finally look back on some of the good times we shared together. It's been…" She trailed off, searching for the right word. "Nice," she said at last, then smiled, adding, "I may not be able to have a second chance with my mom, but it makes me so happy to know that others can with their loved ones. And if I can be even a tiny part of it, well, that's even better."

Overcome with emotion, Cassie wrapped her arms around her, pulling her into a quick hug. She couldn't help feeling like God had been extra kind to her when He'd given her a friend like Kat. And the thought of her child having such an incredible aunt, friend, and mentor brought tears to her eyes.

"Cassie!" Penny called from across the room, her voice brimming with excitement. "Lucy solved our last clue!"

Cassie stepped back, drying her eyes with the sleeve of her cardigan. Gathering their cups of coffee, they rejoined Penny, Lucy, and the guys back at the table. "Really?" Cassie settled in her seat, her pulse thrumming at the possibility. This was the last clue, which meant she could be holding the diary in her hands any moment now.

"I'll read the riddle again and let Lucy explain it." Penny laid the slip of paper flat on the table, smoothing out the creases. "'You've made it this far, the end is in sight. You'll find the diary second to the right. Keep going till you reach morning light. Then I'll bid you farewell; it's been a delight.'" When she finished, all eyes turned to Lucy in anticipation.

"It's a quote from the children's book *Peter Pan and Wendy*," Lucy told them. "Second to the right and straight on till morning are the directions to Neverland."

"Wait." Cassie scrunched her forehead, recalling the framed literary quote she'd seen online recently and saved as an option for the nursery. "Isn't it supposed to be the second *star* to the right?"

"They added that part in the original Disney movie, but in the book, it's exactly like this." Lucy pointed to the note. "So, I suspect you'll find the diary somewhere near a copy of *Peter Pan and Wendy*."

"But which one?" Cassie asked.

"My guess is the library," Penny said, then frowned. "Which means we'll have to wait until it opens in the morning."

"I can get us in," Colt offered. He leaned back casually, one arm draped over the back of Penny's chair. "I've jimmied the lock before."

Penny bolted upright, swiveling to face him. "*You're* the one who moved all the romance books into the science fiction section during our senior year!"

"That was before you showed me love was real." He leaned in to steal a kiss.

Penny swatted his arm. "*I'm* the one who helped Beverly move all of them back. It took us an entire evening after school." She gave her husband a stern glower of disapproval, but Cassie noticed the blush dappling her cheeks. Like a classic romance novel, the shy, straight-A student had fallen for the rebel prankster, helping him to reform his ways.

She hid a smile and reached into the pocket of her cardigan. "No need to break and enter. Beverly gave me a key this afternoon so I can start storing the silent auction items in the back room." She dangled the tiny brass key ring. "Anyone care for a late-night field trip?"

Rejuvenated by the sense of adventure, they traipsed across the town square to the library like Peter Pan's merry band of lost boys.

Penny led them straight to the row of classic children's literature, trailing her finger along the faded spines until she paused at two identical copies. "That's strange. They have the same binding, but this one has a call number, so we know it's been cataloged in the system. But this one is blank."

"What about the diary?" Lucy side-stepped around her brother's massive frame to get a better look. "Do you see it?"

"No," Penny admitted. "But I have a hunch." She slid the duplicate copy off the shelf. "Just like I thought. It feels odd. Lighter than it should." She flipped open the book, revealing a hollowed-out center. A crude leather journal rested inside, bound by a matching cord.

"Cool." Colt leaned over her shoulder. "It's like a turducken."

Jack snorted. "Did you really just compare it to a chicken stuffed inside a duck stuffed inside a turkey?"

"Tell me it doesn't remind you of one," Colt retorted.

"I'm more surprised you think it's cool." Penny raised an eyebrow. "I thought you said it was creepy."

"It *is* creepy. And also kinda cool."

"Can I see it?" Cassie asked, her voice a reverent whisper. She hadn't been able to take her eyes off the diary since Penny uncovered it.

"Of course." As Penny lifted the delicate object from its resting place, a slip of paper fluttered to the floor. She handed Cassie the diary then stooped to retrieve it.

A shiver ran up Cassie's arm as she caressed the worn, feather-soft binding. What secrets awaited her inside?

"What does the note say?" Luke asked, drawing her attention back to Penny, who read it aloud.

"'Well done, you've solved all the clues. The diary is yours, it's long overdue. Thank you for playing along with my game. You've brought honor upon your father's good name. If you're ever in need, simply send me a line. From this day forward, you're a friend of mine.'"

"That's so sweet." Kat rested a hand on her half sister's arm. "I can see why your father liked him."

"Are you going to read it?" Lucy asked Cassie, nodding at the diary.

"I'd really love to," Cassie confessed, unable to hide the depth of her interest. "But we decided to auction off the chance to read it. I'll have to bid on it like everyone else."

"Uh-oh," Colt teased, elbowing Luke in the side. "There goes your kid's college fund."

While they bantered about how much money they thought the diary would raise, Cassie carried it to the back room for safe keeping. She held it close to her chest, her fingers splayed against the cover. There was something about the feel of the velvety leather, made soft and pliable over time, that spoke to her heart, as if there was some truth or whisper of wisdom within the worn pages she desperately needed to know.

CHAPTER 20

DONNA

Donna stared at her cell phone, her fingers poised over the keys. Once again, Steph hadn't called like she'd promised, and Donna had a disheartening suspicion that she'd missed another meeting. She'd already left two voice mails asking Steph to check in, but she composed a short text that simply said *Call me* and sent it, too.

Feeling helpless and emotionally exhausted, she sank onto the edge of the bed. The strange string of events that evening, from Frida's unexpected appearance, to sharing her story during the meeting, to winding up alone with Rhett again, had worn down her defenses. She'd wanted to tell him every-thing—things she'd never told another living soul. When Vick appeared, she wasn't sure if she felt disappointed or relieved. Or a confusing combination of the two.

A *thwack* against the French door leading to the balcony startled Donna from her thoughts. It sounded like a wayward bird confused by the transparent window pane, but that seemed unlikely at this time of night. Curious, she tugged open the door and stepped into the moonlight.

A small red and white fishing float glinted at her feet. She crouched, inspecting a slip of paper attached to a hook at the end of the line. Her heartbeat thrummed erratically as she read the scrawled handwriting.

Meet me on the lawn behind the gazebo.

Her pulse quickened, skipping a few beats, as her gaze followed the line over the railing to an abandoned fishing rod below. Whoever had wielded it must have waited for her to open the door before disappearing from sight. She squinted in the distance but couldn't see beyond the garden's murky periphery. Who awaited her in the darkness? She knew who she *wanted* it to be, but there was one other possibility. In truth, ever since she'd arrived in town, she'd wondered if this moment would come. If she'd finally have to face her demons.

She shrugged on a light sweater, anxiety churning in her stomach. What would she do? What would she say? She'd envisioned this scenario before, rehearsing every word, every line until she knew them all by heart. Of course, it was always a one-sided conversation. A cleansing release in the safety of solitude. She never anticipated they'd reach their intended audience.

Her slip-on sneakers barely made a sound as she padded across the plush grass in the dim moonlight, but her heart pounded loudly in the silence, nearly bursting when she rounded the gazebo. Her steps stalled, relief spilling from every pore at the familiar silhouette before her.

Rhett reclined on a wool blanket, both arms propped behind his head like a pillow as he stared up at the stars.

When he heard her approach, he scrambled to a seated position.

She couldn't help the smile in her voice as she asked, "What are you doing here?"

"I thought we could try again. Since my son has a habit of interrupting us." He gestured to a Coleman thermos nestled on the edge of the blanket. "I brought hot chocolate."

"You drive a hard bargain," she teased, easing down beside him.

He stretched onto his back again, and she followed suit, careful not to lie too close. But even two feet apart, his pine-scented soap mingled with the faint aroma of sweet vanilla emanating from the nearby clematis blossoms, tempting her to distraction. She kept her gaze pinned overhead, studying the swathe of midnight-blue sky dotted with stars. A tiny spark of light shot across the expanse, catching her eye before it fizzled from existence.

Rhett must've witnessed it, too, because he smiled and said, "Make a wish."

Donna closed her eyes, but not to make a wish. She hoped to suppress an unwelcome memory before it crowded her mind. But as she lay still, her palms grazing the soft wool, she could hear her father's comforting voice rousing her from sleep. She could feel his large, calloused hands tugging her out of bed, guiding her down the stairs then out to the front lawn. They'd lain side by side, gazing upward as meteors danced across the sky in a shower of sparkling light. Her heart had ached as each falling star seemed to represent the fragility of life. If the doctors were right, her father's light would soon follow their lead, vanishing from the world.

With every falling star, he'd told her to make a wish. And

with every falling star, she'd made the same one. But not even the most skilled oncologists could make it come true.

At the telltale tightness in the back of her throat, Donna quickly diverted the discussion away from stars and wishes. "It's so peaceful out here. I could fall asleep like this." Crickets chirped a melodic lullaby, and the cool, crisp air swept across her cheeks like a gentle caress.

"I often sleep outside," he admitted. "In a nylon hammock. It's one of the only things that helps my insomnia."

Donna turned her head, studying the shadowy outline of his profile. "You have trouble sleeping?"

"Ever since the robbery." His words escaped in a hushed confession, and she once again marveled at his openness. No topic seemed off-limits, as if he wanted her to know him, deep down to his core. And it made her want to be equally forthcoming in return.

"I'm so sorry," she told him sincerely. "I don't know how I'd function without sleep." She'd had her fair share of nights she'd lain awake, agonizing over her guilt and regrets, and the following days were all the more miserable.

"It's not as bad as it used to be." His tone took on a far-off quality, as if he'd momentarily revisited the past. "My first week in prison, my cellie—"

"Cellie?" she asked.

"Prison slang for cellmate," he clarified. "He went by Spider, although I think his real name was Carl. He wasn't horrible, all things considered. Could've been a lot worse. But he's the one who got me hooked on—" Rhett paused, shifting his weight before adding, "Sleeping pills."

Donna turned her gaze back to the stars, sensing he needed a moment to gather his next words. But she scooted a few inches closer, letting him know she wasn't going anywhere.

"I declined the first time he offered, not wanting to get mixed up in his shady side business. Besides, I had no way of knowing the brand, correct dosage, if they were laced with something dangerous, or anything pertinent someone should know before taking a prescription medication. All I knew was that he had someone smuggle them in somehow, then he'd use them as currency to buy protection and other harder drugs. I didn't want any part in it."

"What changed?" she asked gently.

A long pause followed her question, punctuated by the occasional rustling of the trees. When Rhett finally spoke, his voice resonated with a raw, gravelly edge she'd never heard before, as if the words scratched his throat on their way out.

"Everything. The day I got divorce papers from my wife, I knew I'd never see her or my son again. It was all over. In an instant, I'd lost everything that ever mattered to me. And I stopped caring. About anything. At first, I started taking the pills to sleep. Then I'd take half a pill in the morning, too. It made me numb to the world, able to function but never fully present." Pain etched his features, and she scooted next to him, instinctively placing a hand over his. His skin felt warm against the cool night air, and as he laced his fingers through hers, she sensed his need through his touch—the need to be known by another sentient soul, wholly and completely.

She didn't pull away, surrendering to the intimacy of the moment, and he gave her hand a grateful squeeze. "I honestly think I would've lived my entire life that way—not really living at all—if it weren't for Chaplain Dan. He made me believe I wasn't beyond saving. That I was *worth* saving."

"It's funny, isn't it?" she murmured, lost in her thoughts.

"How another person can have so much influence over us, for better or worse."

He shifted onto his side, still holding her hand. She felt his gaze on her face, studying her. "During the meeting, you said the night of your father's funeral changed everything. But it was more than the alcohol, wasn't it?"

She nodded, tears suddenly burning her eyes.

"What happened, Donna?" Compassion flooded his voice. And something else. Something deeper. For reasons she didn't think she'd ever understand, this man cared about her. Well-honed instincts developed over years of self-loathing told her to resist, to dissuade his misplaced affection. But for the first time in her life, she didn't want to listen.

Relishing the snug, secure sensation of her hand in his, she exhaled slowly, releasing her confession in a single breath. "That was the night I became pregnant with Cassie."

She watched as a microcosm of emotions flickered across his face. Surprise, concern, sadness, and finally, as realization settled, unbridled empathy.

"You were just a kid."

"Seventeen. But I turned eighteen by the time Cassie was born."

His gaze searched hers—warily, tenderly—as if he could detect signs of undisclosed sorrow in the depths of her eyes. "Were you—? Was it—?" He struggled to finish his thought, but she knew what he was trying to ask.

"Consensual?" His troubled expression told her that she'd guessed correctly. "I suppose it was. Although, neither of us was sober."

His grip tightened, which oddly brought her comfort, as if to say if he'd been there, he would've looked out for her.

"I'm sorry, Donna. Having a kid that young must've been

tough. Did the guy do the right thing, at least?"

"You mean marry me?" she asked wryly.

"I mean, did he take responsibility and pitch in? Has he been a good father to Cassie?"

Tears pooled in her eyes, spilling down the sides of her temples onto the warm wool blanket.

As if he knew exactly what her tears meant, Rhett pulled her against him, hugging her close as she cried softly. Cried for her younger self, scared, ashamed, and achingly alone. For so long, she'd wondered how their lives would've turned out if Cassie's father had been someone different. What if he'd loved her? What if he'd wanted to raise Cassie together? Would her mother still have begged her to consider adoption?

Her mother's features, pallid and wrinkled like worn, rumpled linens faded from drying too long in the sun, stared back at her from the past. Ever since her father's death, her mother had withered to a lifeless imitation of her former self, slowly crumbling to dust from her own heartbreak. Heartbreak she wouldn't share with Donna, even though they'd both lost someone they loved.

To make matters worse, Cassie had been a colicky baby, crying all hours of the night. After trying everything—feeding, changing, rocking, singing, and pacing the entire house—Donna had finally coaxed her daughter into dozing off. Exhausted, she'd collapsed onto the couch with Cassie in her arms, too tired to make it back to her own bed. Her mother had perched on the cushion beside her, her long flannel nightgown hanging from her too-thin frame.

Donna's muscles had tensed in defensive anticipation, mentally reciting her mother's words before they'd left her mouth. They were always the same; only the order changed.

She was too young for a baby. Too inexperienced. She needed to finish school, to go to college and see the world. While her mother was too old, too tired, and too unwell to raise another child. Cassie needed a mother and a father. She needed the kind of life they couldn't provide. She'd be better off with another family. Wasn't it time she did the right thing?

The right thing...

Donna had heard those words over and over, and yet, she couldn't wrap her head around them. All she knew was that if her mother tried to take Cassie away, she didn't think she'd survive. Her daughter was a part of her, as integral as her own pulse.

If only she'd known what the future held, maybe she wouldn't have run away. Maybe if she'd known her fear and depression would lead her back to the bottle, she would have realized her mother had been right all along.

Right...

There was that word again. One syllable. So simple in sound yet so complex in meaning. Deep down, despite all the years of turmoil and her own remorse and misgivings over the choice she made, she still wasn't sure what she should've done. Without the past, every dark moment and brief glimmer of good, they wouldn't be together now. This slice of joy—reconnecting with her daughter, the thrill of a granddaughter, and a new, better life—wouldn't exist.

She'd grown accustomed to carrying her regrets. Resigned to shouldering the weight without complaint. But what would it feel like to finally let go?

She found herself relaxing against Rhett's chest. Her breathing slowed. Cocooned in his arms, she felt safe for the first time in years. And against all logic and reason, a reckless thought flickered through her mind.

What would happen if she decided to stay?

CHAPTER 21

DONNA

D onna flipped the switch, and the shiny copper machine purred, forcing water through the compact grinds in the portafilter where it transformed into a dark, velvety shot of espresso. She barely noticed the rich, earthy scent as the aromatic liquid pooled in the tiny porcelain cup, her mind replaying her favorite moments from last night with Rhett.

They'd talked until sunrise, sipping hot chocolate, swapping childhood stories, and sharing their hopes for the future. Something about the stillness of the stars and Rhett's calming presence had quieted her heart, allowing a release of thoughts and emotions she'd long kept locked away. She'd even confided that part of her wanted to stay in Poppy Creek, to rebuild her life alongside her daughter and newfound friends. But whenever she allowed herself to dream, the bright, happy visions vanished almost as quickly as they appeared, obscured by bleak, ever-present clouds from her past. There was only one scenario in which she could safely stay in town, and in the clarity of daylight, she knew it was impossible.

"Mom." Cassie's voice invaded her thoughts. "I think it's done now."

Her daughter reached past her and flicked the lever, drawing her attention to the over-extracted espresso spilling into the drip tray.

"I'm so sorry." Donna grabbed a clean rag from beneath the counter, but Cassie smiled and waved her aside.

"Don't worry about it. It happens." She deftly stepped in and started a fresh shot. "Are you okay? You looked miles away."

"I'm fine. Just tired." She forced a playful lilt into her tone as she added, "They say you're not supposed to operate heavy machinery on too little sleep, and I think this vintage behemoth definitely counts."

Cassie laughed. "Is it still okay if I head to Eliza's for a bit?"

"Absolutely. It's nothing a little caffeine won't fix." She lifted the watery espresso and downed it in one gulp before summoning a smile. "Maggie and I can hold down the fort."

Since Cassie and Eliza both needed a few hours off that afternoon, they'd asked Maggie to fill in for Eliza in the kitchen while Donna handled things out front. She'd internally balked at first, not thrilled by the prospect of working side by side with Maggie, then chided herself, determined to bury her pettiness once and for all.

"And don't forget Ryder will be here soon," Cassie reminded her.

When Donna started helping at the café, Cassie had explained how Poppy Creek High let Ryder use his free period to leave school early since he was gaining valuable work experience. Somehow, the teen managed to juggle homework, football practice, and a part-time job, while at his age, Donna could barely get out of bed thanks to extreme morning sickness.

She shook away the melancholy thought as Cassie finished preparing the Americano and handed the paper to-go cup to the gentleman waiting at the end of the counter with his young daughter.

The little girl, who appeared to be five or six, tugged on her father's hand, pointing animatedly to a cupcake in the glass case. Eliza's pretty spring-inspired creation had thick pink frosting and pastel-colored sprinkles shaped like delicate daisies.

The man bent down and gently explained how they'd carefully budgeted each meal on their road trip, and they'd already splurged when she'd asked for a sarsaparilla float with lunch yesterday. The girl nodded in understanding, but her once-excited expression fell.

"May I?" Cassie asked, gesturing to the cupcake. "My treat."

The father looked taken aback, then smiled gratefully. With his permission, Cassie reached into the case, and the little girl's eyes widened with delight as the sugary treat landed in her outstretched hands. She thanked Cassie and gifted her with a gap-toothed grin before gobbling the mound of frosting, which incidentally wound up all over her face.

Donna's heart warmed at the touching exchange. Between her boundless generosity and sweet, nurturing spirit, Cassie would make an incredible mother, and she still couldn't believe she was back in her daughter's life to watch her thrive in the role.

Father and daughter left hand in hand, leaving them alone for the first time that morning. Cassie's gaze followed them out the exit, and Donna's happiness waned at the wistful glimmer in her daughter's eyes.

"It's sweet, isn't it?" Cassie said softly, still watching them through the window. The father held the girl's cupcake while she clambered into the back seat of their Subaru piled high with camping gear bound on top by bungee cords. "When he ordered his coffee, he mentioned that he goes on a special trip with each of his kids once a year. Isn't that amazing?"

"It is." Donna tried to swallow past the lump of apprehension in her throat, afraid of where the conversation might be headed.

Cassie turned toward her, meeting her gaze.

Donna's chest cinched, stealing her breath as she caught her reflection in her daughter's burgeoning tears.

"Please," Cassie whispered, her voice a raspy plea. "Please, tell me something. *Anything.*"

She didn't elaborate, but Donna knew exactly what she meant. Cassie had asked before, but never with this much need and urgency.

Donna stood frozen, each heartbeat a sharp pang of regret. She'd do anything for her daughter, sacrifice her very life, if needed. But she couldn't give her the answer she so desperately sought. She couldn't break her heart even more than she already had. Even if it meant pushing her away again.

"I can't." She winced as the words left her lips, knowing they'd wound the one person she loved most in the world.

A single tear tumbled down Cassie's cheek, and Donna felt a sudden shift between them—a tenuous fissure cracking the fragile bond they'd painstakingly pieced together.

Cassie whirled around and tore off her apron, erecting an invisible barrier with each step she took toward the door.

Donna wanted to stop her, to cry out, to fight her way back into her daughter's heart and mend what she'd broken. But what could she say? The only card she had left—the identity of Cassie's father—would bring the entire house tumbling down around them. And she couldn't let that happen.

"Are you okay?" At the soft, compassionate question, Donna turned to find Maggie standing in the doorway leading to the kitchen, holding a tray of fragrant raspberry Linzer cookies.

Donna shook her head as a sob rose in her throat, strangling her words.

Just then, Ryder strolled through the entrance, whistling as if he didn't have a care in the world.

Maggie intercepted him. "Ryder, dear, would you mind putting these in the display case while Donna helps me with something in the kitchen?"

"Sure thing, Mrs. D." He snatched one of the buttery morsels and placed it between his teeth for safekeeping before taking the tray from Maggie.

With a gentle grip on her elbow, Maggie guided her into the kitchen and settled her on a barstool before filling a glass with cold water.

Donna blinked at the ceiling, determined not to cry.

"You think parenting will get easier when they're all grown up," Maggie said as she placed the glass in Donna's hand. "But the truth is, in some ways, it gets even harder."

"Not for you." Donna took a sip, thankful for the cool liquid on her raw, swollen throat. "You make it look so effortless."

Maggie offered a kind smile. "Many things look different from the outside. That's why it's best not to assume what's behind a door before we've taken the time to open it."

Donna took another sip, mulling over Maggie's words before she set her glass on the counter. Maybe it had something to do with the woman's benevolence, or the way her time with Rhett had lowered her walls, but a sudden urge to finally clear the air overtook her reservations. Expelling a deep breath, she said, "Maggie, I owe you an apology."

"For what, dear?"

"For the last two and a half years, I've envied your relationship with Cassie. And I let it come between us, which wasn't fair. All this time, I've been fighting my jealousy when I should have been thanking you." Her voice broke, but she forced herself to continue, sharing a sentiment long overdue. "Thank you for being the mother I wasn't. The mother I should have been." The tears fell freely now, and she didn't bother hiding them. Embarrassing or not, the words needed to be said, and she felt a strange sense of relief in the wake of her confession.

Maggie took her hand, cradling it between both palms. "You'll always be Cassie's mother. But not by birth alone." She held her gaze, and Donna glimpsed a fierceness in her eyes that she'd never seen before. "You've earned the title. You never gave up, no matter how difficult the road became. Which is why I know that whatever happened between you and Cassie, you'll find a way to work things out. Your daughter not only needs you, Donna, she *wants* you in her life. Just as much as you want to be in it."

With a surge of overwhelming gratitude, Donna stood and embraced the woman she'd once viewed as a rival. Even as an adult nearing half a century of life experience, she struggled to sift through her fears and uncertainty to find the truth. For years, she'd missed out on this woman's friendship thanks to her misplaced insecurities.

What else had she gotten wrong?

CHAPTER 22

CASSIE

Cassie tightened her grip on the steering wheel, her eyes burning as she blinked back tears. She'd been so foolish, believing her mother would finally be forthcoming simply because they'd grown closer over the last several days. But she shouldn't have pushed. Deep down, buried beneath her hopefulness, she'd had an inkling that despite their progress, her mother would never give her the answer she craved. Like all the times before, the fruitless conversation left her more confused and conflicted than ever.

In all her futile attempts to uncover her father's identity, she'd learned only two things: that her conception hadn't involved an assault or a drunken blackout resulting in memory loss. Which meant Cassie had ruled out the only two reasons she could fathom for her mother's closely guarded secrecy. Nothing else made sense.

Her thoughts flickered back to the father-daughter duo from the café, and a familiar ache wrapped around her heart. Did her father ever think about her? Did he wonder what she looked like? Or where she lived? Did he want to know her favorite book, how she took her coffee, or if she preferred mustard on her fries instead of ketchup? Basically, all the things she'd pondered over the years about him. He could literally be anyone—and any*where*—in the world. And he could be searching for her as desperately as she sought after him. Why did her mother insist on keeping them apart?

For a brief moment, a cynical suspicion slithered through her mind. What if her mom didn't want her to know that for all the years she'd suffered in the shadow of her addiction, she could have lived a better, more stable life with her father? As soon as the misgiving pricked her subconscious, the tears fell harder, drowning her in grief.

"That's not true," she murmured in the silence of her car, banishing the ugly thought. For all her mother's faults, she knew she loved her. Which is why she couldn't understand her stubborn concealment. Whatever her mother was hiding, didn't she trust her to handle the truth?

Cassie parked beneath the shade of a sweeping oak tree, wiping the dewy trail of tears from her damp cheeks. The sight of the cozy, moss-green farmhouse bathed in warm, golden sunlight soothed her throbbing heart. And even more comforting was the couple swaying side by side in tandem rocking chairs.

Beverly spotted her in the driveway and waved.

Cassie returned her welcoming smile then composed a quick text to Eliza, letting her know she'd arrive a bit later than expected. Eliza immediately responded, telling her to take her time. With one last sniffle, Cassie slipped from the driver's seat and ambled toward the broad front steps flanked with red and purple pansies spilling from terracotta pots.

She gave Frank and Beverly each a kiss on the cheek hello

before settling on the porch swing, sinking with a sigh into the plush cushions.

"To what do we owe the lovely surprise?" Beverly asked. "Are we all set for the festival?"

"Almost. I have pledges for all the silent auction items, but I still have a few left to collect." She hesitated, not sure how to proceed. The second she'd climbed into her car, she knew she'd arrive on Frank and Beverly's front porch. They'd become like grandparents to her, a safe harbor and wellspring of wisdom. Frank's blunt, no-nonsense insights on life paired perfectly with Beverly's sweet, more subtle advice. They always seemed to know exactly what to say. Or when to say nothing at all.

"Actually, Beverly," she began, pushing her heels against the knotted-pine planks, setting the swing in motion. "I was hoping I could ask you something."

"You can always ask me anything." Beverly gifted her an encouraging smile.

"Did you…" Cassie's voice fell away, replaced by the gentle squeak of the springs. This was going to be harder than she anticipated. Gathering a breath, she tried again. "Did you know my mother? When she was growing up?" She'd done the math, and knew Beverly would've been a librarian during her mother's school years. Their paths must've crossed at some point.

Beverly exchanged a furtive glance with Frank before meeting Cassie's questioning gaze. "Yes, I did. Although, not well. She'd come into the library from time to time to work on a school project."

"Did you ever see her with anyone in particular?" Cassie asked, then decided to be more direct. There was no point in being coy. "I mean, with any *boy* in particular? I'm trying to find my father, and I thought that if my mother had a boyfriend in high school, that might give me a place to start."

"I see." Beverly's features softened, and she studied her for a moment, as if debating her next words. "Have you asked your mother?"

Cassie felt the familiar tingle of tears again, and she pinched her bottom lip between her teeth to keep them at bay. "I have. Multiple times. But she refuses to tell me anything. And the worst part is that she won't explain *why* she won't tell me. I'm starting to wonder if she even knows."

Beverly silently contemplated her admission before she planted both feet, stilling the gentle glide of her rocker, the one lovingly built by Luke. "I know this isn't the answer you'd hoped for, sweetheart, but I don't recall your mother having a suitor at that age. She mostly kept to herself." She leaned forward, her pale blue eyes brimming with tenderness. "Perhaps it's less about what a person says and more about what they don't say."

"What do you mean?" Cassie asked, too emotionally exhausted to solve any more riddles.

"Once you know something," Frank interjected in his gruff, gravelly voice, "you can't *un*know it." He paused and wrinkled his forehead before adding wryly, "Until you're my age. Then you start to forget more than you ever knew."

Cassie glanced between them as understanding slowly dawned. What if her mother was trying to protect her from something? Once she learned her father's identity, she could never return to a state of innocence. In this case, was ignorance bliss? Or did she want to know the truth, wherever it led? Moments earlier, she thought she knew the answer to that question with absolute certainty. But now? She wasn't so sure.

"It's ready!" Vick rounded the corner of the house from the direction of the roastery in back, his tone bright with excitement. He smiled when he spotted her. "Hey, Cass. Are you here to try the special blend? The beans just cooled enough to grind them."

Cassie tucked a strand of hair behind her ear, simultaneously sweeping aside her troubles as she tried to match his enthusiasm. "I'd love to." She stood, sharing a look with Frank and Beverly that wordlessly expressed the depths of her gratitude before accompanying Vick to the kitchen. Although she hadn't received the information she'd hoped to uncover, as usual, they'd given her the gift of a new perspective—one that would help her reconcile with her mother. Which, she realized, was what she needed most.

While Vick ground the beans and prepared the French press, Cassie arranged three mismatched mugs on a serving tray—one for Frank, Vick, and herself, since Beverly didn't drink coffee. Although Frank had cut back on regular coffee, substituting a few cups a day with decaf—not without grumbling—she knew he'd make an exception this time. As would she, since she couldn't resist sampling such an exquisite blend, despite her conviction to cut out caffeine.

From the corner of her eye, she watched Vick's fluid movements as he seamlessly flowed through each step of the brewing process like a natural-born dancer. He'd come a long way in a few short months under Frank's tutelage, and it warmed her heart to see how both men—hardened by their years in the military and subsequent lives of solitude—had helped soften each other's steely exteriors.

Vick caught her staring and flashed a shy smile. "It's strange, isn't it?"

"What is?" Cassie asked. Deciding to brew some Earl Grey for Beverly, she reached into the cupboard for a teacup.

"You know, how if things work out with our parents, we'd kinda become siblings."

Cassie jolted in surprise, and the dainty porcelain cup slipped from her fingertips, shattering across the counter and onto the floor. "I—I'm so sorry," she stammered, gaping at the mess in shock while she breathed a silent prayer of thanks that the cup wasn't one of Beverly's favorites.

"Are you okay?" Vick sidestepped the broken shards littering the scuffed hardwood and grabbed a broom from the pantry.

"I'm fine. I just—" She shook her head, as if the jerking motion would rearrange his words and somehow make sense of them. "What did you mean when you said *if things work out with our parents*? Are they dating?"

Vick's eyes widened, and the broom stilled in his hand. "You didn't know?"

"No. She never mentioned it." What else had her mother been keeping secret? "Is it serious?"

"I can't speak for your mom, but my dad sure seems like a goner."

Cassie leaned against the counter, too dazed to support her own weight. Her mother had feelings for Rhett Douglas? She supposed that would explain her mysterious plans the other night.

Before she could mentally process her emotions, a smile swept across her face, revealing the silent hope hidden within her heart.

Would Rhett give her mother one more reason to stay?

CHAPTER 23

DONNA

D onna stood on the gravel walkway, a jumble of emotions as she stared at the beautiful Queen Anne Victorian looming before her. The pristine white siding, fanciful gingerbread trim, and winsome red door created an idyllic facade, masking the painful memories preserved inside. Her gaze drifted up the round turret, pausing at the second-story window. A lace curtain fluttered in the breeze like a specter of her former self, sending a shiver skittering up her spine.

Her heart hammering, she hastened up the porch steps, eager to speak with Cassie, then put distance between herself and the place she'd once called home. She raised her fist and rapped twice, ignoring the strangeness of knocking on her own front door. Or, rather, what *used* to be her front door.

"It's open!" Eliza shouted from somewhere inside.

Donna's fingers wound around the cold brass knob then curled back as if she'd been burned. Her pulse pounded, filling her eardrums with the deafening sound. This was a mistake. She shouldn't have come.

Closing her eyes, she inhaled deeply through her nose then exhaled in a slow, deliberate breath as she pictured her daughter's face. The hurt etched into every feature left a sharp ache in her chest, and with a quick twist of the handle, she thrust open the door.

She expected to be greeted by the familiar scent of lavender and lemon polish, but it had long since faded, replaced by the sweet, homey aroma of vanilla bean and warm butter, no doubt from Eliza's endless baking. As she stepped inside, she noted that much of the furniture remained the same—the well-worn loveseat with soft, lumpy cushions, the vintage hall stand housing Ben's sneakers and baseball caps, the matching wingback chairs by the fireplace.

The fireplace. A memory slammed against her so forcefully, she stumbled backward. Tears instantly filled her eyes, blurring her vision. And yet, every detail of that evening came back to her with such oppressive clarity, she felt as if she were standing in the room two and a half years ago, watching the agonizing events unfold.

It was the year of her mother's passing, when all hope of reconciliation had been ripped from her hands. Why had she clung to her bitterness so tightly? For decades, she'd dismissed any attempt her mother made to mend the past. And as each day passed, she added another brick to the wall she'd built around her heart, using her grief and resentment as mortar.

That December, as she faced another Christmas alone—the season of Santa, sleigh bells, and a sorrow she could never escape—she'd learned her mother had bequeathed her inheritance to the granddaughter she'd never even wanted. Was it a final peace offering or an act of spite? The letter her mother left her—the one she now kept close at all times—had explained everything. But in the thick of her pain, she'd assumed the latter.

Donna brushed a tear from her cheek, fighting a surge of shame as she relived her reprehensible choices. Once again, she'd tried to drink away her heartache, which had only led to even worse decisions. She never should've showed up on her daughter's doorstep that night, wallowing in too much booze and bitterness.

Spotting the Christmas Calendar on the coffee table had tipped her over the edge. The list of festive tasks for each day in December had been her father's idea—a way to celebrate his final holiday season to the fullest—and her parents had made it together. That fateful Christmas morning, she'd woken before the sunrise, her heart bursting with hope, believing in miracles with her entire being. But as she'd skipped down the staircase, she hadn't found her parents gathered around the tree, happy and healthy as they waited to open stockings and gifts together. She'd found the pastor and his wife, her father's doctor, and her mother, sobbing uncontrollably.

How could her mother use the Christmas Calendar as a clause in her will, making Cassie's inheritance contingent on its completion? At the time, it had felt like a cruel slap to the face. In her drunken anguish, she'd thrown the calendar into the fireplace and watched it incinerate in the flames. As the scorched remnants fluttered up the chimney, she hadn't known they'd become part of the catalyst for her recovery.

"Cass, we're in the kitchen!" Eliza's boisterous voice broke through her reverie, yanking her into the present with an abrasive jolt.

Donna quickly dried her eyes and composed herself before putting the fireplace—and the memories it evoked—behind her. Tracing an imprinted path through the house, muscle memory led her to the modest kitchen.

Eliza stood at the butcher block island, wrapping floral ceramic dishes in newspaper before gently setting them inside a cardboard box.

Beside her, Grant presented two nearly identical cookbooks. "Are you sure we need both? I've already filled four boxes with cookbooks, and one of them is dedicated entirely to Betty Crocker. How many more do you need?"

Eliza planted a hand on her hip. "They're two completely different editions. That's like me asking you to choose between crimson and vermillion. How many tubes of red paint do you need?"

Grant sighed, but Donna spotted a small grin tugging the corner of his mouth. "Fair enough." He set them in a large box on top of the kitchen table before closing the flaps.

She cleared her throat, catching their attention.

"Hi!" Eliza greeted her in surprise. "I thought you were Cassie. She volunteered to help us pack today."

"But we'll take any pair of willing hands we can get," Grant teased, hefting the heavy box laden with cookbooks. "I'm going to run this load over to the new house. A couple of the guys said they'd be over soon to help. I may or may not have bribed them with the promise of brownies."

"I'll see what I can do." Eliza laughed.

As Grant lugged the box out to his car, Eliza tapped a large Tupperware container resting on the counter. "My motto is always *B* prepared. And the *b* stands for brownies." She grinned, peeling back the lid.

The enticing aroma of rich chocolate escaped the cracked seal, but Donna couldn't concentrate on food, despite Eliza's tempting offer. "You're moving?"

"Sadly, yes."

"Sadly?" Donna couldn't think of a reason why Eliza and her family would need to move. Cassie owned the house, and she knew her daughter was happy for them to stay as long as they liked.

Eliza concentrated on wrapping a set of nesting mixing bowls, the crinkling newspaper filling the conspicuous silence.

Was it her imagination, or did she detect a slight tremble in Eliza's lower lip? "Are you okay?" She stepped closer, and Eliza set down the smallest bowl to swipe a fingertip beneath her lash line, catching a wayward tear.

"Ugh. I'm so embarrassed." Eliza attempted a wry smile, but Donna recognized the glint of sadness in her dark eyes. "I promised myself I'd keep it together today."

"Thanks to years of group therapy and AA meetings, I'm a pretty good listener." Donna hoped a little self-deprecation would break the ice, and it appeared to work.

"It's silly, really. I should be happy," Eliza admitted, using a scrap of paper as a makeshift tissue to blot her damp cheek. "We're moving into our dream home. A gorgeous four-bedroom farmhouse on Willow Lake."

"It sounds lovely."

"Honestly? It couldn't be more perfect. It has a wrap-around porch, an enormous kitchen with double ovens, and the back lawn slopes down to our own private dock. Ben's already planning on spending the entire summer swimming and fishing. I've never seen him so excited."

Donna waited as Eliza twisted the crossword section into a pretzel, grappling with her conflicting emotions. "I should be happy," she repeated, her voice a wistful murmur. When she glanced up, her once-vivid gaze looked hollow, dimmed by a deep-rooted sorrow. "We bought the house when we started trying for another child. It needed some work, but we figured by the time we finished renovations, our new baby would be on the way." She looked away, staring blankly out the window. "It seems foolish now."

Donna's heart ached for the younger woman—a woman who, in some ways, reminded her of herself. They'd both had children too young and chosen to raise them without their fathers, though for drastically different reasons.

After she'd mistakenly revealed Cassie's pregnancy in front of Eliza, her daughter had explained her friend's emotional reaction. And now that she'd put the pieces together—that Eliza and Grant had bought a bigger house for the large family they may never have—Donna wanted nothing more than to wrap her in a giant hug. "I'm so sorry, Eliza." She gently rubbed her back, hoping the gesture would provide comfort her words couldn't.

"I've made so many mistakes raising Ben," Eliza confessed in a hoarse whisper. "Especially keeping him from his father for so long. That's by far my biggest regret."

Donna involuntarily winced, trying not to draw comparisons. Her situation was completely different. Grant was a good man. A loving father. While Cassie's dad—

"I'm so glad you're still here!" Her daughter's breathless voice interrupted her thought. "I went back to the café so we could talk, and Maggie said I might find you here. I was afraid you'd already left until I saw your car out front." Cassie's gaze darted between them, settling on Eliza's tearstained face. "What happened?"

"Nothing." Eliza sniffled, managing a smile. "Your mother is kindly listening to me lament my life choices, but I'm beginning to sound like a broken record. I really thought I'd moved past it all. Grant and I have built a healthy marriage. A happy family. I thought we'd healed and grown closer together, but with everything we've been going through lately, it's all bubbled up again. I keep wondering what I'm going to tell Ben as he gets older. What am I going to say when he starts asking questions?"

She fixed her beseeching gaze on Cassie, and Donna held her breath as a dizzying wave of anxiety swept over her. She'd hoped to bridge the divide, but Eliza's question would only widen the gap, forcing them further apart.

"You'll say you're sorry," Cassie said softly. "And you'll remind him that you love him more than anything in the world. Ben may not like or understand the decisions you made, but he knows you never meant to hurt him. You're his mother, and he'll always love you, no matter what."

While Cassie spoke, Donna's heart broke and mended all at once. Because Cassie's words weren't meant solely for Eliza.

They were also meant for her.

CHAPTER 24

RHETT

Rhett slid the gooey golden marshmallow off the end of the stick, sandwiching it between two graham cracker squares and a hunk of chocolate. Beside him, Vick, Luke, and Landon egged on Jack and Colt as they competed to see who could stuff the most marshmallows in their mouths at once. Rhett smiled in bemusement. Although his son and his friends were in their late twenties and thirties, in some ways, they were still big kids at heart. A fact he found oddly comforting, as if he could still witness a tiny glimpse of Vick's childhood.

Even though he'd spent the better part of his evening assembling a jungle gym and swing set for Ben in his family's new backyard—and had a few splinters to prove it—he was grateful to be included. He'd been able to spend a lot of time with Vick over the last few days. That is, whenever he wasn't at work or with Donna.

Donna... Her name still made his heartbeat stutter like an engine operating on too many cylinders. Ever since their late-night rendezvous, when they'd connected over their troubled pasts, they'd settled into a comfortable rhythm of simply being together, whether it was attending a meeting or sharing a meal. He didn't know if people still asked each other to "go steady," but he wanted to lay it all on the line with Donna. He just wasn't sure how to tell her.

"Ben wanted to make you all something special as a thank-you." Grant's voice carried down the walkway leading from the house.

Two steps in front, Ben precariously balanced a large tray piled high with paper plates, plastic cutlery, and what appeared to be a cake of some sort. As Ben drew closer, Rhett noticed the elaborate chocolatey drizzle on top and fancy mint and raspberry garnish. Whatever it was, the attention to detail rivaled anything he'd seen at a professional bakery.

"I made tiramisu cheesecake," Ben announced proudly, his enormous grin glowing in the firelight. "Without any help."

"Wow, Bud, I'm impressed." Luke stood to give Ben's masterpiece adequate praise.

"Dad said I can cut it by myself, too." He eased the tray onto the picnic table, and, as promised, Grant handed him the serving knife.

Ben wielded the long blade with careful precision, clearly feeling all grown up as his father supervised from a close distance.

As Rhett observed the father-son bonding moment—one of many similar rites of passage he'd never experience—he realized the sharp spasm of regret and disappointment had waned to a dull, almost imperceptible ache. Spurred by his conversations with Donna, he'd started to focus less on what could've been and more on the present. Although, the future also occupied many of his thoughts these days.

Rhett and Vick hung back by the campfire while the other

men gathered around the table, good-naturedly jostling for the biggest slice of cheesecake.

"I've been meaning to go check out the dock," Rhett said by way of casual invitation.

"I'll join you." Vick rested his roasting stick on the edge of the firepit before rising to his feet. "Save us a slice, would ya?" he asked Jack, who flashed a teasing grin.

"No promises, Johnson."

"I'll save you one, Uncle Vick," Ben offered.

"Thanks, Ben. You want one, too, Dad?" Vick evoked the moniker with ease, which made it all the more meaningful, as if he'd called him Dad for years.

Rhett cleared his throat, expelling a sudden surge of emotion. "Yeah, please. That'd be great."

They thanked Ben then walked to the water's edge in companionable silence. Dusk fell across the lake, casting shades of indigo and violet on the mirrored surface, while tall pines dotting the shoreline, interspersed by beautiful custom-built homes, created a rugged frame.

They strolled to the end of the dock and sat, dangling their feet over the side. A cool breeze kicked up across the still surface, stirring gentle waves that lapped against the wooden beams.

"This is quite the place." Rhett kept his tone even and nonchalant despite the tenuous topic waiting on the tip of his tongue.

"It is. They got a good deal, too, since it needed some work when they bought it."

"That was a smart move. That's a great way to build equity."

Vick nodded in agreement, and the comfortable silence returned. Only this time, Rhett racked his brain for a way to keep the conversation going without being too obvious. "So," he said, stealing a sideways glance. "You ever think about buying your own place?"

"Sure. I've been keeping an eye out. Might be a while before I can afford something like this, though."

Rhett reached into the side pocket of his cargo shorts—the supposedly outdated pair his son had razzed him about earlier. His fingertips met the creased edge of a blank envelope, and he hesitated, unsure how his son would react. He fidgeted with the unsealed flap, debating his next move, then, with a deep breath, he withdrew the envelope. Before he could chicken out, he handed it to Vick.

"What's this?" Vick stared at the object in his hand as if he'd never seen anything like it before.

"Well, son, it's called an envelope. It's used to contain other items like documents and letters." He hoped his teasing tone would lighten some of the tension that was sure to follow.

"I know what it is. But what's in it?"

"You'll have to open it and find out."

Casting him a curious glance, Vick flipped up the flap.

Rhett's pulse pounded in time with the lapping waves, loud and punctuated, spaced evenly with his measured breaths. *Stay cool. It's going to be fine.*

"I don't understand." Vick gawked at the check, his gaze glued to the hefty sum. "What is this?"

"It's a form of currency us old-timers use."

His son shot him a look that said it was time to cut the jokes. "It's a check," Rhett told him in a more serious tone. "And I want you to have it."

"Where'd you get this kind of money?"

"Don't worry, it's not loot from a bank heist." He couldn't

resist one last wisecrack. All his nervous energy needed somewhere to go.

"I know that. That's not what I was implying." Vick met his gaze, searching for an explanation.

"It's money my dad left me in his will. I've been sitting on it for about a year now."

"Your dad? But I thought he left when you were a kid."

"He did." Rhett's gaze wandered to the hazy sky, spotting dark clouds converging above the mountaintops. "My suspicion is that including me in his will eased some of his guilt. Like maybe leaving me money meant I was still his kid." Rhett knew from experience how easily a person could rationalize horrible decisions. "It's not a lot," he said, glancing back at his son. "But it can help toward a down payment. Or a ring."

Was it his imagination, or did Vick's eyes look misty all of a sudden? His son closed the envelope and held it out to him. "Dad, I can't accept this. This money is yours. Use it toward your own down payment."

For a moment, Rhett merely stared back at him. He still wasn't used to Vick calling him Dad, and it gave him a thrill every time. "Honestly, I like my current setup. It suits me." His thoughts flew to Donna. Someday, he'd need a new arrangement, but for now, this was his priority. He nudged the envelope in Vick's direction. "I want you to have this. Think of it as back pay for all the allowance I never gave you. With interest."

This earned him a grin, but Vick still didn't look convinced.

"Listen. It would mean a lot to me if you'd let me do this for you. Not as a way to buy your affection, but simply because I'm your dad. And it would make me happy to help out."

Vick considered this for a moment then dipped his head in a conceding nod. "Thanks." His voice sounded hoarse, and he cleared his throat.

Rhett smiled to himself, and just when he didn't think his heart could hold any more happiness, his son placed a hand on his shoulder and leaned in slightly for a pseudo side hug.

In turn, Rhett slung his arm around Vick's shoulders, and they sat together for an indiscernible amount of time that simultaneously felt like forever and far too short.

"Better hurry!" Ben called from the top of the slope. "Uncle Jack's trying to eat your cheesecake!"

"Guess we'd better head back," Vick chuckled. He stood and stuffed the envelope in his pocket before reaching down a hand to help him up. "Besides, it looks like some bad weather might be headed our way." As if on cue, a clap of thunder rumbled in the distance.

Rhett grabbed hold, and as Vick lifted him to his feet, a cynical thought darted through his mind. Between his ever-growing relationships with Donna and Vick, was life flowing too smoothly? Was this state of bliss simply the peaceful lull before the storm?

CHAPTER 25

CASSIE

A crack of thunder rattled the windows, and the group of women gathered in Cassie's living room echoed her startled gasp.

Eliza set down the gold ribbon she'd been fashioning into a large bow and raced to the window, searching the dark sky for signs of rain. "I hope this doesn't ruin the boys' campfire."

"I love the rain." Lucy joined her on the window seat, her gaze soft and dreamy.

"That's because you and Vick shared your first kiss in the rain," Sadie teased.

Lucy blushed but didn't deny it. The conversation spun into tales of favorite first kisses, which involved a lot of flushed cheeks and laughter as Eliza, Penny, Kat, Olivia, Lucy, and Sadie all took turns regaling each other. Even Maggie joined the fun, sharing her more comical memory with her late husband that involved an accidental headbutt and bloody nose.

Cassie noticed that while her mother partook in the merriment, laughing along with the others, she didn't share her own first-kiss story. A few days ago, Cassie would've been disappointed, hoping to glean a clue about her father. But since her talk with Frank and Beverly, she'd settled into a comfortable acceptance of the unknown, albeit not an entirely contented one. At least, not yet. She'd come to a patient understanding that her mother would share if and when she was ready. For now, Cassie was just happy that she'd come tonight. They'd all gathered on the eve of the festival to arrange miscellaneous donation items into themed gift baskets for the silent auction, and when she'd invited her mother to help, she'd expected her to decline. Cassie had been overjoyed when she'd accepted and even more thrilled to see her finally bonding with Maggie.

"Sadie, your first kiss with Landon couldn't have been more romantic," Penny cooed, pulling Cassie's focus back to the discussion. "I still can't believe he flew you to New York and kissed you on the top of the Empire State Building just like in the movies."

"He's your very own Tom Hanks," Eliza teased. "When are you going to lock that man down already?"

"First," Sadie said with feigned disapproval, "he's a man, not low mortgage rates. I don't need to lock anything down. And second, we just started dating."

"True," Eliza conceded. "But you two are perfect for each other. Plus, I've seen the way he looks at you. Trust me, the man's ready to buy monogrammed bath towels."

Sadie's cheeks turned two shades redder, but her eyes glowed with happiness. Trying to deflect some of the attention, she asked, "What about Vick and Lucy? They've been dating longer than we have."

"Only by a few months!" Lucy retorted, then grinned as if a pleasant memory flitted to the surface. "Remember when we were kids and we'd daydream about a double wedding?"

"And a double proposal," Sadie added with a nostalgic smile. "Was there anything we didn't want to do together?"

"Maybe our honeymoon," Lucy laughed.

"Speaking of honeymoons," Eliza interjected. "Have you seen Landon's donation to the silent auction?" She waved a paper certificate embossed with gold lettering. "Ten days at his villa in Greece. It includes plane tickets and a sunset cruise on his private yacht. One of you should bid on it," she told Kat and Olivia, who both had honeymoons on the horizon.

"Greece," Penny sighed. "I would love to go back someday."

"Isn't that where Colt proposed?" Kat asked.

"In a secluded cove," Maggie said, her eyes twinkling. "Colt put me in charge of arranging a romantic dinner for the two of them when they got back from the beach."

"It was the most magical summer of my life," Penny said dreamily.

"Then you should definitely bid on it," Eliza told her, and Penny laughed.

"Colt barely has time for a cup of coffee in the morning, let alone a trip to Greece." The amused glint in her eyes gave way to a glimmer of disappointment, one she quickly tried to hide. "Where are you two going on your honeymoon?" she asked Olivia, changing the subject.

"We haven't decided yet. There are so many lovely options in the fall, it's hard to choose. Although..." She trailed off, dropping her gaze to the basket of theater tickets, opera glasses, and a gift certificate for improv classes donated by Eliza's mother, Sylvia.

"Although, what?" Lucy prodded.

"Some days I wish we'd planned our wedding for the

spring instead," Olivia admitted. "We'd both love to attend the Rose Festival in Morocco. It would be the perfect honeymoon, but it's held in May."

"Can't you move the wedding up a few months?" Eliza asked with a grin.

"Not without making a lot of vendors very unhappy." Olivia tried to sound lighthearted, but Cassie caught a glint of uncertainty in her eyes. Did she still have doubts about the wedding details?

"I know this sounds strange," Kat began in a tentative tone, as if she was almost too embarrassed to finish her confession. Cassie caught a brief glance between Kat and her mother, and, curiously, the latter's encouraging smile seemed to give Kat the courage to continue. "I'm actually glad Jack's mother has taken over most of the planning for our wedding. She actually enjoys it, while I find the limitless choices far too stressful. There's only one decision I want to make. Well, besides picking the groom," she said with a playful laugh, adding, "And that's the dress."

Her admission sent the women into a boisterous discussion of styles, fabrics, and necklines, and the gift baskets were forgotten in favor of bridal fashion trends.

Cassie stole away to the kitchen and set a kettle on the stove to start a pot of tea. A gentle rain tapped against the windows, and the crackle of thunder punctuated the conviviality in the other room. Her mother's laughter carried above the rest, and Cassie's chest squeezed at the pleasant, lilting sound. It was a sound she barely recognized, due to its scarcity. And yet, she heard it more and more frequently these days, a realization that warmed her heart.

"Would you care for some help?" Maggie didn't wait for a response and began arranging oatmeal cookies she'd brought on a serving plate while Cassie prepared the teapot. When she'd finished, Maggie reached into her large tote bag resting on the counter. Cassie expected her to produce another container of snacks, but instead, she withdrew a small ivory blanket with tiny red poppies embroidered along the lace border.

"I've been meaning to give this to you," Maggie said softly.

"Maggie, it's beautiful." Cassie gently grazed the soft, creamy fabric that was clearly a blanket intended for a baby girl.

"Of course, I realize you don't know if you're having a boy or a girl, but I have my suspicions. And I have quite a knack for these things."

Cassie caressed the delicate crimson petals painstakingly stitched with love as tears sprang to her eyes.

A daughter... Somewhere, deep down, she'd had the same feeling, but she hadn't wanted to say it out loud. Boy or girl, she'd love her child the same, but she couldn't shake the inkling. "Did you make this?"

"Several years ago. Decades, really. In some ways, it feels like another lifetime."

"I don't understand." Cassie met her gaze. Why would she make a baby blanket for a granddaughter that didn't exist yet?

Maggie's features softened, and her voice escaped in a faint, wistful breath. "I made it for our daughter, Hope."

"Oh, Maggie." Cassie's heart broke in two, and her hand instinctively fell across her stomach, as if the act were a silent prayer of protection.

"It was a long time ago. A miscarriage. I never even got to hold her." Maggie's eyes flooded with tears for a lost child she still loved dearly. "In many ways," she whispered, "I imagined she'd be a lot like you."

A whimper caught in Cassie's throat, and she flung her arms around Maggie's neck, dampening her soft silver-streaked curls with her tears. "I'm so, so sorry, Maggie," she murmured.

"Thank you, sweet one. While I still think of her often, the Lord has comforted my grieving heart." Maggie leaned back and lovingly brushed a tear from Cassie's cheek. "He's also given me two more daughters to call my own."

Cassie blinked back a wave of intense emotion, knowing Maggie meant her and Penny. In turn, Maggie had become a mother to her in every sense that mattered, permanently sewn into the fabric of her life.

Growing up, she'd often prayed for a family, daydreaming not only about her mother's sobriety, but finding her father and extended relatives like grandparents, aunts, uncles, and too many cousins to count. Maybe even siblings.

Lately, those dreams materialized less frequently, and not because the desire had waned, but rather, because it had been fulfilled by the people around her. People like her husband, Maggie, Frank, Beverly, and the women in the next room.

On the same wavelength, Maggie said, "Over the years, the Lord has taught me that not all families are related by blood, but they're no less real."

Cassie smiled through her tears, believing with every fiber of her being that Maggie's words were true. Another clap of thunder shook the windows, but Cassie didn't flinch. The people in her life—her found family—helped her weather the storms, both real and metaphorical. With this much love surrounding her, was there any hurdle she couldn't overcome?

CHAPTER 26

DONNA

Donna popped a morsel of hand-pulled honey taffy into her mouth, smiling as she chewed the buttery-soft sweetness while she observed the unusual relay race unfolding in the town square.

Jack and Colt had chopped a pile of tree rounds into neat logs, which they then loaded into wheelbarrows. At that point, their respective teammates, Luke and Reed, took over, careening the wheelbarrows through a winding course before reaching the next leg of the relay where Grant and Landon unloaded the logs, stacking them in a neat pyramid. Until finally, Rhett and Vick now competed to start a campfire in a stone pit using only the materials around them—twigs, leaves, and pine needles—and an old-fashioned flint kit. The first team to ignite a steady flame would win.

There were several such relays throughout the first day of the Founders Festival, all mimicking survival skills the miners would have needed in the mid-1800s. Donna remembered competing in a few with her dad, and watching Rhett and Vick now, lobbing good-natured heckles back and forth as sparks flew into the late afternoon sky, wrapped her in a nostalgic embrace.

Spending time with Rhett over the last several days had started to soften her heart toward the past, helping her look back with fondness and gratitude for the time she'd spent with her father rather than dwelling on his death. She still missed him terribly, but holding on to her sorrow meant she was missing out on all the wonderful memories, too. They were a blessing, a gift she'd neglected for far too long. And she owed her epiphany to a man intent on creating new memories. A man who'd seen her worth when she no longer could.

Throughout the morning and afternoon, they'd strolled the festival, mingling with volunteers clothed in period costumes, sampling delicious food inspired by hearty gold rush fare, and participating in the quirky fun and games.

For a fleeting moment, she'd felt like a part of the town again, as if a fresh start hovered just beyond her reach. But no matter how desperately she longed for a second chance, she couldn't shake the dark cloud looming over her shoulder, its oppressive weight felt but never seen. She knew it was only a matter of time before she had to face the past. Especially now, with the entire town converged in one place.

A collective cheer erupted in the air, dragging Donna from her melancholy musings. Rhett tossed her a grin as the opposing team celebrated their victory. He may have lost the relay, but from the look on his face as he congratulated his son, he'd won in all the ways that mattered.

He trotted toward her, beaming broadly, and she loved the way it illuminated his handsome features. "Did you save me any?"

She glanced at the empty bag of taffies. "Apparently not.

But in my defense, it took you eons to get that fire going." Her lips twitched.

"Hey, have you ever started a fire using a flint? It's one step above rubbing two sticks together." He flashed a good-natured grin, more playful than defensive.

Not for the first time, Donna's appreciation for his sense of humor deepened. He knew how to find joy in life, even when it felt elusive—one of the many reasons she'd fallen for him.

The unexpected realization startled her, and heat blazed across her cheeks. She admired Rhett. She respected him. She even enjoyed spending time with him. But had she *fallen* for him?

"I hope you saved room alongside all that taffy for some hand-cranked ice cream," he teased, snapping her out of her trance.

She summoned a shaky smile. "Always."

"I'll stand in line if you want to save our spot to watch the next relay. I think it involves hauling buckets of water through an obstacle course, which is bound to be entertaining. What's your favorite flavor?"

"Lemon."

He closed his eyes and tapped the left side of his temple.

"What are you doing?" she asked.

"Making a mental note for the next time I buy you ice cream." He opened his eyes and grinned again, making her stomach spin.

As he strode toward the homemade ice cream stand, her heart performed a funny little flutter, leaving no doubt in her mind. For the first time in years—no, for the first time *ever*—her fears had dissipated long enough for love to sneak through the crevices. Genuine, life-altering, soul-bearing love.

The kind of love she found equal parts thrilling and intimidating. And she had no idea what to do about it.

Reeling with a disorienting mix of anxiety and exhilaration, Donna dug her hand into the brown paper bag containing their most recent snack purchase. They hadn't shown much restraint when it came to the plethora of historically inspired treats and had readily agreed it was all part of the experience. With other men, she might've tried to suppress or minimize her appetite, but with Rhett, it never even occurred to her.

She tore off a chunk of warm, spongy sourdough, barely registering the tangy medley of flavors as it melted on her tongue. Falling for Rhett wasn't in the grand plan. Not that she had much of a plan, to be honest. She still hadn't decided when to head home, but she couldn't impose on Kat's generosity much longer. Not to mention, she lived with a constant knot in the pit of her stomach, a physical manifestation of a niggling feeling that Stephanie needed her. Their phone calls had become even shorter and more infrequent, and whenever they did talk, she couldn't shake the unsettling suspicion that Steph wasn't being completely honest with her.

Donna cast her gaze around the festive town square, alive with laughter and merriment. Vendor booths lined all four streets, offering locally made gifts and wares, and the silent auction was in full swing in the library, drawing an eager crowd. Along the creek bed behind Main Street, a live reenactment of a mining camp offered visitors a rare glimpse into the life of a miner as well as an opportunity to partake in immersive activities like gold panning. The whole affair was vibrant, boisterous, and more than a little bit unusual. And Stephanie would love it.

Impulsively, Donna pulled out her phone, her pulse quickening with each unanswered ring.

"Hello?" Stephanie groaned, hoarse and groggy.

"Did I wake you?" Donna asked in surprise. It was almost four o'clock.

"I had a late night. What's up?"

"A late night?" Donna echoed warily. "Anything fun?"

"Just hanging out with some friends. Are you still in Mayberry?"

Donna couldn't help but smile as the next round of relay racers were handed metal buckets. They'd have to draw water from a large barrel then haul two buckets filled to the brim through a series of obstacles without spilling or sloshing. Whoever had the fullest buckets by the end would win. If only Steph could see the accuracy of her joke. "I am. And I was thinking, why don't you come visit?"

"Visit?" Concern crept into Stephanie's tone. "But I thought you were coming back soon. Weren't you just going to help out for a few days?"

Donna winced against a sudden pang of guilt. While the length of her trip had always been indeterminate, she had alluded to it being short-term. She'd imagined visiting sporadically, as needed, then maybe staying a bit longer when the baby arrived. The shorter her stay, the fewer opportunities for her past to catch up with her. A reality she seemed to have forgotten lately.

"You've been gone for ages," Stephanie continued, cementing her point with an exaggerated whimper. "Nothing's the same without you. At the last meeting, Margery monopolized nearly an entire hour with a eulogy for her Chia Pet. And the snacks weren't even that good. I honestly don't know how I survived."

Donna wanted to simultaneously laugh at Stephanie's lament and weep with relief. The last time she'd asked about her meeting attendance, Steph had avoided her question.

"That's another reason for you to visit. Our meetings have the best food, by far." And, she mused but didn't say out loud, they'd helped her more than she could've imagined. She hadn't craved a single drop of alcohol in days.

"You have meetings there?"

"Yep." So far, everyone but Frida had shared, and they'd remarked on what a blessing the tiny, close-knit community had become in such a short amount of time. Mac not only threw out his last pack of cigarettes, he'd even stopped selling them at the Mercantile, removing the temptation entirely. The first time his wife noticed, she'd cried happy tears—a moment he said he'd never forget.

Donna caught sight of Rhett walking toward her, an ice cream cone in each hand. Her spirits lifted, buoyed by gratitude and affection. And something deeper—an overwhelming sense that, no matter what happened, he would always hold a piece of her heart.

"So, you'll come?" she urged, glancing back at the relay.

A long silence ensued, and she checked their connection before Stephanie finally mumbled, "I'll think about it."

Donna blew out a breath. Although it wasn't a yes, she'd count it as a win for now. They exchanged a brief goodbye, promising to talk soon before Donna ended the call and stuffed her phone back in the pocket of her jeans, feeling hopeful for the future.

"Everything okay?" Rhett asked as he handed her a generous scoop with spirals of candied lemon peel sprinkled on top.

"Everything's perfect." She inhaled the sweet citrus scent,

almost leery of her own happiness. How much longer could it last?

"Want to try our hand at gold panning after this?" Rhett asked. "I'm feeling lucky these days." He met her gaze, and the meaningful glint in his eyes flooded her entire body with warmth.

"Me, too," she murmured, forgetting to breathe when he held out his hand.

As their palms pressed together, time slowed to a standstill, capturing every nuanced detail in her mind, like his rough calluses against her smooth skin and the way he applied gentle pressure with his thumb. He laced his fingers through hers, and she marveled at the way they seamlessly melded together.

As they strolled toward the creek hand in hand, without a single concern about who might see them together, Donna savored the sensation of being wholly and blissfully content for however long they had left.

CHAPTER 27

RHETT

R hett tried to focus on the task at hand, but his gaze kept drifting to Donna, mesmerized by the hypnotic dance of sunlight against her dark, glossy hair. She always looked beautiful, but as she knelt by the water's edge, her pan dipped in the shallow current, she transcended every earthly comparison. He fully admitted he had ulterior motives when he mentioned the excess of other gold panners farther up the creek and led her downstream to a secluded cove.

All day, he hadn't been able to shake the overpowering desire to kiss her. The impulse besieged him each time she laughed or teased him or gifted him with her breathtaking smile, complete with the sexy crinkle across the bridge of her nose. And when he noticed a smear of ice cream on her bottom lip, he'd expended every ounce of self-control resisting the urge to cup her chin and tenderly kiss it away.

Now, sheltered in the tranquil shade of tall, tapering pine trees, they had all the privacy in the world. He'd managed the perfect opportunity to transform his first-kiss fantasy into a tangible reality. Except, he hadn't kissed anyone since his late wife, and *rusty* didn't even begin to describe his ineptitude. He had zero clue how to make the first move. Was he supposed to ask her permission? Or simply sense an opening? And how would he know for sure?

Suddenly, he felt like an awkward kid again, all racing pulse and sweaty palms. Only, this time, it wasn't over a pretty girl in the schoolyard who made him wear a construction paper tie for their pretend wedding. He could see himself spending the rest of his life with Donna—for real. This wasn't a childish crush or immature infatuation. Donna was a woman of substance, of grit. She was worthy of more than he had to offer, but he'd fight his absolute hardest to deserve her, every single day and then some. If his hopes came to fruition, this could be his last first kiss. And he didn't want to mess it up.

He cast another surreptitious glance in her direction. She smiled the kind of cute, slightly quirked smile that made his mouth go dry, as if she sensed his thoughts. Losing his balance in his miner's squat, he teetered forward, barely catching himself before spilling headfirst into the creek. His pan slipped from his grip and plopped into the water, dousing his shoes.

Donna laughed. "You have no idea what you're doing, do you?"

Sacrificing his already-damp sneakers, he inched into the icy creek bed to retrieve his pan. "Is it obvious?"

"Painfully," she teased.

"Care to show me how it's done?"

"I thought you'd never ask." She set her pan on a mossy log before borrowing his. "The whole idea is to separate the pebbles and silt from any gold that may be buried underneath.

So, first, we scoop up the sediment," she said, demonstrating as she explained, "and shake the pan from side to side."

Her movements were fluid and graceful, and once again, he found himself staring, captivated by the smooth curves of her arms and the tempting way her lips parted in concentration.

"Then," she continued, drawing his attention back to her soft, skillful hands, "we want to dip the front edge into the water and give a gentle flick so the top layer washes back into the stream. Any gold nuggets will remain in the bottom, since they're heavier. Does that make sense?"

She met his gaze, and a zing of electricity shot from his head to his toes, which had gone numb inside his soggy socks. Her lips were mere inches away. What if he bent down right now and kissed her? *Focus, Rhett. She asked you a question.*

He cleared his throat. "Yeah, it does."

"Great. Now you try it." She passed him back the pan, and their fingers grazed, igniting the spark of electricity into a full-blown blaze.

Could she feel the heat radiating from his body? He contemplated plunging into the water to cool off but focused on mimicking her movements instead. "Like this?" Rocks rattled and scraped against the metal bottom as he jerked the pan back and forth.

"Not quite," she said with a playful smirk. "You're trying to remove the rocks, not polish them. Although…" She peered over his shoulder, and he caught a whiff of her sweetly scented shampoo. "Look what you uncovered." She plucked a chunk of rose quartz from the murky sludge and held it up to the light, admiring the pink sheen. "It's beautiful. My dad used to joke that I cared more about finding quartz than gold. Rose was always my favorite. According to lore, it represents unconditional love."

Was the sunlight playing tricks on him, or did her cheeks suddenly look flushed as she handed him the stone?

"Keep it." He passed it back, holding her gaze a second longer than necessary.

Kiss her, an inner voice whispered, growing more insistent the longer he waited.

"Thank you." She looked away and set the stone behind her on a smooth patch of sand on the embankment for safe keeping.

Rhett groaned internally. What was wrong with him? He wouldn't get a better chance than the one he'd just wasted.

"Let's try again," she said, refocusing on their task. "Only this time, I'll help you." Kneeling beside him, she placed her hands over his around the rim of the pan.

His pulse slowed to a standstill, and his lungs depleted his entire air supply as she leaned into him, moving the pan back and forth in a smooth rhythm.

"Now you're getting the hang of it." She offered an encouraging smile. "Shake, shake, shake, wash, wash, wash." With each repetition, the amount of debris diminished, as did his ability to concentrate.

This was it. He needed to take his shot before the opportunity slipped away again.

A bright glimmer in the bottom of the pan caught his eye, but he didn't care, too intent on a treasure of much greater importance. "Donna," he murmured, his throat thick and raspy.

She turned her head to face him, and the instant their eyes locked, heat shot through him like a flame. The hunger in her eyes matched his own. Only a breath away, he lowered his lips to hers, his heart bursting at the overwhelming intensity of finally tasting her.

The pan tumbled from his grasp, meeting the water with a splash. As it sank to the bottom, gold nugget and all, he didn't have a single regret.

Here, in this moment, he had everything he wanted.

CHAPTER 28

DONNA

Soft morning sunlight dappled the footpath as Donna made her way back to the secluded cove. Laughter and merriment carried above the rustling of the trees, reverberating from the town square where the second day of the festival was already in full swing.

Today, they'd find out if the silent auction and raffle tickets raised enough money to save the library. A few weeks ago, she cared about the outcome merely for her daughter's sake. But now? Now, she had a more personal investment.

Somehow, this town had wrapped itself around her heart, weaving an inexplicable tether that transcended the pain from her past. Her whole life, she'd stacked the blocks of her resentment, building an impenetrable wall. But through kindness and patient, unconditional love, the people of Poppy Creek had removed them one by one.

Unconditional love... A pleasant warmth crept up her neck, sweeping across her cheeks. Instinctively, she pressed her fingertips to her lips, smiling at the memory of Rhett's kiss. Both tender and passionate, the spine-tingling zing had traversed every inch of her body. She could still feel the aftershock.

They'd been so consumed in each other, by the time they realized they were late to the town-wide baked potato pit— where they baked tin foil–wrapped potatoes in the coals of a firepit before adding all the fixings like bacon, scallions, and hand-churned butter, which was made during yesterday's reenactment—she'd accidentally left the quartz behind.

She wasn't normally sentimental, and apart from the sparrow pendant she'd given Cassie, she didn't keep mementos. But something about the quartz compelled her to go back for it. And the reason may or may not be related to a certain man and his toe-curling kisses.

Blissfully lost in her thoughts, Donna rounded a large redwood then stopped cold, her gut wrenching as a familiar voice slithered through the crisp air.

"Tarence, trust me. I'm a man of my word. The library is yours. We can finalize the deal today."

The ground swayed beneath her feet, and she slammed her palm against the rough bark of the redwood for balance, barely registering the sharp pang of a splinter piercing her skin. She needed to leave, to scramble up the pathway without looking back. She needed to be anywhere but standing here, overhearing Bryce's phone call. And yet, she couldn't move.

"Oh, you heard about that?" A twinge of irritation marred his typically cool, measured tone, but he quickly recalibrated. "I assure you, Tarence. You have nothing to worry about. It doesn't matter how much money they raised. I know what's best for this town. We need developers like you to bring us into the twenty-first century. They may not agree at first. But in time, they'll see I'm right."

An icy dread gripped her chest, squeezing the air from her

lungs like a clenched fist. He never intended to honor his agreement with Cassie. Her daughter had been working tirelessly on a fundraiser that never stood a chance. Heartache, outrage, and helplessness flooded her all at once, leaving her light-headed and sick to her stomach.

"That's the beauty of being the mayor," Bryce said with a callous laugh. "They'll believe whatever I tell them. I'll give some spiel about code violations and mandatory renovations and how I can't handle the undertaking. Plus, I'll assure them you plan to preserve the historical heritage of the building." He laughed again, and the eerie, unctuous sound crawled up her spine like a spider. "Of course, mistakes and miscommunications happen in construction all the time. So, we can hardly be to blame if the preservation goes awry, can we? Now, do we have a deal?" He nodded, keeping his back to her. "Excellent. I'm working with a lawyer out of San Francisco. I'll have him get in touch this afternoon."

As Bryce wrapped up his phone call with more high-handed pleasantries, Donna begged her feet to work. This was her last chance to extricate herself before he saw her. Why couldn't she move?

He slipped his cell into the breast pocket of his slick black suit jacket then turned toward the trail. Shock registered on his face when he spotted her, followed by a flash of anger. "Are you spying on me?"

An inexplicable wave of shame crashed over her, and she dropped her gaze. Suddenly, she was seventeen again, shrinking beneath his disdainful glower. She shook her head, still staring at the ground.

"Good. Whatever you think you heard, you'd do well to forget it." He walked up the path toward her, pausing at her side. The overpowering stench of his expensive cologne elicited another wave of nausea as he leaned in and whispered, "I've stayed out of your way, and I suggest you stay out of mine."

The heavy thud of his soles and snapping of twigs echoed in her ears as he left her standing there, trembling.

"Morning, Mayor!" Rhett's jovial greeting was met with a curt hello as the two men passed each other, but it didn't dampen his bright mood. "Fancy meeting you here. I take it we came for the same thing." His smile vanished the second he saw her ashen face. "What's wrong? Are you okay?"

"No," she whispered, a sob rising in her throat as the adrenaline fled her body. "I'm not." Her knees weakened, and Rhett gathered her in his arms, cradling her against him as she wept.

He stroked her hair, silently holding her while she cried tears she'd hoarded for years. When her sobs finally subsided, he asked, "What happened? Was it Burns? Did he say something to you? I've never liked that guy."

The protective growl in his voice both soothed and saddened her. What she wouldn't give to have had similar support thirty plus years ago. But he was here now. Maybe it was time she finally told someone the truth. The whole truth.

"He's Cassie's father." The words escaped in a weighty exhale, as if she'd been holding her breath her entire life.

Rhett stiffened, and his fingers tensed, briefly digging into her back before they relaxed, as it they'd coiled on reflex. He didn't strike her as someone who resolved his anger physically, but she wondered what he would've done if Bryce had been standing in front of him at that moment.

"I'm sorry, Donna," he murmured, his voice hoarse as he hugged her tighter. "Why didn't you say something sooner?"

"Because I—" She hesitated, drying her eyes. How could

she explain choices she simultaneously regretted and would probably make again? "Because we didn't want anyone to know."

At her confession, she flinched as a memory forced its way into the forefront of her mind—a memory of a time when the decision of secrecy had been made for her.

How could you let this happen? Bryce's seething accusation had dripped with derision, as if getting pregnant had been solely her fault. *You need to take care of it.* He'd spat the command like a manager ordering a clumsy employee to clean up their mess.

They were standing in the rosebushes behind his house, illuminated by the porch light. She could see every spark of contempt cross his face, and his dark eyes burned through her, completely devoid of affection or compassion.

When she told him she wanted to keep the baby, his posture had shifted to one of defense, as if her motivation was purely to attack his flawless character and ruin his chance of becoming mayor after his father.

"I'll deny it," he'd hissed with a vicious sneer. "And who do you think they'll believe? The golden boy who can do no wrong? Or a screwup? No one's going to believe I'd go anywhere near someone like you."

At his heartless words, hot tears had scorched her skin, but they served only to deepen his disgust.

"If you tell anyone," he'd warned, "I'll make your life even more miserable than it already is."

In that moment, she knew she'd never tell another living soul, and especially not her child. But not because of his threat. She wanted to destroy any connection to someone who could be so cruel.

"Does Cassie know?" Rhett asked softly, tugging her back to the present.

She shook her head again, a fresh wave of guilt washing over her, so deep and all-consuming, she could drown in it. All she'd wanted was to protect her daughter, to shield her from a truth more painful than uncertainty. In Cassie's mind, her father could be anyone. She could create any story she wanted. She could dream, wish, and hope, all tenuous like a gossamer thread, but far less damaging than the ugly, unalterable reality. But what if, after all this time, her lie of omission turned out to be her greatest regret?

Her thoughts flickered to her conversation with Cassie and Eliza, and what her daughter said about Ben. *You're his mother, and he'll always love you, no matter what.*

Did Cassie really believe that? Would their own mother-child bond transcend a betrayal of this magnitude? Was it a possibility she could risk?

As if he could glimpse her innermost thoughts, Rhett brushed aside a strand of her hair. Meeting her gaze with unwavering empathy, he said gently, "You should tell her."

"I know," she whispered. Swallowing against the rawness in her throat, she added with fearful resolve, "But there's something else I need to tell her first."

CHAPTER 29

CASSIE

C assie's heartbeat quickened with each new dollar amount as she read the winning bids off the silent auction sheets, pausing for Beverly to add them to the tally. They sat side by side at the vintage executive desk in the back office of the library, Cassie's favorite room in the historic brick building. The mahogany shelves boasted a breathtaking collection of rare books and special editions that lent a comforting scent of aged leather to the elegant room. An oil painting of the founding fathers hung above the marble mantelpiece, their stoic stares ever vigilant. Her gaze settled on the dark-haired man in the center, Chadwick Burns. What had he been like? And what would he think of his descendant and predecessor's former plans to sell out to a developer with deep pockets?

Her gaze flitted to the humble diary resting in a glass case for safe keeping. What had Lydia Burns written all those years ago? What secrets had she shared? And would she ever find out?

She'd placed a generous bid yesterday afternoon during

the silent auction but had been pulled in so many different directions throughout the day helping Olivia manage all the events, she hadn't had an opportunity to add a final bid before the auction closed. Based on the amount of interest the diary had evoked, she'd lost all hope of winning.

"This can't be right," Beverly murmured, interrupting her thoughts. She tugged on the roll of tape protruding from her ancient calculator, squinting at the sum. Her eyes widened, meeting Cassie's in disbelief. "I couldn't resist sneaking a peek at the subtotal, but this can't be correct. We couldn't have possibly raised this much money, could we?"

Cassie stood and peered over Beverly's shoulder, her pulse thrumming with anticipation. She gasped at the large number staring back at her. It was above and beyond what they needed. She scanned the previous entries, and at a glance, everything looked in order. "We should add it up again, but it looks accurate."

Beverly grasped her hand, giving it a squeeze. "You did it, sweetheart. You saved the library."

"You mean *we* saved the library," Cassie amended, glowing with joy and gratitude. "It may have been my idea, but it took all of us together to make it happen."

"They would be proud." Beverly nodded toward the oil painting, and tears pricked Cassie's eyes at the tender sentiment.

Compared to most of the residents, Poppy Creek had been her home for only a short time, and yet, she felt intrinsically connected to its history, as if she'd always belonged here. Like the oak tree in the town square, firmly planted in the rich soil for over 200 years, she'd cultivated roots that ran deeper than she ever could have imagined.

"We have two bid sheets left." She returned to the stack of

papers. "Let's add those, then we can tally them all one more time before we make the big announcement."

She was supposed to meet Burns on stage shortly to go over a few last-minute details before his big tribute speech paying homage to the town founders. He gave the same one every year, and based on the level of pageantry, you'd think he was giving the Gettysburg Address. He'd even commissioned Luke to build a new sign to welcome visitors to town and specifically asked for something striking and grandiose. Luke had presented several sketches, and Burns repeatedly told him to *think bigger*. The end result was a massive concave design with hand-carved lettering and enormous, eye-catching poppies that Grant embellished with splashes of color. Although a bit more ostentatious than strictly necessary, Cassie couldn't deny its extraordinary artistry and charm, and she was proud of her husband's work.

For dramatic effect, Burns planned to reveal the sign during his speech, and had it hidden on stage behind a makeshift curtain he could dismantle with a single tug of a silk cord. The whole production felt a little garish, but she'd come to expect pomp and circumstance when it came to Burns. It would all be worth it the moment she announced to the entire town that they'd raised enough money to save the library. Her heart warmed at the thought.

Toward that aim, she settled her attention on the second to last bid sheet—the one for Landon's villa in Greece. She did a double take at the winning bid. The name printed beside the generous figure was the last one she'd expected to see, but she couldn't be more thrilled. With a giddy grin, she read off the dollar amount.

The soft click-clack then gentle whir of the calculator filled the air as Beverly added it to the tally.

"Last one." Cassie buried a pang of disappointment as she flipped to the final item—Lydia's diary. Whoever won, she'd be happy for them. She dragged her fingertip down the list of entries, stopping cold on the last one. Her breath caught. Tears muddled her vision as she gaped at the neatly printed name.

Sprinkles.

Surprise and affection bubbled to the surface, spilling from her lips as she laughed through her tears. Her sweet, adoring, ever-supportive husband had bid on the diary for her. And she suddenly couldn't think of a single thing save for showering him with appreciation.

"Is everything all right?" Beverly asked, confused by her abrupt burst of emotion.

"Everything is wonderful." Cassie sprang from the chair, wiping her eyes. "Do you mind double-checking the total without me? I need to find Luke."

"Not at all." Beverly stole a glance at the bid sheet, her lips curving into a knowing smile.

Cassie barely felt the floor beneath her feet as she flew out of the library and skipped down the steps. The sun shone brightly across the town square buzzing with festivalgoers gathered on the lawn. A collective aura of excitement and merriment permeated the warm spring air thickly scented with sugary funnel cake and cotton candy.

She wove through the throng, searching for Luke, but paused when someone tapped her arm.

"Can we talk?" her mother asked.

"Of course. But can it wait a few minutes? I'm looking for Luke." Cassie kept one eye on the crowd. If she didn't spot him soon, she'd call his cell.

"It can't wait." Her mother's strained tone drew her gaze,

and Cassie abandoned her search the second she glimpsed her pained expression.

With a flood of panic, Cassie followed her away from the commotion in the town square, behind Mac's Mercantile. "What's wrong?"

The momentary silence felt like an eternity, and her mother's anxious energy only added to her alarm. "Mom, what's going on?"

Donna gathered a deep breath then winced as she exhaled, as if the movement had caused her physical pain. "Bryce plans to sell the library to a developer."

"You mean he *planned* to, past tense. If we didn't raise enough money." Cassie smiled, figuring she could share the good news with her mother to alleviate her concerns. "But you don't have to worry. We raised more than enough."

"No, you don't understand. It doesn't matter how much you raised, he still plans to sell. He's going to blame unforeseen repairs and expenses and claim that selling is in the best interest of the town, but he never intended to honor your agreement. He wants the big payday."

For a moment, the ground seemed to spin, and Cassie closed her eyes, trying to regain her equilibrium. "How do you know all this?"

"Because I just overheard him on the phone with the developer, finalizing the deal."

Cassie's pulse quickened, blood pounding in her ears as her perception of the truth morphed into a gnarled, repugnant vision of reality. All this time, he'd lied to her face. He'd allowed her, and every member of the community, to work tirelessly toward an unattainable goal. But the grief and distress coursing through her body causing her hands to shake wasn't solely about the library. It was about a corrupt, dishonorable man wielding his unbridled power over a trusting town—*her* town. And she wasn't going to stand by and let it happen.

She whirled on her heel, barely hearing her mother's plea to wait as she strode back into the bustling square. Burgeoning tears blurred the faces around her—faces of people she loved dearly and wanted to protect at all costs—and she bit her bottom lip, determined to keep her wits about her.

She found Burns exactly where she'd expected, pacing behind the curtain on stage, mentally rehearsing his speech, and she breathed a silent prayer of thanks for the privacy provided by the curtain on one side and the enormous sign on the other. Bursting up the steps, she headed straight for him.

"There you are," he greeted her with impatient annoyance. "I've been waiting for you to go over the order of events."

"My mother told me everything," she blurted, indignation tumbling out of her, unrestrained. "How could you do this? All this time, you let me believe a lie. You let the *town* believe a lie." The betrayal tasted bitter on her tongue.

Burns's entire body stiffened in shock. "She told you?" His meticulously maintained composure fell away like a mask being ripped from his face. But almost as quickly, he regained his footing, slapping on his well-polished facade. "I never lied to you, Cassie," he said coolly. "I merely withheld the truth. Your mother and I agreed not to tell you, since I never wanted kids. We thought it would be best, and easier for all of us to coexist, if you didn't know I was your father. And clearly, we were right. Look at how much the truth has upset you."

He gazed at her with cold, impersonal pity, like a casual, uncaring observer watching a stranger trip and scrape their knee.

Cassie stared back, unable to breathe, while the invisible walls of her safe, familiar world came crashing down around her. She reached for a stronghold to steady herself, disoriented as her pulse pounded, loud and oppressive, drowning out every sound save for a shrill ringing in her ears. Her hands met nothing but air, and she stumbled backward, reeling at a reality that didn't seem possible.

This man—a man not worthy of her respect let alone her affection—couldn't be her father. Her mother wouldn't let her live in this town, inhabiting the same space with the very man she'd begged to meet, without saying a word. Donna Hayward had made a lot of mistakes, but this was too cruel to even consider.

"I don't believe you." The whispered words barely made it past the sob welling in her throat, and the second they escaped her lips, a terrifying awareness gripped her heart, solidifying an agonizing truth.

She did believe him.

Which meant everything she knew before this moment—about herself, her mother, and the life they'd lovingly built from the broken pieces of their past—had been the real lie all along.

CHAPTER 30

DONNA

Donna scurried down the side street after Cassie, hoping to stop her before she confronted Bryce. No good could come from an altercation between them. She quickened her pace, spilling into the crowd. As she scanned the array of faces searching for her daughter, fear overwhelmed her, bordering on crippling panic. Her breath came in short, ragged bursts as the countless outcomes raced through her mind, all of which led to Cassie being deeply hurt.

"Hey." Rhett placed a hand on her shoulder, gently grounding her. His eyes scanned hers, reading the situation. "I take it the conversation didn't go well?"

Compassion coated his words, soothing her racing heart. After she told him about Bryce's phone call, he'd agreed that Cassie needed to know as soon as possible. And to avoid over-burdening her daughter with a barrage of devastating news, she'd wait to tell Cassie about Bryce once they resolved the pressing issue of the library. "She's on her way to confront him right now. Can you help me find her?"

"Of course."

They split up to maximize their search area, and Donna instantly missed his calming presence. The familiar loss of control and petrifying helplessness consumed her, dragging her thoughts to a dark, ominous place—a place ruled by the numbing effects of alcohol. She fought the urge to run away and seek refuge in the bottom of a bottle.

All these years, she'd kept their secret. Yes, to protect Cassie. But in doing so, she'd also protected Bryce. She'd shielded him from having to take any responsibility for the role he'd played. And for the role he hadn't—as Cassie's father. He'd convinced her that her voice didn't matter, that compared to his, it didn't count. And maybe to some people, it didn't. But it mattered to her. And to her daughter.

Donna spotted Bill Tucker on stage, adjusting the stand of a microphone. The edge of the crimson curtain fluttered in the breeze, and she instantly knew where she'd find her daughter. Bryce would undoubtedly be rehearsing his big speech.

Fueled by adrenaline and protective maternal instincts, she made her way through the crowd, barely registering the people around her as she bobbed around the milling bodies standing in wait. She ducked behind the curtain just in time to see a flash of Cassie's stricken features before she stumbled down the steps on the other side of the stage.

Ignoring Bryce, she moved to follow her daughter, but froze the second he spoke, lobbing his accusation like a poisonous barb. "This is your fault. If you'd kept your mouth shut like you were supposed to, this wouldn't have happened."

"What did you say to her?" A sickening dread slithered up her spine, answering her question before he had a chance.

"You only have yourself to blame." He doubled down on

his excuse, his voice rising in agitation. "I thought you told her."

He had the audacity to curl his lip in disgust, and something inside her snapped. Cowering at his feet all those years ago had crushed her, breaking her spirit and devastating her already-fragile self-worth. Was she willing to give him that power again? Or did they both need to face the consequences of their decisions? "That's not going to work this time, Bryce." She surprised herself with the steadiness of her own words. "You can't hide behind my fears and insecurities anymore. I won't let you."

"Oh really?" He cackled in amusement, not seeming to notice or care the way his voice carried, as if he felt untouchable. "And what are you going to do? Tell the town I'm Cassie's father? Tell them I reneged on my deal to protect the library? Tell them they're gullible sheep for trusting me?" He laughed again, delirious with power.

"She doesn't have to." The deep gravel of Rhett's voice startled them both, but the second Donna turned and saw him standing there like a pillar of protection, her heart soared.

"Ah, the delinquent boyfriend," Bryce jeered. "A felon dating a drunk. You two make quite the couple."

Rhett's fist coiled at his side, and Donna held her breath, praying he wouldn't let Bryce's taunts get to him.

"I hate to break it to you, old boy," Bryce snickered with a scornful sneer, "but no one's going to believe you, either. I think the word of the respected mayor carries a little more weight than an ex-con's."

"That's exactly what I'm counting on." Rhett yanked the silk cord, and the curtain toppled to the stage, revealing a sea of shock and outrage. Between the microphone and the echoing curvature of the sign, the crowd had heard every incriminating word.

Bryce paled as he realized what he'd done in his arrogant carelessness. "It—this—it's not what it looks like," he stammered.

"It looks like you're a fox guarding the henhouse," Frank snarled from the front row. "And do you know what happens when we catch a fox in our henhouse?"

Bryce instinctively inched backward as Luke stepped forward in the crowd, flanked by his closest friends. More than half a dozen men stood shoulder to broad shoulder, staring Bryce down like a battalion. And perhaps even more intimidating were the women who'd crowded in front of them, led by Eliza, whose fiery glare made her look ten feet tall. Donna pressed a palm to her chest, her heart bursting at the sight of so many people poised to protect her daughter.

"This has all been a simple misunderstanding. A harmless mistake." Bryce tried to backpedal, but Donna noticed the beads of sweat on his brow.

"The only mistake," Frank grunted, "is letting you be our mayor. But you know what they say. Fool me once, shame on you. Fool me twice, and I'll run ya out of town." He turned to his wife, trying to keep a straight, menacing face as he asked, "Can we still tar and feather, Bevy?"

"I'm afraid not, darling."

"That's a shame." Frank pinned Bryce with a withering scowl. "You know what else is a shame? Having a daughter like Cassie and being too brainless to see how lucky you are."

"If you've hurt her…" Luke growled, taking another step toward the stage.

"Hey, listen." Burns held up his hands in a gesture of capitulation. "Things are getting a little carried away. Remember, you need me. According to the bylaws, the mayor has to be from one of the founding families."

"Bylaws can be changed, right, Luke?" Eliza asked, keeping her gaze narrowed on Bryce.

"I don't think they have to be," Donna blurted before the thought had fully formed. All eyes turned in her direction as the townspeople waited for her to elaborate. As the impulsive idea coalesced, she realized it made all the sense in the world.

"What do you have in mind?" Rhett prompted, standing beside her for support.

"I know exactly who our new mayor should be."

"*Our* mayor?" he said softly, as if he didn't dare hope.

She smiled, tears welling in her eyes as she swept her gaze from Rhett to the familiar faces beaming back at her in accord as they realized who she meant. "Shall we take a vote?"

"Hold on! You can't do this—" Bryce protested, then snapped his mouth shut at Frank's warning glower.

"All in favor?" Donna asked, ignoring Bryce's objection.

Every hand shot into the air followed by celebratory shouts and cheers.

Donna wanted to share in their happiness, but with one hurdle overtaken, her focus shifted to a more challenging one that lay ahead—seeking her daughter's forgiveness. Again.

Only this time, the damage might be too great to overcome.

CHAPTER 31

CASSIE

Cassie's shoulders shook with each sob as she lay facedown on the mahogany desk, her head propped on both forearms, blocking out the world that hadn't stopped spinning since she'd learned the truth.

The truth... Normally, such a comforting word. Noble. Freeing. Worthy of pursuit. But this time, she wasn't so certain. Had her mother been right to keep it from her?

She lifted her heavy gaze to the portrait above the mantel. The stalwart black eyes of Chadwick Burns met hers, but this time, they didn't belong to a stranger from the past. They belonged to her great-great-great—she wasn't sure how far removed—grandfather.

At one time, she would've been thrilled to discover she had ties to one of Poppy Creek's founding families. But now, she felt nothing but heartache. Heartache over a man who was so disinterested in being her father, he'd lived in the same town for over two years without ever striking up a single conversation.

Grief and a wave of humiliation she couldn't explain

washed over her, churning her stomach. Had he known she was looking for him? Had he heard the rumors and laughed, thinking if only she knew? Or was he so indifferent he didn't think of her at all?

Another sob rose in her throat, and her chest heaved as she struggled for air. How could he look her in the eye—his own flesh and blood—and feel nothing?

"How?" she asked out loud, imploring the stoic figure of her forefather who bore a remarkable resemblance to Burns. They shared the same dark hair and eyes, and boasted a similar sharp, angular jawline and broad nose. Had Chadwick been just as callous and unfeeling as his power-hungry predecessor? Would he be proud of Burns or ashamed? There was so much she didn't know about her ancestry. Was her entire paternal family line just as reprehensible?

Her gaze flitted to the glass case. Lydia's diary lay inside, calling out to her. With trembling fingers, Cassie lifted it from its resting place and settled on the window seat, tucking her feet beneath her. The soft, aged leather smelled earthy and faintly sweet, and she gingerly turned to the first page, slipping into the past.

Lydia's sloping cursive told of intense hardship and innumerable sacrifices but also of resilience as a brave band of men and women sought to build a better life. As she read, Cassie cried solaced tears, sharing in their triumph as they overcame countless obstacles to erect an entire town from the harsh, unforgiving soil beneath their worn soles.

Through Lydia's raw, vulnerable writing, Cassie caught a glimpse of hope in the future. Her tears waned and her spirits lifted, ever so slightly. Until it all came crashing down on the page.

A forest fire had blazed through the town, reducing their

dreams to a pile of ash and cinder. Lydia's sorrow soaked deeper than the ink stains, and Cassie's heart broke anew.

Pushed to the edge of grief, her throat sore, eyes aching and tender, Cassie closed the book, unable to bear any more sadness. But as quickly as she slammed it shut, she eased it back open, driven by a desperate need to know how they persevered through such unthinkable anguish.

Chadwick says we can rebuild, even greater than before, but I do not share his idealism or his fortitude. It is clear to me now. God has abandoned us. There is no good here.

A tear slid down Cassie's cheek and onto the page, dampening a water stain that marred the yellowed paper. Had Lydia shed her own tears as she wrote these words?

I took a constitutional walk this morning at Chadwick's urging. He said the Lord would meet me among the trees. I remained silent, too fatigued to argue, but I knew I would be alone.

With each step, my soul grieved the devastation around me. Mighty redwoods stripped of their glory, regal pines snapped in two. I could go no further. The grief had become too heavy a burden to bear.

Then I saw it, like a vision from heaven. A sea of gold among the ruins. Sunlight streamed through scorched branches, unfurling the velveteen petals, so supple yet strong. They had survived the unspeakable, unafraid to bloom again.

At that moment, I recalled a verse from the Holy Bible my mother made me memorize.

"Wherefore, if God so clothe the grass of the field, which today is, and to morrow is cast into the oven, shall he not much more clothe you, O ye of little faith?"

That morning, the Lord gave me a promise in the poppies. No matter what troubles unfold, He is with us. His love covers all trials and transgressions, and His strength, perfected in our weakness, will always be enough.

I do not have to wither in adversity. Like the flowers of the field, I can bloom above the ashes.

Cassie read Lydia's words again and again, her quiet wisdom like cool water on a blistering burn. As she faced the wreckage of her own heart, she had a similar choice. Wither or bloom?

She gently turned to the last page, hoping to find another

wise maxim—a line, a phrase, anything—not yet ready to say goodbye. But instead of sage reverie preserved in ink and paper, she discovered a dried poppy pressed between the pages, safeguarded for over a century.

With the lightest, feather-soft touch, she caressed the brittle edges, a smile curling her lips. Her father may not be a man worthy of her heart, but he wasn't the only branch of her family tree she'd unwittingly uncovered. And not all of them lived in the past. Perhaps there was some good to be found after all.

The creaking of hinges disrupted her thoughts. She tore her gaze from the pressed poppy to find her husband standing in the doorway with a look on his face that said he knew everything.

As their eyes met, a surge of love and affection barreled through her, stealing her breath. Before she could say a word, he'd covered the distance and gathered her in his arms. For several minutes, she merely clung to him, cocooned in his embrace, inhaling his soothing, familiar scent as his chest rose and fell in a comforting, steady rhythm. No matter how far off-kilter her world became, her husband remained a refuge, fixed and unwavering.

"I'm so sorry, Ru," he murmured, caressing her hair at the nape of her neck. "Do you want to talk about it?"

She tilted her head back, locking eyes once more, communicating in a single glance that, although wounded, she'd be okay. "Yes, but not now." Her gaze drifted to the diary, nestled on the cushion beside her. In a way, she'd worked through many of her feelings with a woman she'd never met. A woman with whom she now felt intrinsically connected.

"How did you find out?" she asked, adding, "Does anyone else know?"

His features softened as he held her hand, tracing his thumb in gentle circles across her skin. "Most of the town knows. Your mother confronted Burns on stage while we all waited for his keynote, not realizing we could hear them."

Cassie winced, fighting a sudden surge of embarrassment. But was it so terrible they all knew? These people were her family. Wouldn't she tell them, anyway? She thought of the tremendous amount of love waiting for her, and Maggie's words from the other night tiptoed into her foremost thoughts. *Not all families are related by blood, but they're no less real.*

In the quiet corner of her soul, beyond the pain and betrayal, in a place that believed in redemption and miracles, she still prayed for a different ending—for a chance at reconciliation with her father and maybe, one day, a relationship. Perhaps she always would. But for now, she'd grieve the loss of what could have been and find comfort in her greatest blessing—the people of her heart who remained by her side through both the fires and the fields of flowers. And she could only hope that she enriched their lives as much as they did hers.

"What about the library?" she asked. "Did you hear about that, too?"

"We did. And let's just say, it didn't go over well." Luke's lips twitched ever so slightly. "I think Burns is afraid of Frank. He canceled the deal with the developer. On speakerphone, thanks to Frank's insistence. And he's leaving town." Luke squeezed her hand, regarding her with earnest empathy. "Are you okay?"

"I think so," she said slowly. "Or at least, I know I will be."

He pressed a tender kiss to her temple, and she savored the

simple gesture that spoke volumes to her wounded heart. "What about the town? We don't have a mayor now."

"About that…" Luke trailed off then cleared his throat. "Your mother made a nomination, and there was a unanimous vote in favor of her recommendation."

"Who was it?" Cassie asked, racking her brain.

"Who do you think?" The way Luke looked at her—with a meaningful twinkle in his hazel eyes—momentarily stole her breath.

"Me?" She blinked, completely taken aback.

"Don't sound so surprised." He chuckled softly. "You're the obvious choice. No one loves this town more than you. You care about its history and its future. And more than that, you care about the people."

"But—" Every word vanished from her vocabulary, leaving her too stunned to speak. They'd all voted to make her Poppy Creek's new mayor? It didn't seem real. Even as her mind tried to make sense of the outlandish proposition, other thoughts crowded her subconscious. Her thoughts filled with ideas she could implement as mayor… like an annual coffee festival.

Before her excitement took over, she tugged her daydreams back to reality. "Luke, how can I be mayor? We're having a baby. I own a business. Even if I wanted to accept, I don't see how it's possible."

"I know. It's a lot. But we can make it happen. Together." He glanced at the door, adding softly, "And there's someone else who would love to help."

Cassie knew who she'd find before she ever followed his gaze. But there was one thing she didn't know… Was she ready to forgive her?

CHAPTER 32

DONNA

As Luke slipped out of the office, leaving them alone, Donna's heart warmed with gratitude. Her daughter had married a good man. He'd known exactly where to find her, and every decision he made—even in supporting the repair of their fractured relationship—he prioritized Cassie's needs and best interests. While she wanted to make peace with her daughter more than anything, at least she could take comfort knowing that no matter what happened between them, Cassie couldn't have a better teammate than Luke.

Gathering every ounce of courage, she settled on the window seat beside her daughter, whose gaze remained fixed on her hands clasped tightly in her lap. Tension strained between them, but Cassie remained seated, which Donna took as an encouraging sign.

"I should have told you the truth." Donna spoke above the knot in her throat, knowing her words would never be enough. "I'm so deeply sorry I kept it from you."

There was so much more she wanted to say, to try to explain. But as she sat there beside her daughter, watching her knuckles turn white as she pressed her palms tighter together, all justification and reasoning fell away, leaving only sincere, soul-searing contrition. Her apology needed to speak for itself. No excuses to smooth the rough edges of what she'd done.

She held her breath as if letting the air settle would give Cassie space to process her emotions.

After an interminable silence, her daughter's hands relaxed on the smooth cotton folds of her sundress, and she slowly lifted her gaze. "I think I understand why you didn't."

Donna exhaled, supremely thankful for the olive branch. "No more secrets. If there's anything you want to know —*anything*—all you have to do is ask."

"Did you love him?" Cassie's question floated from her lips, faint and ephemeral, like a whisper's shadow.

She hesitated, resisting the urge to sugarcoat or spin the truth, answering with a simple but honest "No."

"Then why... *him*?" The word escaped with a wince, as if Cassie couldn't bring herself to say his name.

"Honestly..." She released a slow, ragged sigh, pained by her admission. "Because he was there, during a moment when I so badly wanted to escape my own heartache, I completely shut down. At that moment, nothing mattered."

"Do you regret it?" Implicit in her daughter's question was something deeper and more profound. Did she regret *her*?

"No," Donna said again, this time without hesitation. Tears pooled, collecting in her lashes as she fought for control of her emotions. How could she explain the depths of her love when her actions over the years seemed to be in direct contradiction? "I know it didn't always seem like it," she said, her voice trembling, "but I've always loved you. I've always wanted you. You are the best thing in my life, and I'm so sorry I didn't make that obvious every second of every day."

Her own eyes glistening, Cassie gathered a shaky breath, as if preparing to unburden a weight she'd carried for years. "The day I checked you into the Snyder Sobriety Center, I thought you genuinely wanted to get better. But you didn't even stay forty-eight hours. I never understood why you left."

Donna slumped into the cushions, no longer able to fight gravity. The night she left rehab had been one of her lowest points, and an enormous source of shame, but Cassie deserved to know the truth—every ugly, unpleasant part of it. "Because I was scared."

"That it wouldn't work?"

"That it would."

"I don't understand."

Donna swallowed, her voice raw and raspy as she confessed, "When I drink, I become someone I despise. Selfish. Cold. Unkind. It's as if too much alcohol taints my soul. And I was afraid—" She closed her eyes. "I was afraid my heart would be just as repulsive sober. That nothing would change beyond my blood alcohol content." When she opened her eyes, a tear spilled down her cheek. "I realized it was about more than getting sober. My soul needed healing first. And I wasn't sure I was ready."

"What changed?" Her daughter's soft gaze exuded the kind of compassion Donna couldn't always comprehend—the kind that sprang from somewhere within her being, not from personal experience or intimate understanding.

Donna shifted, reaching into the back pocket of her jeans to pull out her phone. For a moment, she merely held it in her hand, facing the magnitude of sharing this piece of her heart for the first time. Pinching the thin slip of paper, she pried it from the crevice of her phone case. "This." She handed the neatly folded square to Cassie. "It's the letter my mom left me after she died. The first time I read it, I was so angry. Angry at my mom. Angry at myself. The night I left rehab, I hit rock bottom. I got so drunk, I nearly died."

"Your friend Gretchen saved your life," Cassie whispered, and Donna nodded, remembering the first time she'd told her daughter the story—how Gretchen and her AA sponsor never left her side through her withdrawals, supporting her as she took her first real step toward recovery.

"This is the part of the story I left out." She nodded toward the letter.

"And you want me to read it?" Cassie held it in her open palm tentatively, as if it were a butterfly that might flutter away with the tiniest movement.

Donna offered a small smile as her consent, and Cassie gingerly slid her finger into the crease, unfolding the letter.

As her daughter silently absorbed the words on the page, Donna mentally recited each one from heart.

My darling daughter,

As I write this, my heart breaks that I never got to hold you one last time. But even in my sorrow, I understand why all my letters went unanswered. I wasn't there for you when you needed me, when you were hurting as much as I was. I had succumbed to my grief, and it took the grace, patience, and unconditional love of steadfast friends to help me see that I'd lost so much more than your father. I'd lost myself. I'd lost you. And I'd lost my granddaughter.

By the time I realized to what depths my despair had driven me, I could no longer repair the damage I'd caused. I'd pushed you too far to ever forgive me.

Please, my darling, don't make the same mistake. The only thing worse than living with regret is facing death, knowing you've run out of time for a second chance. Your daughter needs you to fight for her. Whatever it takes. I should have fought for you sooner—for both of you—and I'm so deeply sorry I didn't.

In my passing, there will be some things you won't understand. Please know that there are reasons for every decision, each one guided by love.

Lastly, dear one, don't look to the past through the bottom of a bottle. It only distorts and magnifies our pain. People—even people who love us dearly—can let us down. Sometimes, we can feel alone. But don't lose heart. Stand rooted in hope without fear of the future, for if the Lord takes care of the sparrows, how much more will He take care of you?

All my love, always,
Mom

"The sparrows," Cassie murmured, grazing her fingertips across the handwritten letters, as if they spoke to her heart with special meaning. A tear slid down her cheek, and she gently brushed it aside. "When she mentioned the things you won't understand, do you think she meant the clause in her will stipulating I had to complete the Christmas Calendar to inherit the house?"

"Yes, I do," she admitted as a surge of gratitude crashed into her. "I think, in her own strange way, she was hoping we'd both wind up here. Together."

"That we'd find our way back home?" Cassie whispered, meeting her gaze.

Donna nodded, too overwhelmed to speak. Just when she didn't think she could handle another drop of emotion, Cassie slipped her arms around her neck, burying her face in her hair. "I love you, Mom."

Her heart bursting, Donna returned her daughter's embrace, savoring the same sweet, delicate scent forever imprinted on her memory. "I love you, too, sweetheart. Always."

CHAPTER 33

CASSIE

Clasping Luke's hand, Cassie ambled along the well-worn path, her heart soaring so high, her feet barely touched the ground. Luke lugged their picnic basket laden with chicken pesto paninis and enough pasta salad to share. With the plethora of special Poppy Creek events to choose from, Cassie found it difficult to declare a favorite, but the Butterfly Stroll came close.

That morning, on the final day of the Founders Day Festival, they'd met their friends and family in the town square and departed, as a group, to the trailhead just beyond Main Street. Cassie couldn't help stealing periodic glances over her shoulder at her mother and Rhett, who walked close behind them, lost in their own intimate microcosm.

As they traversed farther into the forest, sunlight dispersed through the treetops like soft golden rays guiding their path. The sweet melody of songbirds echoed in the branches, serenading the day's adventure, and the babbling stream accompanied their journey until they crossed the footbridge, heading east toward Larkspur Meadow.

When they reached the clearing and stepped from the tree line into the grassy field, Cassie's breath caught. A blanket of gold poppies, dotted with swaths of purple lupine and baby blue eyes, spread out before them.

"Are you okay?" Luke asked when she halted abruptly. "Are you tired? We can take a break."

"I'm fine. It just—" She paused, uncertain how to describe the sudden burst of emotion.

"Reminds you of Lydia's diary?" Luke smiled as he squeezed her hand, and she met his loving, understanding gaze. He knew her so well.

Last night, as they lay in each other's arms, in the sweet, tender moments before sleep, she'd shared Lydia's words, processing more of her thoughts. Somehow, merely by listening and offering his support, he'd helped her make sense of her new, upside-down world. And he'd opened her eyes to a beautiful vision of what the future could hold if she embraced her newfound opportunities. Opportunities like mayorship. And meeting her grandmother, Anne Burns.

"Yes, it does," she admitted. "I don't think I'll ever see a poppy the same way again."

"Neither will I." He tucked her hand into the crook of his arm, helping her over a fallen branch as they resumed their trek.

When they reached the other side of the meadow, they entered another cluster of trees. The trail narrowed, leading beneath a wooden archway with the words Monarch Butterfly Reserve engraved on a rustic sign. Two by two, they ducked below the wild roses dripping from the rough-hewn beams and entered another world. In the shade of towering sequoias and sugar pines, hundreds of monarch butterflies performed a mesmerizing dance. Their brightly hued wings in varying shades of honey, marigold, and tangerine mingled with the vibrant poppies, as if the petals themselves had taken flight.

Although Cassie had witnessed the stunning sight before, it never ceased to steal her breath, as if it became more captivating each time. And this year, she admired the tableau with added appreciation. She'd learned from Frank's book, *The Mariposa Method*, that a butterfly—or *mariposa* in Spanish—symbolized rebirth. In so many ways, that's exactly how she felt. Like everything had changed.

As she watched the butterflies flit and flutter, finally free from their chrysalides, they gave her hope that the next chapter of her life could be just as beautiful.

They strolled silently through the reserve, peacefully reflecting as they carefully kept to the trail, until they reached a twin archway on the other side. The end of the path spilled into a second meadow with picnic tables and a simple outhouse maintained by a team of volunteer conservationists.

As the tables filled with townspeople, blankets were spread on the ground and baskets and coolers were unpacked. Bill Tucker pulled out his penny whistle, and the light, lyrical sound accompanied the songbirds. The entire vignette couldn't have been more perfect.

Cassie glanced over her shoulder as the last couple exited the reserve. Reed and Olivia paused under the archway, holding hands while they enjoyed one last glimpse of paradise. In her white eyelet sundress, framed by fragrant wild roses, Olivia could be the cover model for Bohemian Bride.

The same moment an audacious, completely outlandish idea struck her, Olivia caught her eye. A look passed between them, and without a word, Cassie knew an identical thought had crossed Olivia's mind.

Olivia's gaze bore through her, questioning, as if searching for a sign of encouragement. Cassie's giddy grin must have given her friend all the confidence she needed, because Olivia turned to Reed and blurted, "Would you like to get married?"

"Yes, I would. I thought the ring made that clear," he teased, rubbing her engagement ring with his thumb.

"No, I mean, would you like to get married right now?"

Reed blinked in surprise. "I—I'm not sure I understand what you're asking."

"I know this sounds rash," Olivia said in a rushed breath. "I know we already have a wedding planned for the fall. But something has felt... off. I couldn't put my finger on it until just now. This—" She swept her gaze over the idyllic setting and their friends and family gathered in one place. "*This* is us. And if it's okay with you, I'd like to marry you right here, right now."

Reed recovered from his shock, chuckling softly. "Liv, I've wanted to marry you since the day you moved next door. If you want to move up the wedding date, you don't have to ask me twice."

With a cheer of delight, Olivia threw her arms around him, kissing her soon-to-be-husband with so much fervor, they almost toppled over.

"Easy, you two," Cassie said with a laugh. "Save it for the ceremony."

In under thirty minutes, Cassie had gathered a wildflower bouquet, recruited Pastor Bellman as the officiant—with the agreement they'd procure the official wedding license soon— and organized a few special ceremony details for the couple while they announced their impromptu decision to their friends and family. The air buzzed with excitement as picnic tables and blankets were rearranged and everyone took their seats.

In her smoky alto, Kat sang an enchanting, pared-down version of "La Vie en Rose" in lieu of the classic wedding march, accompanied by Bill Tucker on his penny whistle. As Olivia floated down the makeshift aisle, Cassie grabbed Luke's hand, moved beyond words. The gentle breeze lifted the strands of Olivia's long onyx hair and ruffled the hem of her dress, giving her an otherworldly allure. Barefoot and wearing a crown woven from lavender and yarrow, she resembled a striking wood nymph, almost too exquisite to be real.

Cassie stole a glance at Reed waiting beneath the archway with Pastor Bellman, and her heart swelled at the blend of pure, unbridled love and awestruck wonder in his dark, shimmering eyes. He dabbed at the corners with the sleeve of his pale blue button-down before straightening, holding Olivia's gaze as she closed the gap between them.

Pastor Bellman gave a brief but profound message on love and marriage before asking the couple to share their vows—their unscripted, spontaneous vows from the heart.

"Reed Hollis," Olivia said with a catch in her voice. "You were my first true friend. Someone who made me feel comfortable being myself, with every quirk and imperfection. In a season when other kids and their unkind words tore me down, you made me feel invincible. You made the whole world seem safer and more magical, like every good thing was at my fingertips." Her words faltered, and Reed tightened his grip, sharing a reassuring smile meant only for her.

Visibly bolstered by his touch, she continued with a shaky breath. "At the lowest point in my life, you came back into it, like an act of God's grace. You helped me see that my worth isn't defined by others, that there's hope in the midst of heartache, and that faith can move mountains." A tear tumbled down her cheek, but she let it fall, clinging tightly to Reed's hands. "From this day forward, I vow to be your help-mate. To encourage, support, and embolden your endeavors as much as you have mine. I promise to be a faithful wife and to never, ever stop being your friend."

Cassie wiped a tear from her eye as Reed cleared his throat, struggling to steady his emotions enough to speak.

"Liv—" His voice cracked and he cleared his throat again. "I used to pray so hard for this moment. Then, when the day came that my dream ended, and I lost you to another man, my prayers changed. I prayed he would love and cherish you and give you a life filled with laughter and treasured moments. Now…" He paused, collecting his composure. "Now, I say those same prayers every night, except this time, they're for me. Liv, you're the most incredible woman I've ever known. And I vow to spend the rest of my life showing you just how special you are."

Cassie sniffled as they exchanged temporary rings made from braided blades of grass, overwhelmed by happiness—and possibly a surge of pregnancy hormones.

She tilted her chin, affectionately regarding the man who'd not only become her husband, but her best friend and father of their child. When they met a few years ago, she couldn't even fathom where they'd find themselves today. The next two, ten, and twenty-plus years awaited them with an equal amount of uncertainty, but she no longer feared what lay ahead or behind.

She glanced at the familiar faces around her. Frank and Beverly, a love story unlike any other that inspired her endlessly. Eliza and Grant, a sweet testament to second chances born from the healing power of love and forgiveness. Penny and Colt, an unexpected but unshakable couple who truly brought out the best in each other. Kat and Jack, a pair of generous and compassionate hearts that grew exponentially when melded together. Olivia and Reed, two childhood friends, reunited after years apart, who found love, redemption, and renewed purpose in one another's arms. Lucy and Vick, so different yet so perfectly suited, like puzzle pieces, balancing and complementing each other to create a more beautiful picture. Sadie and Landon, once enemies who learned to let go of their assumptions to not only find love, but a teammate in all aspects of life. Maggie, Dolores, Bill and Irene, and now her mother and Rhett, two wounded hearts, mended by an outpouring of grace, empathy, and humble bravery.

So many people who had impacted her life in innumerable ways. And it was thanks to each one of them—the family of her heart who loved one another faithfully—that she could look toward the future with hope, courage, and a smile that reached all the way to her soul.

CHAPTER 34

DONNA

"Are you sure about this?" Donna asked from behind the brocade curtain.

"Positive," Penny assured her. "I knew the moment I found that dress at an estate sale that it was meant for you."

"Come out so we can see it." Cassie's voice rang with excited anticipation.

Donna sighed and stepped out of the dressing room at Thistle & Thorn and was met with enthralled gasps from Cassie, Penny, and Kat. All three women sat side by side on a plum-colored chaise lounge, gazing at her with the dreamy-eyed delight of bridesmaids saying yes to the dress. Except, Donna wasn't modeling a wedding gown. Although, she realized with startling surprise, the idea wasn't wholly unappealing. She'd donned the 1950s swing-inspired dress for her date with Rhett at tonight's end-of-the-festival dance.

"Are you sure it's not too much?" She smoothed the fitted sweetheart bodice that cinched at her waist before flaring into a full skirt that fell just above her knees.

"It's perfect." Penny sprang from the couch to finish

buttoning the back of the dress. "This sage green color makes the combination of your light eyes and dark hair pop. And since tonight is more of a barn dance aesthetic, we'll tone it down with simple hair and makeup and these." She held up a pair of cream, ankle-high cowboy boots with subtle floral embroidery. "What do you think?"

"They're beautiful." Donna caressed the buttery-soft leather before she slipped them on.

"I think Rhett's going to be the luckiest guy at the dance," Kat told her with a bright, sincere smile.

"You look stunning, Mom." Cassie pressed a hand over her heart, beaming like a mother admiring her daughter all dressed up for her first date.

Donna smiled at the sweet irony. The sharp trill of her cell phone disrupted the winsome mood, and she ducked back inside the dressing room to check the caller ID.

Her happiness soared as she read the name on the screen. Stephanie was checking in of her own accord, without Donna having to leave several messages first. If her luck continued, Steph would be calling to say she finally agreed to come visit. "Hi!" she chirped, twirling in the mirror as she spoke. "How are you?"

"Fa-fan-tab-u-lous," Stephanie slurred into the speaker. "Ne-ev-er better."

Donna's heart froze as icy fear careened through her. "Are you drunk?"

"To-tally tanked."

"What happened?" She tried to keep her voice steady despite the panic gripping her throat.

"I just wan-ted one drink, ya know? I—I thought I could han-dle it." Stephanie's words came in a garbled, staccato rhythm, each stuttered syllable like a stab to the heart.

If she'd been there... if she'd never left... this wouldn't have happened. "Where are you?"

"At a fr-friend's h-house."

"Where? What's the address? I'm coming to get you."

When Stephanie didn't respond, Donna pressed the phone harder to her ear, as if somehow that would force sound to fill the silence. "Steph," she said as calmly as she could manage. "Tell me where you are."

"I—I don't know. But I'm f-fine. D-don't you worry about me, 'kay? I'll call you l-later."

The deafening click ending the call reverberated in her eardrums, and Donna slumped to the floor. As the adrenaline fled her body, it gave way to an uncontrollable sob. Guilt and gut-wrenching sadness overcame all other senses, and she curled into herself, hugging her knees to her chest as she wept.

"What happened?" Cassie cried with shocked concern as she dropped to the ground beside her.

Donna heard movement in the dressing room, as if Kat and Penny had crowded into the small space around them. Unable to stop the wave of sobs, she managed to expel only a single word—Stephanie—but Cassie seemed to understand exactly what it meant.

"Oh, Mom. I'm so sorry." Cassie slipped a comforting arm around her shoulders. "What can I do to help?"

The same question had tumbled through her own mind, over and over like pummeling fists against her temples. Stephanie must subconsciously want help, or else why had she called? But without knowing where to find her, what could she do? Hopelessness consumed her, dragging her into the darkest corners of herself. "I need a meeting." The whispered statement sounded more like a desperate plea—one that didn't seem possible.

But within an hour, she found herself in the town hall, seated in a circle of folding chairs, still wearing the pale green dress. Rhett, Irene, Mac, and even Frida faced her, all clothed and coiffed for tonight's dance.

Donna gazed at each one in turn, her red, swollen eyes dry of tears. They all had somewhere else to be, and yet, they'd chosen to sit here, content in the stillness, simply because she needed them. She didn't think she'd ever be able to express the depths of her gratitude, but shouldn't she say something? The silence couldn't go on forever, but words escaped her.

"I'm Frida Connelly. And I'm an addict." Frida's placid confession startled everyone in the room, and Donna gaped at her in disbelief.

Not once in a single meeting had Frida uttered a syllable. Donna could never figure out why the woman showed up night after night only to sit there like a statue.

"Hi, Frida." Irene smiled while everyone else wordlessly waited, too stunned and incredulous to speak.

"I'm Frida," she said again, staring at the wall directly behind Donna's head. "And I'm addicted to quilting."

Mac sputtered as he took a sip of water, chuckling at what he assumed to be a joke.

Frida whipped her head around, pinning him with a withering glare.

"Sorry," he mumbled, shrinking into his seat.

"It started when I was a young girl," Frida continued, directing her dismissive gaze back toward the wall. Although she sat with shoulders back and chin raised, Donna noticed a slight tremble in the woman's hands. "Most nights, my father stopped at the pub after work. Just to grab a pint or two with the lads, he'd say. But by the time he came home, he'd become a completely different man than when he left that morning."

An ominous haze permeated the room, as if they all knew too well what that meant. Donna swallowed a sickening dread rising in her throat like bile.

"I'd hide in the sewing closet until it was over," Frida confessed with a calm, practiced passivity, although Donna knew, deep inside, the woman's heart was breaking anew. "I'd pass the time by stitching scraps of fabric together in the light of a single flickering bulb. I liked turning the discarded, damaged remnants into something beautiful and useful." Her harsh features softened a moment before returning to their former stoic state. "As I got older, the habit transcended my hiding place. Whenever I succumbed to stress or anxiety, I'd quilt to calm my nerves. My coping mechanism became a crutch, then a vice. And I cannot abide a vice. It's a weakness." Her piercing eyes flashed with self-reproof.

"It will come as no surprise that my father died of liver disease," she said with a matter-of-fact finality. "The doctors warned him, given his propensity to drink to excess. On his deathbed, when we all faced the inevitable, I asked him why he simply didn't stop drinking. You know what he said?" Frida met her gaze with an unnerving intentionality. "He said it was easier to die drunk than live sober." Something shifted in Frida's eyes, like a veil lifting, revealing a secret sentiment Donna had never seen the woman bestow on anyone before, let alone on her. In the woman's open, vulnerable gaze, she glimpsed raw, unadulterated respect.

After gifting her with a short, almost imperceptible nod, Frida glanced around the circle. "Those of us in this room know that the easiest choice isn't always the right one. We also know that when we make the hard choice—sometimes more than once—we don't have to do it alone."

A wave of affection and appreciation washed over Donna, directed at the most unlikely person. She'd been drowning, and Frida Connelly had reached out her hand, offering a lifeline not only to her, but by proxy, to Stephanie, as well.

She may not know where Stephanie was at this exact moment, but she wouldn't give up until she found her. Because if her daughter, and this town, had taught her anything, it's that love always hopes and always perseveres.

CHAPTER 35

RHETT

I rene was the last to leave the town hall, slipping out the front door and down the ramp Bill and a few others had constructed recently. In her absence, the door hung slightly ajar, and boisterous, twangy music heavily featuring the banjo and fiddle carried through the crevice.

"How are you doing?" Rhett asked, his arm looped around Donna's waist as they stood in the stillness of the empty room.

"Better. But it's hard not knowing where she is."

Rhett drew her closer, his chest heaving as she rested her head on his shoulder. Even in hard times like this—battling the worry and frustration over not being able to find someone who needed their help—he recognized the gift of going through it together. Donna had invited him into her life, both the good and the bad, and in doing so, into her heart. He never wanted to take the privilege for granted.

"We don't have to go to the dance, you know," he told her. "We can stay here or go somewhere quiet."

"Thanks." She smiled up at him, and the sight made his

heartbeat stop. "But I think I'd like to go. There was a time when I never thought I'd say this, but I'd actually like to be surrounded by friends right now."

"Then, allow me." He removed his hand from her waist, holding out the crook of his elbow instead.

With another smile, she linked their arms, and they strolled toward the door together.

"I've been meaning to tell you," he said in a soft, low whisper, leaning in close enough to smell her sweetly scented hair. "You look incredible."

"Thank you." She tucked a silky strand behind her ear, blushing beneath his compliment.

It took considerable effort to take his eyes off her long enough to push open the door, plunging them both into the warm glow of golden, twinkling lights, laughter, and a spirited display of do-si-do.

Throughout the night, they joined in the breathless dancing and mingled among friends, sipping sarsaparilla and munching Eliza's Motherlode Mounds, which were essentially enormous brownies with gold nuggets—aka caramelized hazelnuts—hidden inside. Most of the conversations revolved around Reed and Olivia's impromptu wedding that morning and their subsequent plans to honeymoon in Morocco for the Rose Festival in May.

Periodically, he'd noticed Donna staring into the distance, her expression pensive, and he'd squeeze her hand, silently checking in, making sure she was okay. Each time, she'd meet his gaze with a grateful smile, and the rest of the world would disappear. No matter what the future held, he could say with unwavering certainty that he'd met the person he wanted by his side through it all.

He had an inkling he wasn't the only one having similar

thoughts when the band abruptly stopped midsong and the lively music gave way to a dulcet penny whistle solo by Bill Tucker. Rhett recognized the tune of "True Love Ways" by Buddy Holly as the cluster of dancers backed away, forming a circle around Irene and her current dance partner—her son, Landon—in the center of the town square. Landon bent and kissed his mother's cheek, whispering something in her ear, before slipping away to stand beside his girlfriend, Sadie, who watched the unfolding scene with happy tears in her eyes.

"Is what I *think* is happening really happening?" Donna murmured, sounding a little nonsensical in her surprise.

"I think so." He grinned at Irene's expression of incredulity as Peggy Sue waddled through the crowd, pausing obediently by her side, her curly tail wiggling in excitement as if she knew what came next.

Irene bent and unfastened something tied to Peggy Sue's collar, and at her audible gasp, Rhett could guess what she found.

Donna reached for his hand, her eyes wide and shimmering, and his heart warmed at her obvious delight for her newfound friend. One day, it would be their turn. He had no doubt.

When the song concluded, Bill stuffed the whistle in his back pocket and stepped off the stage. He strode toward Irene with purpose, never taking his eyes off her face, and dropped to one knee. With a flourish, he whipped off his cowboy hat and pressed it to his chest.

A hush of anticipation swept over the square as enraptured onlookers held a collective breath.

Bill's tanned, ruddy face reddened even deeper. He clearly wasn't used to an audience when it came to more private matters. "I'm not good with words, like some folks, so I'm just gonna say what's in my heart, if that's okay." He cleared his throat, grounding himself in Irene's gaze. "Irene, before we met, I didn't think I'd ever find love again. And that was all right with me. I'd had my fair share. I could be happy on my farm, keeping the critters company, counting down to my final days. Then I met you, an angel who could talk to the animals, and something in my heart changed. I didn't want to be alone anymore. Because everything in my life was better when you were there. Even doing nothing, I wanted you there by my side to do nothing with me." He cleared his throat again, flustered. "I guess what I'm trying to say is, what do you think about tying your reins to this old hitching post?"

"I think," Irene said, smiling through her tears, "that I've never heard a better idea. I'd love to marry you, Bill Tucker." She handed him the ring, and amid a swell of cheers and applause, he slid it onto her finger before leaning forward to kiss her, creating a semblance of privacy with the wide brim of his cowboy hat.

"I don't think I've seen a sweeter, more heartfelt proposal in all my life." Donna beamed at the newly engaged couple as friends and family crowded around to offer congratulations.

"You don't mind that it's simple?"

"I think the proposal should fit the couple. For some people, big and flashy is perfect. Personally, I love when they're intimate and from the heart."

"Noted," he said out loud, without thinking.

His face heated when she looked up at him in surprise, but he shrugged away the momentary embarrassment. Why hide his feelings? Turning toward her, he took both of her hands in his. "I'm not saying I'll follow Bill's lead tomorrow, but I do want to tell you this." Time stood still, pressing pause on the world around them, and Rhett savored the sensation of complete and utter peace. "I've fallen in love with you, Donna Hayward. With your courage, compassion, and tenacity, even against overwhelming odds. Borrowing a line from Bill, I didn't think I'd ever find love again. Or that I even wanted to. But now that I have, it's deeper, richer, and more soul-satis-fying than I ever thought possible. And in some ways, this is only the beginning." He hesitated, wrangling his thoughts as he added, "I know you're not sure how long you'll stay in Poppy Creek, but I want you to know that, when it comes to us, I'm not going anywhere. I'm afraid you're stuck with me."

Donna laughed softly—the sweetest sound he'd ever heard. "You're stuck with me, too, Rhett Douglas. And so is Poppy Creek. Despite my best self-sabotaging attempts to resist, I've fallen in love with this town. And with you." She rocked onto her tiptoes and pressed her lips to his, stealing every thought from his mind save one.

He couldn't wait to see what the future held.

CHAPTER 36

DONNA

"What are we doing here?" Still buckled in the passenger seat of her daughter's Prius, Donna gazed at the cottage in confusion. A fresh spring wreath of greenery and lilacs hung on the door. Had Cassie rented the house to someone new?

"I thought we'd make a quick pitstop." Cassie unbuckled her seat belt and slid from the driver's seat, smiling at Donna to follow.

Donna hesitated, one hand on the push-button release. They were supposed to be heading to the town square for Cassie's official inauguration ceremony. What could be so important they'd stopped here first?

As Donna climbed out of the car, she expected to feel the familiar knot in the pit of her stomach that surfaced whenever she revisited her childhood home. And yet, she experienced a surprising sense of calm instead, as if she no longer viewed the memories through the eyes of a lost, wounded teenager.

So much had changed in the last few days since the dance.

Stephanie's so-called friend finally called, begging Donna to come get Stephanie, whose drinking had become a burden rather than an amusement. With Kat's permission, Donna brought Steph to stay with her at the inn. She was currently two days sober, and still experiencing withdrawals, but Donna felt hopeful. She hadn't left her side in the past forty-eight hours, but Frida, of all people, showed up this morning and insisted on sitting by Stephanie's bedside so Donna could watch Cassie be sworn in as Poppy Creek's new mayor.

"Shouldn't you be at the town square getting ready for your speech?" Donna asked, standing beside her daughter in the middle of the gravel driveway.

"We still have a few minutes. And I have something to give you." Cassie reached into the pocket of her bright red blazer— that she'd paired with a pretty floral skirt and silk blouse for the special occasion—and retrieved a small brass key. "I want you to have this." She placed the key in Donna's palm. "And I think Grandma Edith would want you to have it, too." Cassie's lips quirked into a lopsided smile as she added, "To be honest, I think she wanted you to have it all along, and somehow, she knew this was the best way."

Donna's throat closed around a wellspring of emotions as her fingers curled over the cool metal in her hand. Was it possible that after all this time, she could *literally* come back home? Her gaze flitted to the window at the top of the turret. The lamplight no longer glimmered against the glass. But now, going forward, it could burn bright again, like a light-house for other lost souls like her.

For a moment, she stood still, turning the key over in her hand. She could envision making a life here. Brewing enough coffee to be shared around the butcher block island—the same island she'd accidentally nicked at age nine while her father taught her how to filet a freshly caught trout. She could bake scones served with sweet lemon curd every Sunday before church, just like her mother had.

In her visions of the future, Stephanie sat at the table beside her, taking the time she needed to recover, tucked away from temptation, surrounded by people who cared about her well-being. And maybe Stephanie was only the beginning? Other women needed a refuge, too. A beacon of hope when the darkness of their addiction blocked out the light. What if she could help others find the same gift she'd found in Poppy Creek—the gift of hope and second chances?

Rhett also featured prominently in these visions, as did Luke, Cassie, and her future grandchild, plus countless others she'd come to know and love. She'd gone from isolation in a one-bedroom apartment in the city to an abundance of blessings too numerous to count.

"Thank you," she whispered, pressing the key to her heart. How could she ever express to her daughter how much this meant to her?

"There's something else." Cassie slid her hand into her pocket once more. This time, she lifted a delicate silver necklace.

Donna's breath caught as sunlight glinted off the silhouette of a sparrow. "You kept it?"

"I may have stopped believing in its magical powers," Cassie confessed, unclasping the chain. "But I realized it represented something far more important."

Donna swept aside her hair as her daughter draped the pendant around her neck and secured the clasp, meeting her gaze with a look that said more than words. A look that said she understood her gesture of love all those years ago, bestowed in the midst of her brokenness.

With trembling fingers, Donna traced the faint outline against her clavicle, recalling her mother's counsel. *If the Lord takes care of the sparrows, how much more will He take care of you?*

She thought her mother's letter would be the last time she ever heard her voice—their final sliver of connection. But in this moment, a reassuring truth became remarkably clear. A loved one never truly left your side. They remained in the quiet corners of your mind, sheltered in sweet memories, forever nestled in your heart.

As the walls of this home once again reverberated with laughter and the blissful sounds of shared lives, both her parents would be present in the pieces of her soul they'd shaped together.

When it comes to family—both given and chosen—there's no such thing as goodbye.

EPILOGUE

While other wedding guests admired the newlyweds on the dance floor, Cassie couldn't tear her gaze from the beautiful bundle in her arms. Edith Hope Davis, the most breathtaking sight she'd ever beheld.

"She's amazing, isn't she?" Luke murmured over her shoulder. He hadn't been able to take his eyes off their daughter all evening, either, and frequently snuck peeks from beneath the swaddle of warm blankets guarding against the late autumn chill.

"Sometimes, I still can't believe she's ours." Cassie gently stroked a silky wisp of hair, careful not to disturb their sleeping angel who'd managed to doze through an entire wedding ceremony and now, Bill and Irene's raucous first dance song.

"Except for the fact that she has your stunning eyes." Luke's adoring gaze traveled from daughter to mother and back to daughter again.

"And your thick, wavy hair," she pointed out with a pleased smile, convinced they had the most perfect child in the world.

While new motherhood wasn't without its difficulties, and she still had moments of insecurities, wondering how many mistakes she'd make as she figured things out along the way, something had clicked the moment the doctor first laid her daughter in her arms. A connection, overwhelming in its intensity, drew tears that transcended her exhaustion. A connection she couldn't describe, but one that changed everything in the most glorious way possible.

"Let's just hope she doesn't get his bulbous nose, too," Colt teased from beside his brother at the large round table where all their friends had squeezed in together, transforming a twelve-person seating arrangement into a snug fourteen.

"Hush. Luke doesn't have a big nose. And neither will Edie," Penny playfully scolded her husband, although every inch of her body indicated she felt anything but cross with him. With their chairs scooted side by side, she leaned against him, their heads bent together, arms entwined.

Ever since they returned from their anniversary trip to Greece, they acted like two lovesick teens, completely besotted, and Cassie couldn't be happier for her sister-in-law. Before they left, Penny had confided that Colt's surprise bid on Landon's villa had opened a dialogue between them that assuaged her concerns.

Turns out, Cassie had been right. Now that Colt had found his passion in life, he'd put pressure on himself to assure the restaurant succeeded. When he realized his professional ambitions had taken a toll on his loved ones, he bid on the villa, intent on finding a healthier balance between work and family. Especially since they both wanted kids in the near future.

"She's gorgeous," Olivia cooed, leaning over Cassie for a closer look. "And such a good sleeper."

"Ben was like that at this age, too," Eliza said with a smile. "I swear, he'd snooze through an explosion without so much as a fluttering eyelid. I hope his sister is the same way." Beaming, she placed a loving hand on her protruding belly. Thanks to her petite frame, even at five months pregnant, she appeared poised to give birth at any moment, and Cassie could hardly wait to raise their daughters together.

"Either way, we can say goodbye to sleep for a while," Grant teased, looking perfectly content with the impending insomnia.

"That's true," Luke said with a soft chuckle. "I don't think I've slept more than a few hours at a time since this little beauty arrived."

"What about you two?" Eliza asked Olivia. "Now that you've been married a few months, any thoughts as to when you want to start popping out babies?"

Olivia laughed before exchanging a starry-eyed gaze with Reed. "Not yet. I'm still reliving our perfect honeymoon and wedding. It all feels like a dream."

"Your wedding *was* perfect," Eliza admitted. "And this one that you originally planned is surprisingly well-suited to Bill and Irene. Especially once you added a few personal touches."

"I couldn't agree more." Cassie admired the floral centerpieces combining dahlias and roses in shades of burgundy, blush, and mauve with special additions from Bill's farm like miniature white pumpkins and dried wheat stalks. Olivia had even enlisted Grant's artistic expertise to create elegant place cards with sketches of different animals in homage to Irene.

Cassie stole a glance at the dance floor where other couples had joined the newlyweds, including her mother and Rhett. Her mother looked stunning in her maid-of-honor gown of mauve velvet that hugged her curves and paired beautifully with the rose-quartz bracelet gifted to her by Rhett. As they swayed in each other's arms to Neil Diamond's "Forever in Blue Jeans," both their faces radiated happiness.

"You really do have a gift, Olivia," Kat agreed. "Tonight almost makes me want to reconsider and get married here instead of in Primrose Valley next spring."

Jack leaned forward, but before he could speak, Kat laughed and held up her hand. "I said *almost*. The wedding your mother is planning will be equally wonderful. It's just, this night has been so perfect, it's hard to imagine another evening more lovely than this one."

Cassie knew exactly how she felt. Bathed in soft silvery moonlight, the Sterling Rose Estate transcended earthly realms, like a slice of heaven on earth. And the way her daughter's face glowed in the amber candlelight, so sweet and precious, made her heart ache with love. She would echo Kat's sentiments out loud—that nothing could top this moment—except she knew the wonder of the evening wasn't over yet.

At the end of the night, when Irene positioned herself on the edge of the dance floor in preparation for the bouquet toss, Cassie hid a smile as all the single women clustered together. Donna and Stephanie hovered near the back, and when the latter met her gaze, she waved, grinning with bright eyes and cheeks flushed from dancing. Over the last several months, Cassie had come to love the girl like a sister, and although Stephanie's future might take her away from Poppy Creek one day, she'd forever be a part of their family.

With some less-than-subtle urging from Eliza—who was privy to the surprise—Sadie and Lucy found themselves front and center.

With a brief although less-than-subtle glance over her

shoulder, Irene sent her bouquet flying straight at Sadie, who caught it with little effort.

Lucy squealed, hopping up and down in her excitement, wholly unprepared for the second bouquet Irene tossed next. It sailed into Lucy's cheering arms, and she fumbled the poor crumpled flowers, flinging petals like confetti before finally clutching them to her chest. Her startled gaze darted to Irene, questioning if there had been some mistake.

Irene, a gorgeous vision in her ivory satin wedding gown, blew a kiss to both women before gesturing for them to turn around.

Bewildered, Lucy and Sadie turned in tandem to find Vick and Landon down on one knee before them, each holding up a ring.

Lucy gasped and gripped Sadie's hand, and the two childhood friends exchanged a look of delight and disbelief as their youthful daydream came to fruition.

Blinking back blissful tears, Cassie caught Eliza's eye, knowing she shared the same earnest hope that as their daughters grew up, they would forge a similar bond.

And that maybe, one day, the blessing of friendship and community they all savored in this moment would carry on in their children.

THE END....

For now

If you enjoyed your time in Poppy Creek, you may also enjoy a trip to Blessings Bay—an idyllic coastal town with the same quirky charm and close-knit community. Immerse yourself in a new yet comfortingly familiar locale with book 1 in the series, *Blessings on State Street*. Read now or sample an excerpt at the end of this book

As always, thank you for reading. I'd be so grateful for an honest review.

SPECIAL BONUS OFFER

Dear Friend,

Thank you for reading *The Promise in Poppies*. We can't truly say goodbye to Cassie and our friends in Poppy Creek without returning one last time during the season that started it all. Please visit www.rachaelbloome.com/secret-garden-club to download your FREE BONUS SCENE featuring the most magical time of the year.

Thank you again; you truly make writing these stories worthwhile. As always, I would love to hear from you. You can reach me anytime at hello@rachaelbloome.com.

Until next time…

Blessings & Blooms,

Rachael Bloome

BLESSINGS ON STATE STREET: SAMPLE CHAPTERS

CHAPTER ONE

Operation Cancel Christmas would begin as soon as Abby Preston tossed her bags into the trunk of her silver sedan and sped away.

She couldn't wait to see her tires fling the sun-scorched sands of the Mojave Desert into the spiteful sky as Edwards Air Force Base shriveled in her rearview mirror.

"Are you sure you want to do this?" Although an unwilling participant in her Scrooge-like scheme, her best friend and roommate, Nadia Chopra, folded a white T-shirt and placed it on the pile with the rest of Abby's hastily packed wardrobe.

"I'm sure." Abby tugged the handle of her suitcase with as much force as she could muster.

Stuffed to overflowing, the stubborn lid sprang open.

Determined, Abby leaned all 115 pounds of her petite

frame against the bulging exterior, but it barely budged. "A little help?" she grunted.

"Fine. But I still think this is a terrible idea." Nadia put her exquisite curves to use and sat squarely in the center of the soft-shell suitcase, giving Abby just enough wiggle room to yank the zipper closed.

"Duly noted." In truth, Abby expected nothing less. As a professional product reviewer, Nadia shared her opinions as effortlessly as offering someone a stick of gum. But her blunt nature was offset by her big heart. Last year, she'd gathered Abby into her arms—and her stylish apartment—the moment she'd learned about Donnie's accident. The moment Abby became a widow while the rest of the world overindulged on Thanksgiving turkey and pumpkin pie.

Nadia's boyfriend was also one of the rigorously trained test pilots on base, and while both women knew the risks, Abby never expected to lose her husband of only two years in the same amount of time it took someone to order a peppermint latte.

Death, though always cruel, had been particularly heartless that day.

Abby dragged the suitcase to the door where the rest of her belongings waited. Then she turned, surveying the room she'd inhabited for the past year but had never truly made her own.

A comforting ache coiled around her heart, stealing her breath as it cinched tighter. The ever-present pain had arrived the day Donnie died, like a distant family member who'd come to pay their respects but never left. Over time, she'd gotten used to it, both anxious and afraid for the day it finally faded.

If it ever faded.

She reached for her throat, her fingers finding the cool metal chain perpetually draped around her neck. It served as a memento—a poignant reminder—she'd never remove.

"You're really going to do this?" All the disapproval had evaporated from Nadia's voice, unveiling her sadness.

"I have to, Nadia." Whenever she thought about spending another Christmas without Donnie, panic flooded her veins, fueling her impulse to flee like a primal survival instinct she couldn't ignore.

Daily life without Donnie was unbearable, but the holidays? She couldn't handle the haunting memories attacking her at every turn.

No one loved Christmas more than Donnie Preston. He made Clark Griswold from *National Lampoon's Christmas Vacation* look like the Grinch. Not only did he insist they attend every festivity within a fifty mile radius, he'd created their own traditions, from snowman-shaped cinnamon rolls on Sunday morning to special notes tucked inside handmade keepsake ornaments.

Which only made losing him during the so-called Most Wonderful Time of the Year all the more painful.

Nope. She couldn't do it. She couldn't hang around waiting for her heart to crumble like the walls of a stale gingerbread house, forgotten long after the festivities had ended.

Hiding in Blessings Bay until the new year was her only option.

The single stop sign town on the Northern California coast would be the perfect escape. After all, how Christmassy could the coast be? Sandcastles instead of snowflakes? Crab cakes instead of Christmas cookies? The decidedly un-festive locale was exactly what she needed.

Plus, the fully furnished home Donnie's aunt left him in her will would afford her some much-needed privacy and seclusion. The only downside? She'd finally have to face the ugly reality that he'd kept the home a secret from her their entire marriage—an unpleasant truth she'd long been avoiding.

"Abby," Nadia said softly, sympathy shimmering in her dark eyes. "I understand why you want to get away. Honestly, I do. But you don't even know if the house is vacant. It'll take several hours to drive there, and leaving this late, you'll probably arrive in the middle of the night. What if it's occupied?"

"I've looked into it. Donnie hasn't received any rent money since his aunt passed. As far as I can tell, he hasn't done a single thing with the property except pay taxes."

Which also meant, he probably hadn't sold off the furniture or other possessions, either.

"What about electricity and water?"

"I'll figure it out when I get there. It can't be too complicated." Abby slipped on her coat, avoiding the obvious—her impromptu trip lacked planning. But Nadia didn't understand what it felt like to wake up on December 1st faced with the incessant hope and cheer of the holidays, without the man she loved, the man whose death had robbed her of every ounce of joy she once possessed.

She'd worry about the details later. For now, she needed a haven where she could be alone with her heartache without well-meaning friends trying to make her feel better, as if such a thing were even possible.

Besides, she wasn't being completely irresponsible. She could ghost write cookbooks for D-list celebrities and quirky entrepreneurs from anywhere in the world. She'd just turned in the final draft of *Cooking with Cocker Spaniels: Dietary Deli-*

ciousness for You and Your Dog, and didn't expect rewrites until the new year.

A mixture of concern and something deeper flickered across Nadia's flawless features. "I still wish you'd wait until after the holidays so I could come with you."

Abby swallowed, her throat suddenly as dry as the desert air outside, as though an unspoken question had passed between them.

What if the house wasn't the only thing Donnie hid from her?

"I would, but that would defeat the purpose. Besides, I'll be fine." Her words carried a confidence that belied the telltale tension in her shoulders. "I really need to get on the road before it gets too late." She strode toward the bed and knelt on the floor, retrieving a small package wrapped in gold paper— the only festive leniency she'd allowed herself. She handed it to Nadia. "Don't open it until Christmas, okay?"

Tearfully, Nadia drew Abby into a hug that felt painfully close to an indefinite goodbye.

And for the first time since packing her bags, a tiny pang of doubt pierced her heart.

Was she making a big mistake?

Logan Mathews grabbed the plastic elf by the throat and yanked the goofy-looking lawn ornament from the soggy soil.

Fat raindrops pelted his face, blurring his vision and sliding, uninvited, down the collar of his jacket.

One elf rescued, only a thousand more to go.

He should let the unsightly horde of Santa's helpers fend for themselves, considering he loathed the eyesores. In all the years he'd lived across the street from Verna Hoffstetter, she never failed to litter her lawn with the ugly little devils every December, like the holiday version of plastic pink flamingos.

The next elf he came across lay prostrate in the mud, upended by the turbulent wind that seemed personally ticked off by Verna's tacky Christmas decorations.

Blinking against the curtain of rain that careened down his forehead, trying to drown him where he stood, Logan tucked the tiny toy maker beneath his arm with his fallen comrade.

Why exactly had he left the comfort of his home in the middle of a torrential downpour on some misguided rescue mission?

Heck if he knew.

He supposed he wanted to avoid seeing the crushed look on Verna's face when she emerged the following morning to find an elfin massacre on her front lawn.

Okay, so she wasn't his favorite person, always intruding on his solitude with invitations to play backgammon or to borrow some sugar—and one oddly specific request for a whole pineapple. But in some ways, she reminded Logan of his grandmother, and watching her lawn display be decimated by daggers disguised as raindrops seemed unnecessarily callous, even for him.

Although a self-proclaimed recluse, he was a decent enough neighbor. Unlike some clichéd curmudgeons like Mr. Wilson from *Dennis the Menace*, he'd found a healthy balance between privacy and common courtesy.

The wind came at him sideways, knocking him to his knees in disagreement.

His palms sunk into the sludge, his nose pressed against the cheek of an elf with a painted-on smile that appeared to be mocking him.

Ha-ha. Very funny, Wind.

Okay, so maybe he wasn't well-balanced. On the teeter-totter of life, he'd sunk his heels pretty deep into seclusion and self pity.

But it suited him.

Plus, it seemed reasonable considering the crummy discount store playing cards he'd been dealt for thirty-five years.

First, losing his parents at an age when transitioning to the second grade should've been the most traumatic event in his childhood. Then, when he'd finally built a decent life for himself as a fighter pilot in the Air Force, a neck injury ripped everything away, including what little dignity and self-worth he had left.

It wasn't bad enough that he'd had to move to a dinky, backwater town like Blessings Bay, which was basically the coastal version of Mayberry. He'd had to rely on a friend's generosity to make ends meet, the equivalent of rubbing salt *and* lemon juice in a gaping wound.

Sure, some people rose above the hard knocks and toured the country giving perky Ted Talks on overcoming adversity.

Frankly, he found those people more irritating than inspirational.

He'd gone the other direction, embracing the title of town hermit—a respectable role in the ecosystem.

After all, it took all kinds of people to make the world go round.

And he was perfectly content with his choice.

CHAPTER TWO

Abby squinted against the persistent raindrops pelting the windshield, struggling to keep her eyes open after an entire day of driving with minimal breaks.

Thankfully, she'd arrive at her destination any second now.

At least, she desperately hoped so.

She couldn't find the adapter to charge her cell phone, and before the battery died, the squiggly line on the GPS leading to Blessings Bay looked relatively close.

If only she could stay awake.

She tightened her grip on the steering wheel, prying her eyelids open with sheer willpower.

During the last few hours of her drive, the stunning coastline had kept her alert. Like peeking into another world, she'd witnessed towering redwoods on one side and rugged cliff faces on the other. The vibrant cobalt waters had stretched toward the invisible horizon, a breathtaking blank slate of endless possibilities.

That is, before nightfall and an unexpected storm plunged everything into a pitch-black void, leaving her disoriented.

To make matters worse, the rhythmic pitter-patter of raindrops pinging against the roof of the car threatened to lull her to sleep.

She flicked on the radio, scrolling through crackling static until the velvety croon of Judy Garland's "Have Yourself A Merry Little Christmas" stilled her hand.

Donnie used to love the sultry classic, and had added it to

his Christmas Kickoff playlist, along with an eclectic mix of Bing Crosby and Burl Ives.

Abby always thought the song sounded a little sad, as though a tear hid behind each dulcet note.

She should have changed the station or turned off the radio altogether, but she leaned against the headrest, letting the music wash over her.

Her own silent tears slid down her cheeks, the sadness in the song—real or imagined—more palpable than ever.

Lost in the melancholy melody, Abby nearly missed the sign welcoming her to Blessings Bay.

Snapping out of her reverie, she jerked the wheel, veering off the highway down a narrow lane.

Rain pounded the windows even harder now, and the violent wind battered the compact vehicle with shocking force.

With every muscle in her body clenched, Abby searched the darkness up ahead, expecting to see light from the town— a street lamp, glow in a shop window, *something*.

Although her wipers worked tirelessly to whisk away the waterfall cascading toward the hood of her car, she couldn't make out anything save for murky shapes and moonlit shadows.

Had she stumbled upon a ghost town?

A subtle weight of regret settled in her stomach. Why had she been so impulsive? Nadia had tried to warn her, tried to stop her…

She should've listened.

Suddenly, her headlights bounced off reflective paint, and she stomped the brake.

Her heart vaulted into her throat as she lurched forward,

the unexpected stop sign glaring down at her with a disapproving glint.

Where had *that* come from?

Gathering a deep, shaky breath, she steadied her erratic pulse as she eased forward.

"1109 West State Street," she murmured, searching for house numbers within the limited radius of her low beams.

A quick glance at the clock on the dash told her it was almost midnight.

She allowed herself a brief whimper, then bolstered what little energy she had left, determined to see this through. But she wasn't sure how much longer she could last...

On the verge of pulling off the road and crawling into the backseat, she nearly wept when 1109 leaped off the curb in blocky white lettering. She couldn't make out much of the home in the gloomy abyss, but at this point, curb appeal wasn't high on her priority list.

She eagerly turned into the driveway. "Please, please have a warm bed and soft pillow."

Fishing inside the glove box, she found the key that had been included with the paperwork from their lawyer. Clutching it tightly in her palm, she grabbed her purse and overnight bag from the passenger seat, braced herself, and exited the car.

The moment she left cover, merciless raindrops besieged her on all sides, soaking her hair and clothing in a matter of seconds. Sprinting toward the house, she sloshed through several puddles before stumbling up the slippery steps, finding a modicum of refuge on the expansive front porch.

She fumbled with the key a few minutes before bursting inside, slamming the door against the maniacal wind that seemed to have a personal vendetta.

Panting, she leaned against the doorframe in the darkness, collecting her wits as water dripped from her shoulder-length hair, pooling by her wet sneakers.

In the dim moonlight, she could barely make out the ghostly outline of a staircase a few feet ahead. She opened her purse for the flashlight on her phone, then remembered the battery died.

Great.

She fought against tears of exhaustion—tears that would affirm she'd made a terrible mistake.

Nadia was right. She'd been so focused on running *away,* she had no idea what she'd run *toward.*

So far, the trip was shaping up to be a colossal disaster.

After dropping her duffle, she peeled off her drenched jacket.

A loud *thump,* then a *clatter* came from somewhere upstairs.

Abby froze, fear gluing her feet to the floor.

Was someone in the house?

Her breath remained lodged somewhere in her lungs as she dug inside her purse for her Taser.

She'd heard of squatters moving into vacant houses, but the possibility hadn't occurred to her until this moment. Inching toward the bottom of the stairs, she switched off the safety feature, tucking herself against the wall.

Growing up in a not-so-great part of Chicago, Abby wasn't a stranger to taking care of herself. Plus, Donnie had made a point to teach her combat maneuvers. But the reality of executing the self defense techniques in an actual life or death scenario sprouted beads of sweat on her already damp forehead.

More than anything, she wanted to go home.

She wanted Donnie.

A creak on the staircase sent her heart scrambling into her throat, and she fought the urge to squeeze her eyes shut.

Stay calm. Stay focused.

The dark figure slowly descended the steps, and her fear ratcheted with each imperceptible sound—another creak, the thud of a weighty gait.

This was it... the intruder was almost upon her.

No time to back out now.

When the shadow drew within arms length, she inhaled a sharp breath and lunged forward, ramming the Taser against bare flesh.

A man's guttural cry ricocheted off the walls and a heavy body hit the ground.

Logan wasn't sure which hurt worse, the cattle prod to the ribcage or his face getting cozy with the hardwood floor. Either way, he wouldn't let his attacker get away with the cheap shot.

His fingers curled, prepared to fight back.

"Who are you? And what are you doing here?" a strong, yet feminine voice demanded in the darkness.

His assailant was a *woman*?

He hadn't seen that coming. But then, he hadn't seen the electrified metal prongs before they'd zapped him, either.

Whoever this woman was, she had gumption.

Detecting the faintest warble of fear in her words calmed his self preservation instincts and he uncoiled his fist.

"Logan Matthews. I live here. Who are *you*?" He rolled onto his back, but didn't get up, in case the movement provoked her again. While he was pretty sure a standard-issue Taser couldn't cook his vital organs, he didn't want to risk it.

"Abigail Preston. I own this house."

He squinted, straining to glimpse her features in the shadows. But although he couldn't see her face, a clear picture formed in his mind.

Abigail Preston... Donnie's wife.

In all the years they'd served together in the Air Force, no other man had been more proud of his better half than Donnie. Even in bootcamp, he'd taped a photo of her above his bed for everyone to see. Nothing crass or inappropriate, like some of the other guys posted.

In fact, all things considered, the snapshot had been fairly simple—a dark-haired woman at some restaurant—Donnie couldn't remember which one. She held a glass of ice water in one hand, her head thrown back, laughing at something Donnie said. As he told it, late afternoon sunlight had hit her just right, creating a halo effect. She'd looked so beautiful, so captivatingly blissful, he'd snapped a photo to preserve the memory.

What had stood out to Logan the most was the woman's smile—the kind that lit up the world, but also seemed to belong only to you.

While it was a pleasant visual from the past, he had a feeling Abigail wasn't smiling right now.

"I'm a friend of Donnie's. We were in basic training together."

"Really?" She didn't bother hiding her skepticism, and he envisioned her dark eyebrows raised, her lips scrunched to the side. "I've never heard of you."

He sighed inwardly, suppressing a groan.

Of course, she hadn't...

"What about Nugget?"

"*You're* Nugget?"

"The one and only." He rose, stretching to his full six foot two inches, hoping to regain some dignity.

He'd loathed that call sign every single day of his service. If he'd been smart, he would've participated in some good-natured bribery, which was how one of his buddies wound up with the name Shooter.

But no, he'd taken the moral high ground, and they'd named him after the sugary, walnut-laden dessert bar his grandmother sent him in regular care packages. But hey, at least they were delicious.

Besides, if he had a choice, he'd give anything to be back in the cockpit of an F-16, even if it meant reclaiming a call sign as humiliating as Nugget.

"Donnie used to talk about you all the time. And weren't you the one who sent the box of desserts the day of Donnie's funeral?" Her words blended with a mixture of gratitude and something softer, something close to affection.

At the time, he'd wondered if he should've sent flowers instead, but the homemade Nevada Nuggets seemed more fitting, somehow. At least, Donnie would've gotten a kick out of it. "They're an old family recipe. I hope you liked them."

"I did. They were wonderful. So much better than flowers."

Her tone carried a hint of a smile, and he was surprised by how badly he wanted to see it. "Why don't we move into the sitting room? The power's out because of the storm, but there's a fire in there and I can scrounge up a couple of battery operated lanterns."

As she followed him into the next room, Logan mentally rehearsed half a dozen ways to ask the awkward yet all-important question—what was she doing here? And how long did she plan to stay?

But no matter how he phrased it, he couldn't bring himself to form the words, realizing his future hung on her response.

After all, she owned the place. If she wanted to kick him out, she could.

The smoldering embers cast a peripheral glow, allowing Logan to glimpse Abigail for the first time.

Even dripping wet and a little worse for wear, she did something to his insides that closely resembled internal combustion. Only, in this case, it was ignited by striking hazel eyes instead of jet fuel.

Abruptly looking away, he rummaged through a desk drawer for a flashlight, then moved to the closet and retrieved two lanterns.

Clicking them on, he set them both on the coffee table, turning to look at her again.

Her eyes were fixed on his bare chest, and when he caught her staring, she flushed, quickly averting her gaze.

"The fire feels nice." She stepped toward the hearth, stretching out her hands to gather warmth. And maybe mask the sudden rosiness in her cheeks.

"There's a fireplace in the master bedroom, if you'd like me to build one in there for you..." He intentionally let his words trail off, hoping she'd fill in the blanks with her plans for the foreseeable future. When she didn't, he added, "My room is upstairs, so you're not putting me out or anything."

He didn't want to go into the morose psychological reasons of how he'd chosen the smallest room in the house over the large master suite because he didn't feel he deserved it.

Thankfully, she didn't ask.

She stood in an uneasy stance, kneading her lips together as though massaging the right words out of them. "I'm sorry to intrude like this. I had no idea you were living here. How, uh, how long has it been?"

"A couple of years. Donnie didn't tell you?"

Something flashed in her eyes. Embarrassment? Sadness? Perhaps a mixture of the two. She shook her head.

Guilt clawed at Logan's stomach. Why hadn't Donnie told her? Was he worried she wouldn't approve of the arrangement?

Logan always knew his friend had been far too generous. Sure, he paid the utilities and maintained the property, which wasn't exactly easy considering large historic homes needed a ton of work. But Donnie would have made a small fortune selling the place. Maybe he hadn't told his wife to avoid the conflict.

Logan hated the thought of being a wedge in their marriage even more than he hated being a burden.

"I'm sorry for the... *mixup* tonight," he said, putting it mildly. He'd likely have a nasty burn on his side in the morning. "This is your house. If you need me to leave, just say so. Only, I'd prefer to wait until after the storm, if that's okay. Otherwise, the moving boxes might get a little soggy." He grinned, hoping to add some levity to an all around uncomfortable situation.

The corner of her mouth lifted, giving him a small taste of the smile he remembered. "That won't be necessary. Honestly, I don't really know what I plan to do with the place long term, but for now, I was just hoping to get away for the holidays. Or more accurately, get away *from* the holidays." She hesitated, slicking a strand of damp hair behind her ear. "I suppose we could work something out for the next few weeks. Find a way to coexist without getting in each other's way. Would that be okay with you?"

She met his gaze, and his heart rate skyrocketed like the first time he experienced G-force. Coexist? As in, live within the same four walls? He wasn't used to sharing his space with anyone, let alone someone like Abby.

His brain shouted, Eject! Eject!

But the rest of his body didn't heed the warning. "Sure. We can make that work."

"Great. I just have one... request," she said in a tone that indicated it was more of a non negotiable. "I'm skipping Christmas this year. Which means, no decorations, no tree, no holiday music, nothing festive whatsoever. Is that going to be a problem for you?"

"No, ma'am."

He could handle nixing Christmas.

The real question was whether he could handle living with his attractive new house guest.

Read more of Abby and Logan's story in **Blessings on State Street**.

ACKNOWLEDGMENTS

As my fingertips hover over the keys, and I contemplate how many people have contributed to this series over the years, I'm at a loss for words. When I first sat down to write *The Clause in Christmas* in early 2019, I had no idea God would lead me down this road and introduce me to so many lovely, generous, kind, truly incredible people along the way.

But I wouldn't be here at all without my loving, supportive, and unbelievably gracious family. And at the risk of sounding braggy, my unparalleled support system starts with my husband and best friend, Mr. Bloome, and extends to my parents, in-laws, siblings, extended family, and my chosen family of friends, readers, and other authors.

I'm blessed with the most wonderful critique partner, Dave Cenker, who has been by my side since the beginning, and a professional team that has grown over the years—Ana, Beth, Krista, Laura, and Trenda. I can't thank you all enough for helping me craft stories that are the best they can be.

Wendy and Gwenn, you ladies began as readers but have become so much more. You're not only huge supporters of my books and have poured countless hours into helping my business grow, but you've become dear, treasured friends and so much more than I deserve.

To my ARC TEAM, thank you for being the first eyes on my completed work, offering your honest thoughts, catching typos, and celebrating alongside me with each release. Sharing a new novel with the world conjures a certain amount of nervousness and uncertainty, and reading your reviews lends me courage and support, almost as if you're beside me when I press Publish Now. I hope one day I can give you a hug of thanks in person.

To the readers in my Facebook group, thank you for creating the best corner of the internet. Getting to know you, interacting, chatting, and reading your posts and comments has added so much joy to my life. I never considered myself a fan of social media until I met all of you. Now, I look forward to popping into the group and saying hello whenever I can. I wish I could mention you all by name, but the printing costs of a book that large would be astronomical. Just know that you are loved!

And lastly, thank YOU, dear reader. The fact that you're still here, eight books later, is a blessing I can't describe. Thank you for letting these characters into your heart. Time is precious and options are endless. I'm so grateful you chose to spend your time with me. I hope we can connect over the magic of stories for many years to come.

ABOUT THE AUTHOR

Rachael Bloome is a *hopeful* romantic. She loves every moment leading up to the first kiss, as well as each second after saying, "I do." Torn between her small-town roots and her passion for traveling the world, she weaves both into her stories—and her life!

Joyfully living in her very own love story, she enjoys spending time with her loving husband, adorable daughter, and two rescue dogs, Finley and Monkey. When she's not writing, helping to run the family coffee roasting business, or getting together with friends, she's busy planning their next big adventure!

BOOK CLUB QUESTIONS

1. Did you find Cassie's fears about motherhood relatable or understandable?

2. What did you think of Donna? Has your perception of her changed since The Clause in Christmas? If so, how?

3. Which side character's story resonated with you the most and why?

4. Do you have experience with addiction, either personally or with a loved one? If so, did you find the various representations in the novel realistic or relatable?

5. Which aspects of the novel, if any, surprised you?

6. Which of the Poppy Creek couples is your favorite and why?

7. What did you like and/or not like about Donna and Rhett's romance? Are you glad they each found redemption and a second chance? If not, why?

8. Did you suspect Burns was Cassie's father? If so, what led you to that suspicion?

9. What theme/themes did you notice in the book?

10. What did you think of the ending? Were you happy with the conclusion? If not, what do you wish the author would have done differently?

As always, I look forward to hearing your thoughts on the story. You can email your responses (or ask your own questions) to hello@rachaelbloome.com or post them in my private Facebook group, Rachael Bloome's Secret Garden Club.

FREE DIGITAL COOKBOOK

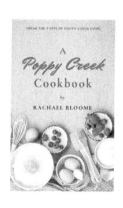

You can now keep all your favorite Poppy Creek recipes in one place. Simply join the Secret Garden Club (a FREE all access pass to exclusive bonus content) to receive a copy of *A Poppy Creek Cookbook* (available as a digital download or printable PDF).

Join here: www.rachaelbloome.com/secret-garden-club

Printed in Great Britain
by Amazon